<u>T A B L E O F C O N T E N T S</u>

DEDICATION

This book is dedicated to anyone injured or damaged through medical incompetence, arrogance, or poor judgement.

ACKNOWLEDGEMENTS

The author would like to thank Bryan Fox, solicitor, for all his generous assistance in helping him through the maze that are the court proceedings when suing for damages and establishing a Ward of Court.

Also, I must thank my wife, Ramona Valentine, BSc. Hon, for her tolerance and patience, and in undertaking quality work in the self-published industry; and for her ongoing technical support in bringing this book together.

INTRODUCTION

This tragic story happened in a Dublin Hospital in the early 1970's. Through gross medical incompetence, negligence, poor practise, and judgement, compounded by denial and arrogance, a young woman is put into a chronic vegetative state from which there is no prospect of ever recovering. She was undergoing a surgical procedure that she did not need when she suffers a cardiac arrest with devastating consequences.

Those responsible for this disaster added to their disgrace by denying their victim her right to die. Rather, by tube feeding her, they locked her into a hideous state of suspense between life and death from which there is no escape unless the doctors say so.

Finally, after almost twenty years, the victim's mother was forced to take a High Court action compelling her daughter's carers to allow her daughter to die with a modicum of dignity. After a long, protracted, and tortious legal battle, she eventually won her case. The artificial feeding was discontinued, and her daughter was allowed to rest in peace at last.

Because these legal proceedings were held in camera the names of the institutions and individuals involved were never disclosed or released into the public domain. Therefore, what's given here is, of necessity, a fictionalized true story.

However, the author, a retired doctor and coroner, was made sufficiently aware of the facts of the case by colleagues involved at the time to be confident in its essential validity.

Finally, it needs to be born in mind that up to quite recently, hospital consultants in Ireland, enjoyed almost Godlike status, where their word was final and their engagement with their patients and their relatives, minimal. To further enforce their position, many of them belonged to right-wing, secretive, conservative clubs like Opus Dei and the Knights of St Columbanus. These in turn enjoyed the blessings of the Holy Roman Sea and The Government of Ireland of the day.

++++++++++++++++++++++++++++++++++++++

CHAPTER 1 - THE CATASTROPHE

Margaret drove her younger sister, Linda, to the hospital on the other side of Dublin. Grey January clouds gathered over The Four Courts, and greater black-backed seagulls perched on the balustrades of O'Connell's Bridge. They pointed their yellow bills into the biting easterly winds coming upriver from Liberty Hall and Butt Bridge. Linda looked very worried and unhappy. She envied these seabirds their freedom.

Being a Sunday evening, the traffic was light. Linda could see a long line of people queuing outside The Carlton Cinema. "The Exorcist" was up in big lights across the front of the cinema. She yearned to have their freedom and leisure. Did they have any idea of just how lucky they were? Couples in the queue necked and French kissed. How much more would she have preferred now to be going to the pictures with Tom or with her own girlfriends rather than be facing into this hellhole of a hospital and a general anaesthetic tomorrow? Linda decided then and there that she abhorred hospitals and anything to do with them.

"Do you know something, Mags?"
"No, what?"
"I absolutely fecking hate hospitals."
"Who doesn't?"

"No, no. I don't mean it just like that. My abhorrence of the places runs much deeper than that. Do you know what I mean, like?"

"Oh, really?"

"Yes, really. If I'm ever terminally ill and can't speak for myself, will you make sure that I'm not left in a hospital?"

"Oh, Linda, will you lighten up for Christ's sake?"

"No, Mags, I'm serious now. You have got to promise me."

The man at reception wore a shiny peaked cap and a shabby dark blue uniform – tunic and pants, shapeless brown shoes. With a lighted cigarette dangling from the right-hand corner of his mouth, he ran a grubby, nicotine-stained index finger down a long list of names he had in front of him. To keep the cigarette's smoke out of his eyes, he held his right eye tightly closed, like a frozen wink.

"Let's see now, Boyle, Boyle, Boyle. Here we are, Miss Linda Boyle. You will be in St. Ann's Ward, Miss Boyle, up two flights of stairs there and first on the left." He pointed with his right index and middle fingers; together, these now secured the half-smoked cigarette.

"Sorry, the lift is out of order," he said nonchalantly.

The two well-dressed sisters trudged up the broad limestone Victorian staircase with ornate cast-iron banisters on each side, topped by a heavy, polished, mahogany handrail. Margaret carried Linda's overnight bag, and Linda followed reluctantly behind. She couldn't stand the smell of this place. What is it about hospitals that they always must smell like this? The hall-porter's cigarette was preferable to this sickly mixture of antiseptics, anaesthetics, bacon, and cabbage.

St. Ann's Ward had only four beds in it, and three of them were already occupied. Staff Nurse Jennifer Ryan greeted the two young women cheerfully.

"Which of you two young women is Linda?" she wanted to know.

Linda, reluctantly, owned up to being that person. Had the ground only opened up and swallowed her at that moment, it would have been a great relief.

"You'll be over there, Linda, that one in the corner. And will you cheer up for God's sake? It's only for one night. It's not the end of the world."

Linda would have preferred if Nurse Ryan allowed her to decide for herself what was and what was not the end of the world. However, under the circumstances, she decided that the best course might be to hold her counsel, at least for the moment.

Her mother, Mary, was on the phone outside at the nurse's station and wished to have a quick word with her:

"Well, have they given you a nice, quiet ward and comfortable bed?" her mother wanted to know.

'Oh God, I do love my mother, but I just wish she would not do this kind of thing – trying to be all jolly jolly in the face of disaster,' Linda thinks before replying with a deep sigh.

"It's alright, Mum. It's in a corner by itself. So far, I have only sat on it, but it seems comfortable enough." Linda forced herself to sound cheerful.

"Anyway, it hardly matters; it will be only for one night."

"That's right, love. Would you like me to go in and see you in the morning before they take you down to theatre?" Mary wanted to know, concern in her voice.

"No, Mom, thanks just the same. You stay warm and cosy there where you are. I'll be fine. They will let you know after the procedure when I should be discharged. Hopefully, it will be late tomorrow afternoon sometime."

"Grand then, so."

"Good night, Mom. I love you."

Mary Boyle quietly replaced the phone back on its cradle and went to join her husband on the sofa before the glowing coal fire. Why is she suddenly filled with strange feelings of deep foreboding?

Margaret then bade her sister farewell, wished her the best of luck, and gave her a peck on the cheek. When she departed, Linda pulled the curtain closed around her hospital bed, undressed, donned her white nylon nightdress, pulled back the curtain, climbed into bed, and sat up to take in her new surroundings.

Directly across from her, a young woman, only a few years Linda's senior, also sat up and looked across at Linda. Her head was totally devoid of any hair, and her face was slightly moon-shaped. These, Linda thought to herself, were the tell-tale signs that she had been given chemotherapy and was on steroids. Despite all of that, she managed to smile broadly across at Linda.

"I see you are a patient of Dr. Newman then, same as me."

"That's right, how did you know that?"

"It's written on the chart there at the end of your bed."

"Oh, of course, how stupid of me."

Soon, supper arrived, brought in by a sullen-looking nurse's aide. It mainly consisted of tea, two pieces of buttered white sliced pan, and two triangular wedges of indifferent white cheese, each wrapped in tinfoil. Out of politeness, Linda nibbled at this offering with little relish.

The two women struck up a conversation and exchanged their reasons for being in the hospital and the events that led up to it. Linda's companion, whose name was Patricia, was from Carlow town. Only three weeks previously, she had been diagnosed with a malignant ovarian tumour. She hoped to go home tomorrow and was looking forward to being reunited with her husband and eight-month-old baby daughter.

"Tell us this much now, how do you get along with Dr. Newman?" Linda wanted to know.

"I like him. Yah, he's alright, a nice enough sort of a man."

What did Newman say about ovarian cancer? One in sixty women have it, with a mortality rate in less than five years, of over 80%. "Scary stuff," isn't that what he called it?

Thinking of this and looking over at her cheerful companion in the bed across the ward, Linda began to feel profound sadness tinged with considerable guilt. Her sadness sprang from the fact that this pleasant and happy young mother, looking forward to being reunited with her baby and husband, should be so cruelly struck down in her prime. Was there any God?

Her guilt stemmed from the trivial nature of her own predicament and how pathetically she was dealing with it. Everything in this difficult life was relative. For the next half hour, Linda did her utmost to cheer up her companion from Carlow by doing a credible take on Peter Newman's 'hot potato in the mouth' accent and what he had said to her. To do this, she had to hold her mouth in a particular way, with lips pursed, to make a funny face.

Linda mimicked Newman:

"Your question is a fair and reasonable one, ah, and I will do my best to answer it as fairly and as reasonably as I can, ah."

Patricia nearly broke her sides laughing at the jest. Soon, the two young women turned in for the night and, despite their worries, slept soundly.

The small side operating theatre in St. Malachi's General Hospital was tiled in white from floor to ceiling. From the centre of the high ceiling hung the main operating theatre light, five feet in diameter and adjustable to every possible angle. Accompanying this were two independent, smaller satellite lamps, each on their own separate mountings and each capable of emitting one thousand watts of shadow-less white light. These operating theatre lights were specifically designed to throw powerful light into every imaginable nook and cranny of the human body, large or small.

The floor was covered in a special green, non-static, non-slip, heavy-duty lino that covered the entire floor and returned up the wall for six inches, where it was fused to the wall tiles. Positioned randomly around the theatre were stainless steel surgical trolleys on large rubber wheels, one to each corner. One of these carried the cautery equipment used to stop small blood vessels from bleeding and to cut through tissue bloodlessly. Another was a crash cart housing a defibrillator and emergency medicines in the unlikely event of a cardiac arrest occurring in an anesthetized patient.

The operating table was freestanding, centre stage, directly under the massive theatre lights. Heavy, it was made of solid stainless steel and was adjustable in every plane – height, list, and tilt. It was dressed in a single white, newly laundered linen sheet, and a thin Styrofoam pillow. Linda Boyle would be next to lie down on it.

Dr. Walter Malone, consultant anaesthetist, sat at the head of the operating table, dressed in a green scrub-suit that seemed several sizes too small for him. He was a heavy, squat man in his mid-forties. On his feet were white wooden clogs with open heels. Around his bare neck hung a black-tubed stethoscope and a loose surgical mask. His cheeks and nose were florid. He had all the appearances of a man who, at least sometime in the past, enjoyed too many whiskies and late nights.

His colleagues also knew that alcoholism was an issue with Walter Malone. They understood he was a member of Alcoholics Anonymous, but nobody was sure, and nobody spoke to him about it. It was, after all, his own business, and doctors did not meddle in other doctors' private affairs. At least, they tried not to.

Anyway, clearly sober now, one day at a time, Sweet Jesus, he had been back working for the last two months after being on a year's paid leave of absence. The hospital administrator had told him to go away and sort himself out. His drinking was endangering patients' lives, and if he did not pull himself together soon, the Medical Council would be after him, and he'd be struck off the medical register, which would almost certainly be the end of his medical career. It happened all the time.

He did, in fact, join the AA for a while but couldn't stand the phony confessional self-flagellation of the whole thing. He was sober now, but unbeknownst to anyone except his long-suffering wife, he had replaced alcohol with self-prescribed Librium, 10mg three times a day. Dr. Malone was fine nowadays if there were no emergencies. He could cope with everything else, but not emergencies.

He was moreover, a staunch Catholic and daily communicant. His colleagues in the hospital also understood that Malone was a member of The Order of the Knights of St. Columbanus. Or was it Opus Dei he was in? Nobody seemed to know for sure, and nobody asked because it was, like his drinking, his own business after all.

What was known for sure was that Walter belonged to one of those charitable, if somewhat secretive, Catholic male-only organizations. The Knights had a meeting house in Ely Place in Dublin since 1923. The Order elected a Supreme Knight every three years to head up the organization. Currently, Malone may have held that position, although nobody seemed to know for sure, nor would they be told should they have the audacity to enquire.

The Order of the Knight of St. Columbanus attracted membership from every profession. This could only be gained on the recommendation of two existing members. Thus, you would find members of the Irish judiciary, the Irish legal profession, members of the Irish Government, high-ranking academics, clerics, civil servants, and of course, top-ranking medical and surgical consultants, might be attending any one of their secretive meetings held every two weeks.

Dr. Malone adjusted the valves and settings on his anaesthetic trolley, checking the pressure reading on the attached gas cylinders. He carefully connected a new facemask that, in a few minutes, would be used to deliver the anaesthetic gases down into the patient's lungs. All connections were doubly checked because Malone was aware that even a simple accidental or unobserved disconnection, for example, could have fatal consequences.

At the other end of the operating table, Theatre Sister Ann Harris was laying out an instrument trolley with the simple sterile paraphernalia required to carry out a hysterosalpingogram. This theatre nurse was masked and gowned in white, scrubbed, and gloved. The equipment required included a vaginal speculum to allow the surgeon to have a clear view of the cervix lying at the end of the vagina. The specula were laid on a stainless-steel kidney dish along with sterile gauze smeared with a blob of KY gel. Along with this was a length of fine clear plastic catheter tubing attached to a fifty-cc glass syringe filled with contrast medium that would soon be used to show up on X-Ray the uterus and fallopian tubes of Linda Boyle.

Outside in the scrub-room, Dr. Peter Newman scrubbed his hands and forearms back to his elbows using a hard, disposable, large nailbrush and a brownish-yellow antiseptic liquid soap called Betadine. This was dispensed from an inverted wall-mounted container over the sink by depressing a floor-mounted pedal with his right foot. Dressed in a dark green scrub suit, on his feet, Newman wore half-length white Wellington-like rubber boots. He whistled tunelessly to himself as he scrubbed away. He stayed at it for a full five minutes or more, soaping, scrubbing, rinsing, and then soaping, scrubbing, and rinsing all over again. Finally, he rinsed off the soapy concoction for the last time, allowing the warm water to flow freely from fingertips to his elbows. He turned off the water by nudging clockwise the solid stainless-steel lever tap with his right elbow. He came backward through the swing doors into the operating room with his hands held high up beside his ears as if surrendering to someone pointing a gun at his head.

"Morning, Walter, and how are we today?"

"Morning, Peter, have often felt better, I have to say. What did you think of the match on Saturday? Didn't Murphy have a crap game? Jesus, that fellow couldn't kick snow off a rope!"

Theatre Sister Mary McGonagall now attended to Peter Newman and stayed with him until he was fully togged out. All the while, the two doctors exchanged views on the first rugby game in this season's Triple Crown. First, she handed him a warm, sterile towel so he could thoroughly dry off his hands and forearms. Then she held out a medium-sized green, sterile theatre gown in front of him and gave it a shake, like a matador goading a harmless bull. Into this, the surgeon dived his right arm, followed by the left, like a man doing the over-arm in a swimming race. Next, she held open a size seven and a half powdered, sterile right-hand surgical glove. Into this, Peter Newman plunged his dainty hand, wiggling his fingers as he got in deeper. The latex gloves made a noise like a worried balloon. This act was then repeated with the left-hand glove. And finally, Sister Mary grabbed and untied the gown strings at the doctor's back and swung each around to the front, first left and then right, requiring surgeon and nurse to move around each other as if in a loveless tango.

The ritual was finished. Peter Newman now stood off to one side with his gloved hands folded in front of him. He stood there like a 'living statue' street performer on Grafton Street. Peering over his surgical mask, he could see the radiographer had now hauled in the heavy portable X-Ray machine into the theatre and was placing a large blank X-Ray plate into the slot in the operating table under where the patient's pelvis was going to be in a few minutes' time. Newman admired her bum and visible panty line as she bent forwards.

A male student theatre nurse escorted Linda Boyle into the operating theatre. Pre-op medications have made her wobbly on her feet. She stumbled a bit. She was wearing a full-length white theatre gown tied at the back, white woolly theatre stockings adorned her feet and, on her head, sat a surgical paper hat. Into this, she had managed to bundle all her long black hair. She was instantly recognisable as the patient being the only one in the room not wearing a surgical mask. The student theatre nurse helped her step onto the low footstool and from there to lying supine on the operating table. In muffled terror, she looked up at the operating lights five feet above her head.

Walter Malone went into his reassuring routine and explained to Linda, in some considerable detail, the sequence of events, as they would occur in the coming minutes. First, three chest leads to the ECG heart monitor will be attached to her chest, one below her left breast, two above. Dr. Malone pointed out the ECG screen to Linda who was a bit too dozy to take it in. Then, he explained, she would be given an IV injection into the vein at the bend of her right arm. This will only hurt a tiny bit and that will be the last thing that she will feel. Within ten seconds of the thiopentone entering her bloodstream, she will be profoundly asleep and totally unaware of anything being done to her.

Newman nodded at Malone. Everything seemed to be in place, and it was time to get on with it. All light-hearted banter about the weather and rugby matches ceased and everybody concentrated on the task in hand. Dr. Malone attached the leads to Linda's chest using adhesive contact disks and looked up at the monitor. The electric pulses generated by a full cycle of her heart's action moved across the green screen from left to right. The normal sinus rhythm of the heart was maintained. With each passing R wave, the machine emitted a high-pitched bleep and a tiny blue light flashed on the top right-hand corner of the monitor.

Dr. Malone moved around to Linda's right arm now been strapped to an arm board by Nurse McGonagall who also had applied and inflated a blood pressure cuff. This made the vein stand out better and Malone had no trouble in finding it. He withdrew a few drops of venous blood back into the syringe to double-check that the needle was in the right place. It was. Now he deflated the BP cuff and proceeded to inject twenty cc's of thiopentone by slowly pressing the plunger forwards.

"Can you count backwards for me, Linda please – ten, nine, eight?"

Linda tried to mutter 'seven' and was suddenly unconscious.

Now the anaesthetist moved back to behind Linda's head again and, grasping her by the mandible, he used a tongue depressor to gently prize her mouth open before sliding the silver blade of a laryngoscope down her throat. This instrument chattered against her teeth and Malone had to be careful not to chip or otherwise damage any of Linda's nice strong white teeth. It could so easily happen. Now he shifted the scope from his right into his left hand and lifted on the handle. By peering down along the curved blade, Malone could now see Linda's vocal cords deep below. Without taking his eyes off them for one second, he held his opened right hand back behind his right ear and Nurse McGonagall placed a red rubber lubricated curved inflatable endotracheal tube between his thumb and index finger.

Now, using the groove along the inside of the curved blade of the laryngoscope to guide him, Dr. Malone passed the endotracheal tube along until it slipped in between the vocal cords and went on another two inches. Held in this position, the doctor inflated the cuff at the end of the tube thus anchoring it safely. All of this had taken less than one minute from the time the IV injection had been given. The anaesthetist had now completed the most difficult art of his task. Intubation had been safely accomplished.

Finally, he connected the endotracheal tube into the anaesthetic circuit. The facemask, which had already been connected to the anaesthetic gases, was then held firmly over Linda's mouth and nose. Within another minute, she was deeply asleep. Malone nodded to Newman indicating that he may proceed.

Linda's heels were then placed up in stirrups and she was put up in the so-called 'lithotomy position'. Peter Newman sat at the end of the operating table between her draped thighs. He waited silently while Nurse McGonagall swung the two satellite lights behind the surgeon's left and right shoulder and directed them to their maximum effectiveness.

The obstetrician now proceeded rapidly to identify her cervix and passed the narrow clear catheter into her uterus. The operating theatre had gone completely quiet. The only sounds to be heard were the rhythmic gushing, popping, and sucking sounds from the Manley Ventilator as it gently pushed air and gases in and out of the patient's lungs. The other sound was the pulsing, steady and regular bleep coming from the ECG monitor accompanied by the reassuring pulsing blue light.

Professor Newman fixed the fifty-cc syringe filled with the contrast medium to his end of the catheter, and the radiographer, now wearing a heavy leaded apron, positioned her mobile X-Ray arm over Linda's lower abdomen. She tilted the machine head slightly towards Newman so that the patient's uterus and fallopian tubes would occupy the centre of the X-Ray film. Newman introduced twenty-five cc's of contrast medium into Linda's uterus. He did this with sufficient force to drive the fluid through the uterus and out into the fallopian tubes.

Then, everybody scattered. Nurses, orderlies, anaesthetists, and the surgeon sought protection from the X-Rays that were then flying about the place. Some escaped into the scrub room, kicking the swing doors open with their feet. The radiographer removed the x-ray plate from under Linda and replaced it with a fresh one. Everyone returned to their positions. Now, Peter Newman pushed home the plunger and discharged the remaining twenty-five cc of contrast medium into Linda's body. All went and hid behind something solid again, and a second X-Ray was taken. The salpingogram was over. Dr. Newman helped lift Linda's legs down out of the lithotomy position, and she was laid flat. The operating table was lowered by a foot.

Then, quite suddenly and without any warning at all, the ECG monitor went completely flat, dead. The anaesthetist couldn't believe what he was seeing and hearing. A straight, lifeless line moved across the green screen, and the blue flashing bleep had turned into a hideous screeching alarm.

'What the fuck?'

Dr. Walter Malone was speaking to no one in particular. His first thoughts seemed to be that some mechanical failure was causing the monitor to behave as it was.

"Has anyone pulled out a line there?"

Malone shouted this with barely controlled panic in his voice. The entire theatre staff looked around them and lifted their feet to see if anyone had accidentally pulled a lead out of the monitor. No, all the leads were intact. Malone lifted Linda's gown in front and checked the chest leads in the forlorn hope that all three of them had somehow become detached spontaneously. All three leads were properly applied and functioning. One full minute had now passed.

'Oh my God. Oh, sweet suffering Jesus, this cannot be happening. Please make it stop, please make it out to be just a bad dream.' Malone was beginning to panic.

He was feeling sick and finding it hard to function. Through his Librium-soaked brain, it was now slowly dawning on him that the horrible noise from the monitor and flat ECG was no mechanical malfunction. Quickly, he placed the earpieces of his stethoscope in his ears and bent forwards over Linda's chest to see if he could hear a heartbeat. There was none. In terror, he wasted more time, now seeking a pulse on Linda's right wrist. There was none. Two minutes had now elapsed, and Malone's behaviour was no longer rational. He was losing control rapidly.

'Oh, Merciful Christ, this cannot be for real.'

He whipped off the gas mask and noted that Linda's lips had now turned a hideous shade of purple, corpse-like. Small bubbles of saliva formed along her lip margins. This was horrible. As quickly as he had taken it off, he slapped the mask back on again. Two and a half minutes were now wasted.

All thoughts in the theatre were the same. A doctor-induced cardiac arrest in a healthy young woman undergoing an elective investigative procedure, that may or may not have been necessary, was just about the worst possible scenario imaginable. If anything, untoward should happen to this lovely, healthy, and vibrant young woman, then it will simply be a tragedy of incalculable dimensions. Everyone's professional reputation will be indelibly tainted for the rest of their lives. Particularly for the surgeon and the anaesthetist, it may take years to assuage their deep feelings of guilt. Some indeed might never recover. Nobody in this operating theatre was in any doubt whatsoever about the dire seriousness of the situation in which they now found themselves. And with every passing second, it got worse. Time was against Linda Boyle. She was already technically dead.

Newman and Malone both knew only all too well that her chances of survival were reduced by 10% for every one minute that passed, and she remained in cardiac arrest. They could calculate that after ten minutes; she will have passed to a point of no return and any further efforts at resuscitation will be fruitless. However, unfortunately, her situation was much, much worse than that.

What was so profoundly worrying for the doctors right then was not whether Linda Boyle survived or not. The real worry right now was what state her brain would be in if she survives. Now, with her heart stopped and no circulating blood, her brain was being starved of oxygen. Of all the organs in the body, the human brain was least tolerant of oxygen deprivation. Brain death starts to occur somewhere between four and six minutes after a cardiac arrest unless the heart is made to start up again. Already, almost three minutes had elapsed since the calamity, and the anaesthetist had lost his head and had ceased to function properly. Normally, it would be his job to start cardiac resuscitation, but he was still flustering and fumbling and had made no move towards the crash cart.

"What in Christ's name are you at, man?"

Newman made no effort to conceal the terror in his voice. He suddenly realised that he had been watching the inept fumbling of a dysfunctional colleague for far too long already.

Peter Newman and Theatre Nurse Ann Harris, instinctively and in harmony, reacted at the same time. Pushing Dr. Malone to one side, Harris pulled back Linda's surgical gown and immediately started external cardiac massage, throwing her weight down on her straightened outstretched arms with the heel of her left hand placed over Linda's lower sternum, her right hand covering her left. After every five forceful downward thrusts, she paused and looked at the monitor. Nothing. The next five thrusts emitted the sound of breaking ribs, but Harris ignored this as a small price to pay if they could bring Linda back to life. 'If you are not breaking ribs, you are not doing it properly,' she had been taught during her CPR training sessions.

In the meantime, Peter Newman rushed to the defibrillator and crash cart, plugged it into a wall socket, and had it turned on and charging. It took twenty seconds to power up, twenty seconds that none of them had to spare, but there was nothing for it but to wait. Meanwhile, he smeared the paddles with a contact-enhancing gel.

The clock on the theatre wall told them that the four-minute post cardiac arrest mark was fast approaching. They were about to enter the brain damage time zone, and everybody in that small operating theatre was only too painfully aware of the potential medical catastrophe that might be unfolding before their eyes. But Ann Harris's efforts were paying off. On the tenth downward stroke, she noticed a faint blip on the monitor. This was followed by another and then another. There was no sinus rhythm, and clearly, cardiac output would be extremely poor, but at least these ECG awakenings showed that Linda's heart was making some sort of an effort to kick back into action.

Peter Newman now approached the operating table, defibrillator paddles in his hands. The machine emitted a long bleep, indicating that it was fully charged up. He placed one of the steel paddles below Linda's right clavicle, holding it tightly against her chest wall. The second paddle, the doctor pressed over the apex of Linda's heart below her left breast.

"Stand back, please, everybody."

He could hear himself giving this order but had no intention of waiting for everybody to get back. Immediately, he depressed the button on the right paddle and discharged the defibrillator, giving off a 'thud' sound as if someone had kicked a bass drum. Linda's body was thrown upwards into a violent jerk as the electric discharge forced every muscle in her young body to contract, including her heart muscles. Peter Newman looked up at the monitor and was greatly relieved to see that Linda's heart had started up again. It was beating strongly with a regular sinus rhythm.

Newman uttered a silent prayer of thanks, tore off his surgical gown, and left the operating room. With any kind of luck at all now, Linda should escape unharmed. But it was going to be a close call. How long had the heart been stopped? Three or four minutes, was it? Too damn long in any case. What was that prick Malone doing in there, fussing about with the leads and wasting precious seconds? Fuck him anyway. Worrying times lay ahead, very, very worrying times.

CHAPTER 2 - A SESSION OF MUSIC

Sunday morning, and the back room of O'Donoghue's Pub was flying. They had reached lift-off velocity. The craic was ninety. The Mecca for Irish traditional music was up and at it. An ad hoc group of like-minded musicians gathered there to belt it out. Jigs, reels, and hornpipes were played in quick succession. Fiddle, flute, tin whistle, uillean pipes, banjo, guitar, and bodhran gathered and fused with the pipe and cigarette smoke, the clatter of bottles, and the occasional yelp from the enthusiastic audience.

The young woman on the tin whistle stood out among the musicians, for she was tall and handsome and seemed to lead the others into each twist and turn. Her whistle sounds were shrill and round, her notes, liquid, popping, and perfect. Her shoulders moved in time to the fast music as she scanned her fellow musicians with her large brown eyes. Bending forward slightly, she signalled the players into the next reel.

It was mid-summer on a Sunday morning. Seven musicians in all showed up. They didn't play together regularly as a group, but they all knew each other, at least by sight, and each had a similar repertoire that they played by ear. Their music was unrestrained and exciting. An old man got to his feet and danced free style in the middle of the crowded little room. His performance brought hoots of delight from his appreciative audience. A few American tourists took photographs with their flash cameras and could scarcely believe their luck at having stumbled upon something so authentically Irish.

Linda Boyle on the tin whistle and her boyfriend, Tom Gilmartin, on guitar led the session. They now started the other musicians into the final set of reels, ending with a tune called "The Foxhunter". The bodhran player now took charge of the rhythm and battered away. The audience could hear the horse's hooves and the cry of the hounds in full chase. The session was drawing to a close. Licensing laws demanded that Dublin pubs close at 2 pm for four hours on Sunday afternoons. Last orders had been called, and most of the glasses on the table in front of them were empty. The audience gave the players a sustained round of applause and cheers, and the session was over.

Tom Gilmartin packed away his guitar in its case that he had stowed under the table, and Linda Boyle threw her tin whistles in beside it before asking:

"Are you hungry, Tom?"

"Am I what? Jesus, I'd ate a Christian Brother's arse through a hedge."

"Try not to be so charming, love, will you?" Linda said, somewhat offended by his coarseness.

"How about Luigi's across the road?" he asked, ignoring her rebukes.

"Yeah, that's fine by me. Nothing like a bit of Italian soakage after a session of music and a few drinks."

Tom and Linda bade farewell to their fellow musicians and made tentative arrangements to meet them all again next Sunday.

Luigi's, across the street, was quiet. Tom and Linda sat across from each other. The small table was covered with a red and white checkered oilcloth. Between them, a candle shoved into an empty Chianti bottle flickered. They were both absorbed in their big menus. Linda was the first to break the silence:

"That was a good session, I thought, Tom. Some great tunes that I hadn't played in ages."

"Yeah, it was alright, except for that silly long-haired bollock on the bodhran. Whoever said that a bodhran should be played with a penknife might have had the right idea."

"Yeah, his timing wasn't great, was it?"

"Wasn't great! Will you come on, Linda? He had about as much rhythm in him as a billygoat trying to get out of a wooden barrel, for fuck's sake. People like that have some neck sitting in on a session and not asking any of us first. And it's always bodhran players, have you noticed? Jayus, do they come out of the woodwork or what? What are you having?"

Linda had to laugh at Tom's notion of awful rhythm — a goat trying to get out of a barrel. He could be very funny at times, and that was what she loved about him. He was crude but funny. She wondered if her mother would approve of Tom and thought it very unlikely.

The waitress materialised beside their table, impatiently tapping her pen on her notepad, waiting to take their orders.

"The spaghetti bolognese, please," Linda said and smiled sweetly up at her. "With lots of parmesan too if you can. What about you, Tom?"

"And I'll try the ravioli, please, and a half carafe of red, and some garlic bread too, if you will, like a decent woman."

They sat in silence while the waiter brought their cutlery, individually wrapped in red paper napkins, and the half carafe and two glasses.

"So, how's the new job going then, Linda?"

"It's brilliant, so far anyway. I'm loving it. Like you know, they are sending two of us to Parknasilla for two nights next week. Imagine getting paid to stay in a five-star hotel, not bad, is it?"

"No, not at all, good old Bord Fáilte. Nice work if you can get it. Nothing quite like working for a State Body, permanent and pensionable as they say. Hey, what am I supposed to do when you're away? I'm going to Miss, you, you know."

"Never mind, Tom, I'll lend you, my Teddy."

"Jaysus, thanks a bunch, Linda, that sounds like a lot of fun."

Their food arrived, and they both set about breaking off chunks of garlic bread that came hot and wrapped in tinfoil. They used these to scoop up their pasta and both ate in silence and with gusto. Linda paused and observed her boyfriend across the table from her. She wondered if she could trust him. Surely, he had noticed anyway, but if he had, how come he had never said anything?

She thought, 'What the hell?' Drawing in a quick breath, she ran her well-manicured index finger lightly across her upper lip and then up to her right earlobe, saying,

"Do you see this, Tom?"

"Do I see what?"

"This, Tom. Don't be so nice all the time. I'd prefer a bit of honesty. Surely you must have noticed these hairs along here!"

Tom, putting down his knife and fork, leaned across the table to see what Linda was on about.

"Jaysus, Linda. I never noticed – seriously though. What is the problem?"

"Well, thanks Tom, but you must be blind or else you're just trying to be nice again. But the last time I looked, I had fine hairs on my upper lip and on the side of my face, all of which I find a tad embarrassing."

"Oh, I don't know, Linda; I mean, it's hardly a big deal."

"Well, it may not be for you, but it's my face for Christ's sakes. I was wondering if I should see a doctor." Linda now regretted bringing up the subject in the first place. Tom was a good guitarist, but a beautician he certainly was not.

A full minute passed while they ate in silence.

"Alright, Linda, you're asking for my advice, so I'll give it. I'm only an agricultural student, but I would stay well clear of doctors if I were you. You're dark-skinned, so it's natural for you to have slightly more visible facial hair than a light-skinned person. Leave well enough alone would be my advice!"

They finished off their food and called for the bill.

The skies were sunny over Sandymount strand with a few wispy clouds floating high above. A cool sea-to-land breeze chilled the two young women who had donned swimsuits but were now thinking twice about taking to the water. They sat on low boulders, their towels wrapped around their shoulders, chatting casually. Linda Boyle and Catherine Maher were on an extended lunch break from the Bord Fáilte offices ten minutes away.

"Linda, are you going in for a swim or what are you doing?" "Ah, feck it, Catherine, it's too cold, we must be mad. They look frozen out there." Linda turned her gaze seawards.

"On the Mediterranean, you get a suntan; in Ireland, you get goose pimples."

"Still, it's nice to get out of that office."

They fell silent for a while. A woman passed by, dragging a toddler by the arm. The child was crying quietly, clearly not enjoying his day at the seaside. Looking after them, Linda said:

"You know something, Catherine? Getting married and having kids may not be all it's cracked up to be. I mean, just look at that woman and her crying kid. They're not exactly the picture of happiness now, are they?"

"No, you're right, I suppose. Still, it must have its moments, you know."

"Catherine, would you know anything about this?"

Linda drew her finger along her upper lip just as she did a few days before when having a meal with Tom.

Catherine leaned forward to look at what Linda was on about.

"Yeah, what about it, Linda? That's just a little facial hair – normal for someone with your dark colouring."

"Do you think so? I'm a little peed off with it, I have to say, and Tom was commenting on it too the other day."

"Well, tell him to go and get stuffed. Jesus, men, they can be so insensitive! I'm telling you, Linda, it's just you; it's normal. Leave it be."

"It's nice of you to say so, Catherine, but I was wondering if I should see a doctor about it."

"Doctor, my arse, Linda. Just use a hair remover. It would be a lot cheaper for one thing."

Catherine looked out to sea, shielding her eyes with both hands, before going on.

"It's up to you, girl, but if it were on my face, I wouldn't bother with any doctors, and that's for certain. They'd just want to do tests and mess you about. Relax, you're grand."

Linda looked across at her friend wrapped in her bath towel and wondered to herself.

"Yeah, maybe you're right."

CHAPTER 3 – VISITING DOCTORS

He listened to the wind throw drizzle against the window of his surgery, the sound of a distant sea. At age 62, Dr. Martin Quinn feels he's getting too old for this racket. General practice is a young man's game. It's hard to keep smiling all the time, and the patients know too much these days. God be with the good old days when they would just do what they were told without all those stupid questions.

The practice had the smell and look of being run down, of being, like the good doctor himself, past its best.

Quinn was a big, unhealthy man and a bad advertisement for his trade. He was obese, tired, and slightly hung-over. Castle Golf Club's annual Christmas outing last night went on for far too long. Those stupid, long, and boring speeches; some people never seem to know when to shut up and sit down. And those last few dodgy Ports? They were surely his undoing.

The second last for the day, thank God – I am bushed. I need a stiff one to see off this hangover. Here she is --- the worried look on her face.

"Ah, Linda, how nice to see you! Please take a seat. What can I do for you this evening?"

Dr. Quinn had automatically slipped into his all sweetness and charm mode. The 'nice to see you' bit was not actually true. He would far sooner be going home right now to watch the new detective series, Colombo, starting on RTE at 8:00 pm. Colombo would have to wait. With two more patients still to be seen, it could be after 9:00 pm before he would be sipping a Jameson whiskey with no ice in front of a log fire at home with Maura. Quinn had a bit of an issue with the demon drink. Tiredness and half a bottle of whiskey at the end of the day sent him off to bed every night half-pissed. And that is why he never wanted to retire. The work kept him half-right.

Closing the door quietly behind her, Linda Boyle crossed the small, untidy surgery and took the seat indicated to her by the doctor. She smelled the medical smells – a mixture of Isopropyl Alcohol, Hibitane, and the doctor's musty aftershave. She noted his roll-top desk was strewn with samples and tablets. These are blood pressure tablets, non-steroidal anti-inflammatories, cough bottles, antacids, sleeping tablets, antidepressants, anxiolytics, beta-blockers, diuretics, tonics, and the medication left on her bedside locker after Mrs. Hannon died suddenly two years ago. Out from this, a small bare island towards the front of the desk is skilfully maintained, whereon to write a note or a prescription.

The chair that Linda occupied was to the left of his old Edwardian roll-top desk, over which the doctor now peered at her, reading glasses perched on the end of his chubby nose. She was embarrassed at being there in the first place. She was never one for going to doctors and would only avail of their services as a last resort. But what made this even more discomforting was the embarrassing nature of her complaint. Should she have come here at all? Perhaps she should leave now and forget about the whole thing. Just offer some apology or other and walk out of this place.

With these thoughts racing through her mind, Linda observed the doctor fidgeting with her family's medical records. Linda's mother, Mary, was a great believer in Dr. Martin Quinn. She said he was an excellent diagnostician, full of sound medical advice and good judgement. Another thing Mary appreciated about Dr. Quinn was that he wasn't always pushing pills and medications. Some doctors were too quick to prescribe antibiotics and tranquilizers when a bit of listening and common-sense advice might be more appropriate.

Linda relaxed a bit. Growing up, she was always considered tall for her age. She stood a good head, and in some cases, head, and shoulders, above most of her colleagues at the Irish Tourist Board Office on Baggot Street. Her hair was long, straight, and strong, combed back into a ponytail held by a purple elastic tie. Her face was oval and angular with high cheekbones and a full mouth. She might be described as handsome rather than pretty. 'Beautiful' wouldn't quite fit. She waited for the doctor to finish with the chart. He finally looked up and asked:

"How's your mom?"

"Fine, she's fine."

"What can I do for you?" He inquired.

Taking a deep breath, Linda began:

"Dr. Quinn, I have two complaints, and I'm not sure if they're connected."

"That's alright, I might know."

"It's a bit embarrassing, to be honest."

Linda paused, expecting the doctor to reassure her. Instead, he simply looked at her, waiting for her to continue. She realized he was eager to finish up. She sat cross-legged, left over right. The toe of her left patent leather high-heeled shoe pointed at the doctor's desk. Her black dress, as short as fashion dictated, revealed a lot of knees.

"The first problem is my irregular menstrual periods. They're patchy and sometimes absent for up to four months. The second problem is this."

Linda pointed to the space between the end of her nose and her upper lip, running her slim finger along the full length of her mouth. The doctor moved his head in to have a closer look. The light in the surgery was poor, but even at that, he could easily see what Linda was concerned about. In fact, he had noticed it while she walked across the room and before seating herself. The area over her upper lip and extending out over the sides of her mouth was covered in fine downy black hairs. In this poor light, it was but a dull shadow. Linda, in fact, had a light moustache. These fine hairs also extended down from her earlobes along her jawline, and she pointed this out to her GP as well.

Now, Dr. Quinn went straight into his 'differential diagnosis' mode. This is the mental exercise that doctors go through when presented with symptoms or complaints. Could these indicate this condition or that malfunction, or that disease? Which was the more likely, and what more do we need to know in order to make a firm diagnosis? Without a diagnosis, there can be no treatment and no resolution other than a spontaneous remission, something that is always possible. Clever doctors will often take credit for a spontaneous remission.

First of all, Quinn needed more details about how long these complaints had been there, were they getting any better, or were they getting worse. He quizzed his patient along these lines. Had she taken anything for the painful periods and, if so, did this make any difference or bring some relief?

He asked her if sexual intercourse hurt, a question that Linda found gratuitously invasive and wondered if the doctor got his jollies from this kind of thing. She answered that she did not have sexual intercourse and therefore she could not really answer the question. He noted her blush while answering.

However, there was something nagging at the back of the doctor's mind. Linda herself suggested that her two different complaints of painful and irregular periods and facial hair growth might have a common link. Had she not made that suggestion, it was likely that the doctor would have been more inclined to deal with both of these things as separate entities. He probably would have treated Linda's dysmenorrhoea with the birth control pill, and her hirsutism might have been dealt with cosmetically and separately, if at all.

"We know of a condition," the doctor explained to the young woman, "but it is an extremely rare one, and it's called hyperandrogenism."

Dr. Quinn scrunched up his brow and closed his eyes tight in a masterful effort to recall didactic lectures from his medical school days thirty years earlier. The word 'arrhenoblastoma' came into his head as if out of the blue. This medical condition was, in effect, the over-production in a female of male hormone, and it just might explain symptoms of loss of regular periods and facial hair growth occurring concomitantly. Another possibility was polycystic ovarian disease. Both were a long shot, and the doctor was tired and somewhat out of his depth diagnostically speaking. It might be time to kick for touch and end the consultation -- it is getting late. Dr. Quinn had already decided to refer his young patient to a Consultant Gynaecologist.

"Linda, sorry, but I am a bit out of my depth here," he confessed, continuing.

"This is a rare situation where tiny benign tumours form beside your ovaries, produce small amounts of male hormone, and this just might be the underlying cause of your erratic menstrual periods and facial hair growth. It is a long shot, but still, it might be a good idea if we referred you to a specialist to have a second opinion."

The doctor now sat back, folded his arms over his more than ample stomach, and awaited his patient's response. The drizzle on the window behind him had changed to a more persistent rain. It was driven by city wind and went pitter-patter.

Linda looked at him and wondered. She does not like the sound of what she has just heard one little bit. She came in here twenty minutes ago fully expecting that her GP would be able to give her some medication to regulate her periods and reduce the facial hair growth. Now here he was suggesting that she visit another doctor, only this time a gynaecologist. How was she to explain this to her mother at home? She had no clear idea of what gynaecologists did for a living, but whatever it was, it sounded nasty, unpleasant, and invasive. She would prefer not to have to go through with any of this.

"Sorry, Dr. Quinn, but is this necessary? I mean, are there not some tablets or something that I could take first?"
"No, Linda, we need a diagnosis first. It's a principle in medicine, you see, diagnosis first and treatment second."

Dr. Quinn was doing his best, though not actually succeeding, to hide his irritation. His mouth went stiff and narky. Patients these days have far too much say in how they are treated. God be with the good old days when they did what they were told to do without all these damn questions. He can forget about Colombo now; he will be lucky if he gets home in time for the nine o'clock news on RTE. It was time to turn up the heat on young mini skirt here. The rain battering on the window had suddenly stopped; the surgery was quiet except for the tap-tapping on a typewriter out at the reception desk. Anne was typing up insurance reports dictated by the doctor earlier that day.

"All it takes is a procedure done under general anaesthetic called a hysterosalpingogram."

Again, the arms were folded over the ample belly. The doctor sat back and waited. The patient was now baited and trapped. She had nowhere to go and no one to turn to.

Linda Boyle suspects that there might be some kind of game going on there, but it is a game that she cannot quite fathom. On the one hand, her GP, Martin Quinn, sitting at his roll-top desk and peering at her over his reading glasses, seems not to have a clue as to what is the matter with her. He seems to have no explanation for her hairy face or for her erratic and painful periods. He mentioned in the vaguest possible terms something to do with male hormone and 'hyperandrogenism' and then went on to mumble something about a remote possibility of her having small benign tumours near her ovaries that could turn nasty, whatever that was supposed to mean.

Could he be manipulating her? What was that he said about the small tumours, that probably do not even exist, turning nasty? This, Linda thought to herself, was putting the ball right back in her court and placing her in a no-win situation. She was damned if she did, and she was damned if she didn't.

And why did she have this distinct feeling that she was being fobbed off by this middle-aged medic? Could the real reason for his wishing to refer her to a colleague be his unwillingness to take on the responsibility for her care himself? Or maybe it had something to do with his wanting to show his gynaecological colleague how clever he, the mere GP, was being in crafting a single proposition for otherwise unrelated symptoms?

While she was thinking over these disturbing thoughts, her doctor was already bent over a sheet of his headed notepaper, with a pharmaceutical industry-donated expensive ballpoint pen in hand.

He scrawled:
Re: Linda Boyle. (22.)
16 Ashgrove Lane,
Rathfarnham, Dublin 14.
Dec 14th, 1973.
Dear Peter,

This young lady is suffering from facial hirsutism and prolonged periods of amenorrhoea/dysmenorrhoea over the last two years or so. She is otherwise in good health and not on any medications. I am slightly worried about the possibility of an arrhenoblastoma lurking somewhere and wonder if she should have some more investigations. Her medical and surgical history are unremarkable. Physical examination is NAD. Thank you for seeing her and for your valued opinion.

Kindest personal regards,
Martin Quinn MD

He handed the note in a sealed white envelope to Linda. He stood up on heavy legs. He wanted to end this consultation. He had had enough for one day. He shook Linda's hand. Both hands were warm.

"Linda, I know by looking at you that you are none too impressed with what you have just heard, and you are disappointed that I could not give you some tablets and make you all better."

"Yes, I am sort of," Linda said.

"But it's a bit more complicated than that. It is not like you just have a sore throat or something. This is different and frankly a bit worrying, and I believe it needs to be taken a bit further."

More vague threats and innuendo, Linda thought to herself.

"I'll tell you what."

Dr. Quinn summed up cheerfully, putting any animosity aside for the moment.

"Why don't you just go home for now and think things over for a few days? Have a chat with that sensible mother of yours and see how she feels about it -- it's just a simple matter of having a salpingogram."

"But this is not a simple matter for me, Dr. Quinn."

"I'm not saying it's simple in that sense." Jesus, will this young lady ever give over? Quinn is beginning to lose it again.

"Simple or not, it needs doing. We need to rule out cancer. Take this note home with you. Dr. Newman's phone number and address are on the front of the envelope here. When you have had a good think about things and have decided on the wisdom of my advice, then give his secretary a call and make your own arrangements."

Now there, he said it at last; the dreaded word was out, Linda thought to herself, the ultimate threat, the thing that everyone dreaded. CANCER. God Almighty, let me out of here. She managed a small smile for the doctor and took her leave.

"Give that mother of yours my best regards, will you!"

The doctor shouted after the retreating young woman in a black mini-skirt and patent leather black high-heel shoes. She promised to do just that.

Number 66 Merrion Square, Dublin 2, like most of the other Georgian houses on that side of the square, presented a formidable front door with an overhead fanlight and ornate side windows. The door was freshly painted a deep glossy black and was framed on each side by freestanding Corinthian columns of yellow-gold Portland Stone. Classically early nineteenth century, this house, like the others around here, would have originally been home to some wealthy merchant or professional who, with their many servants, would have occupied it in its entirety from the large basement below street level up through three stories above. Today, inside, it has been fragmented and broken up into separate offices for medical consultants, orthodontists, clinical psychologists, orthopaedic surgeons, and like-minded serious professionals. This was Dublin's answer to Harley Street in London.

A bitter December wind blew across Merrion Square from the northeast. Linda Boyle moved from one foot to the other on the granite steps outside number 66 in a futile attempt to get herself warmed up. She had just pressed bell number 4 on the central panel of the heavy door, the bell beside the brass strip that declared DR. Peter Newman MD FRCS FRCOG.

Her decision to take her GP's advice and to follow up on her embarrassing symptoms was not as difficult as one to make as she first had thought it might be. When she got home from her consultation with Dr. Quinn at first, she kept her own counsel and divulged as little as she could get away with to her enquiring mother. All she told her in the beginning was that the GP was not particularly helpful and tried to leave it at that. But Mary Boyle was having none of this. She knew all her three grown-up children only too well, and she knew Linda, her second youngest, the best. She was hiding something, and of that, Mary had no doubt whatsoever.

Mary Boyle needed to know. "Come on now, Linda, spit it out. I know Martin Quinn would not just leave things up in the air like that. Tell me what he really said to you?"

In the end, Linda knew in her heart of hearts that, no matter how hard she tried, her mother would eventually whittle it out of her what Dr. Quinn had actually said. She may as well tell her mother the whole truth now rather than later and have to put up with the constant questioning and nagging.

Next morning, after a light breakfast of tea, toast, and freshly squeezed grapefruit juice, Mary was still looking inquisitively at her daughter sitting across the pine kitchen table from her. She was far from happy with Linda's account of her recent visit to Dr. Quinn. For her part too, Linda was getting mightily teed off with the tension that this situation was causing. She decided there and then that it was time to let her mother in on the details of her recent visit to the GP. No mileage was left in holding back any further.

Heaving a mighty sigh, she said, "He told me that both my problems might have a common cause, that the facial hair thing and the erratic periods might be caused by the same thing. He spoke of the possibility of a small and rare tumour beside or on my ovaries and that the only way to find out if this was there or not was to have a special X-Ray thingy using a dye while I am under general anaesthetic. He has given me a letter for a specialist named Peter Newman in Merrion Square who can arrange for me to have this procedure done in St. Malachi's Hospital."

At this stage, Linda decided not to say anything about hyperandrogenism and, of course, she would not dream of mentioning the dreaded C word, knowing how easily her mother spooked.

"Ah, Peter Newman did you say? He is kind of half-related to us, you know. I bet you did not know that. Isn't it a small world now all the same?"

"Oh yes, how is he related?" Linda asked disinterestedly.

"His wife Sheila is a second cousin of your father's. Isn't that a good one for you now? Ah well, keep it in the family I always say. And did you make the appointment to see him yet?"

"No, I did not, and I'm not sure that I want to. I don't want to go rushing into this thing, need more time to think it over."

"That's fair enough I suppose, dear. But still -."

"Something about the way that Dr. Quinn was looking at me, something about his body language that did not seem quite right. At one point he used the words 'remote possibility'. He said that there was a remote possibility that these tiny tumours existed and were causing my problems."

"Still, Linda, remote possibilities have a nasty habit of becoming realities, you know," Mary said while tossing back the last of her grapefruit juice.

Linda looked across at her mother and thinks it is alright for her and said, "Yes, but it occurred to me that having to undergo a general anaesthetic and have this dye put up inside me was an awful lot to have to endure just to rule out something that was a 'remote possibility'."

Mother and daughter sat in silence for a while, both deep in thought.

Linda broke the silence:

"I got the impression that there was something else going on, that there was more to it than I having to have this procedure carried out for sound medical reasons."

"Like what, dear?" Mary looked confused.

"Well, for starters, I wondered if Dr. Quinn was just trying to cover his arse for some kind of medico-legal reason. Alternatively, was he trying to impress Dr. Newman with his brilliance in knowing about these rare tumours. Do you know what I mean, Mum? You never know with these doctors."

Mary observed her daughter across the kitchen table from her and poured herself a second cup of tea to help wash down her blood pressure pills. Yes, she did. She knew exactly what her daughter meant, and she fully supported her deep scepticism about the medical profession and some of the antics that they are capable of.

That on the one hand, but on the other, Mary reminded herself, Martin Quinn had always been a doctor of sound judgement and if it was his view that Linda should have this investigation then it might be best to go ahead.

"I suppose love, the best thing to do would be to go along to old Newman anyway and see what he has to say for himself. Take it a step at a time like that. What do you think?"

"Yeah, I suppose you're right."

"Honestly love; I don't know what to say. Another GP opinion is a thought, but I would hate you to have to go that route in case Martin found out."

"Yes, can I help you please?"

The crackly voice with the refined Foxrock accent seemed to come from deep within the bowels of number 66 Merrion Square.

"Hi, this is Linda Boyle here. I have an appointment with Dr. Newman for two thirty."

The Yale latch made a long buzzing sound.

"Push the door please and come up the first two flights of stairs."

Linda let herself in to a large and empty entrance hall with diamond-shaped black and white floor tiles. She climbed the two flights of stairs to suite number 4 and handed the receptionist her letter of referral.

"Take a seat dear. Dr. Newman will see you in a few minutes." The Foxrock accent grated on Linda's nerves. Were not things bad enough already? She thought to herself miserably.

Dr. Peter Newman was at the height of his profession. Aged fifty-two, he held the appointment of visiting consultant Obstetrician Gynaecologist to St Malachi's General Hospital just north of the river Liffey in central Dublin. He was ex-Master of the nearby Rotunda Lying in Hospital, one of the oldest and most prestigious maternity hospitals in the world. Here he now held the post of visiting consultant Obstetrician and Gynaecologist; he was Emeritus Professor of Obstetrics and Gynaecology at the Royal College of Surgeons in Dublin where, twice a week, he delivered lectures to fifth- and sixth-year medical students. Currently, he was also President of the Irish College of Obstetrics and Gynaecology.

She noticed his impressive array of framed degrees on the wall behind his desk as she entered his plush consulting room. Newman stood up immediately, walked around his enormous reproduction mahogany partner's desk lined with brown leatherette and gold trim and with brass escutcheons.

He took Linda warmly by the hand and bade her take a seat. She thought she caught a faint suggestion of cologne from him. Linda observed him carefully. She sensed an uneasy charm about him, a strange mixture of charisma and cuteness.

A tall and gaunt, bespectacled man, Newman spoke through his nose in what Linda might describe as a Clongowes Wood College accent. Like so many Dublin medical consultants, she knew that Newman was likely to have spent his earlier years in that boarding school in County Kildare run by the Jesuits. Graduates of this institution spoke with a Jesuitical and ever-so-slightly West-Brit accent. Speaking in this practised way tended to convey authority, or so some thought. In order to get people to do as you advised, authority was essential.

She noticed that he dressed impeccably. He made an impressive trim cut figure, she thought, in his three-piece pinstriped dark blue suit, dark blue tie bearing the gold crest of the Royal College of Surgeons where he lectured twice a week during term. Impressive too, she thought, was his matching pinstriped waistcoat, completed by a gold watch-chain running straight across. A small gold fob, a droplet, dangled in the centre line and immediately caught Linda's eye.

Dr. Quinn's letter lay before him on the desk. This he studied for a few minutes, lifting his gold-rimmed glasses for the short-sighted off his nose the better to decipher the GP's scrawl. Outside at reception, the phone purred quietly from time to time. Through the large Georgian windows, Linda could hear the traffic below. A boy selling papers shouted 'Herald or Press' on top of his voice, a car horn occasionally blared out and interrupted the near silence. Given the time of year, the evening light outside was still good.

When Dr. Newman finally finished studying the GP's letter of referral, he put it to one side, replaced his glasses on his nose, placed his elbows on the desk, and leaned across to address his patient. It was only then that Linda noticed he was wearing gold Royal College of Surgeons cufflinks.

Clearing his throat and in his best cultivated, ever-so-slightly English accent, Dr. Newman addressed his patient:

"Linda, I'm sure you know why Dr. Quinn thought it necessary that he should have a second opinion ah. He is concerned about a possible association between your symptoms of facial hair and erratic menstrual periods and the possible presence of a small tumour attached to the ovary called an Arrhenoblastoma. In my view ah, there is some justification for that concern ah. What do you think?"

She feels her heart sink to the bottom of her stomach, and she feels nauseated. Here we go again, she thinks to herself. Of course, he would say that, wouldn't he? I mean to say he is hardly going to say that the GP was an arsehole to refer her there in the first place, now, is he? That is not how the system works. Doctors support each other and try hard not to differ, at least not in front of their patients. They might fight like cats and dogs in the background, but to the great unwashed, they like to present a united front.

Then there were the questions of the fees that Dr. Newman will receive from Linda's private insurers if he goes ahead with the procedure. Might that not have some bearing on his willingness to concur with the referring doctors' concerns? Linda thinks these thoughts miserably to herself in silence. Perhaps it is time to start raising some objections, time to regain some autonomy back from this medical dandy here with his gold watch chain and cufflinks.

"Yes, Dr. Newman, but Dr. Quinn also spoke about a 'remote possibility.' He said, on more than one occasion, that the chances of my actually having this rare tumour were at best a remote possibility----"

Newman was now fidgety and clearly not enjoying this. But Linda pressed ahead: Feck him anyway, she thinks to herself.

"Do you know what I mean, Dr. Newman? Pushing dye into my body under general anaesthetic seems like a radical kind of thing to do for a 'remote possibility,' but then of course you are the expert."

Newman wonders if there may have been a hint of sarcasm in that last bit. For a full twenty seconds, he observes this tall smart, well-dressed, and handsome young woman seated across from him on this December evening. By Christ, he thinks to himself, this young lady is no pushover, is she? It might be time to turn up the pressure a bit.

"You are absolutely right in raising that question, ah," he said with obvious condescension.

"Arrhenoblastoma are as rare as rocking horse droppings and the possibility of you having one are indeed, as you say, remote and -------"

"Then could we not just postpone things for a while?" Linda interrupted the consultant in full fright.

Clearly now he is irritated, not used to being interrupted. He held his dainty hand up as if to impart a papal blessing.

"Sorry now, just a second, Miss, Boyle. I'm trying to help you here. You do have symptoms and this, to some extent anyway, ups your chances and puts you into a category of your own, ah."

Another pause now as the consultant gave his patient a chance to respond. Linda stayed silent.

"And I would go further and say this, ah."
Dr. Newman straightened himself up in his fancy chair as if to better face the challenge before him.

"If you were my wife or my sister, I would be advising her to go ahead with the hysterosalpingogram just as I am now advising you. Because the point about it is this, ah: The only arrhenoblastoma that will ever kill you is the one that is not diagnosed and removed in time. When present it is a benign time bomb. It can sit there for decades, but if it should ever start to spread, then that is it, ah. Curtains, lights out."

Ah yes, Linda thinks to herself, here we go again. The veiled threat, the innuendo.

"Do you mind if I just ask you something, Dr. Newman?" Linda tries another tack.

"No, ask me anything you like, ah."

"How many arrhenoblastoma have you seen yourself over the years?"

Dr. Newman suddenly feels wrong-footed. However, he must not show his irritation. Let's keep this professional, shall we? Let us keep smiling. One should never let one's guard down, now, should one?

"Your question, Miss, Boyle, is a fair and reasonable one, ah, and I will try to answer it as fairly and reasonably as I can, ah."

Linda finds Newman's condescending attitudes just another added annoyance, that and his half-arsed 'hot potato in the mouth' Clongownian accent was enough to make you sick even if you were fine before the consultation.

"The overall incidence of ovarian cancer is roughly one in sixty, ah," Dr. Newman pressed ahead. This consultation is taking far too long. Two more patients were now in the waiting room outside, one of them coughing.

"One in every sixty adult women will get ovarian cancer at some stage during their lives, ah. It is a silent cancer with no symptoms and that is the problem you see. By the time it is diagnosed it is usually too late and it will have metastasized widely, it will have spread all over the place, ah. Thus, more than half the women diagnosed with ovarian cancer will be dead in less than five years. Pretty scary stuff, doesn't you agree, ah?"

Linda chose to ignore Newman's silly question.

"But now, to get back to your specific question, about the incidence of arrhenoblastoma, the male hormone-secreting ovarian tumour? This is an extremely rare bird, it is a blue cockatoo, ha, I would say. As an educated guess, arrhenoblastoma would represent less than half of one percent of all ovarian tumours."

So, there it was at last out in the open. Professor Peter Newman had never seen an arrhenoblastoma in his long distinguished surgical career. The tumour was exceptionally rare with less than half of one percent of one in sixty women contracting it. Could part of Newman's motivation then, in wanting to carry out a hysterosalpingogram on Linda, be his ambition, his drive, and his arrogance? If he were to discover this rarity, this academic jewel lying deep within her pelvis, would he not write it up in the medical journals? Of course, he would. Would he not then advance his career? Was Linda, therefore, at least to some extent, to be used as grist to Newman's personal academic mill?

How was she ever to know? Linda felt defeated. What was the point in any further argument with this pillar of academia? And his talk of giving the same advice to his wife or sister may have been potent and convincing to some but it did not altogether fool Linda. Something a tad phony suggested itself where a consultant hypothetically personalizing an issue to lend weight to his argument. She had heard that kind of old thing before out of doctors.

Linda left the consultation feeling that Dr. Newman may have been sincere and honest but also, he just might have been wrong. His motivations and intentions were at best dubious and spurious. She was to think about it and discuss it with her family over Christmas. She was to get back to Dr. Newman's secretary in the New Year if she decided to go ahead with the salpingogram. And it was Dr. Newman's strong advice that that should be her decision but in the last analysis, it was up to herself.

A cold dampness was in the air outside number 66 Merrion Square; the late December evening was closing in fast.

Angelic voices of carol-singers drifted across the four acres of landscaped gardens that comprise the centre of this fabulous Georgian streetscape. Linda stopped to listen to these gentle distant vocal harmonies and was suddenly filled with an overwhelming sadness. Tears welled up in her lovely eyes and flowed easily down her cheeks. Professor Peter Newman had unnerved her. How was she to enjoy this Christmas with his proposed plans for her hanging over her head?

Hark the herald angels sing, glory to the newborn king.

Linda's older brother, David, is a final-year medical student at University College Dublin. Broad-shouldered and standing at six feet three in height, David played out-half for UCD's first rugby side. He was considered by his peers to be quite bright academically and recently won a gold medal in surgery. Gold medals in surgery were not given out that easily. Recipients were expected to choose one of the surgical disciplines on graduating from medical school. David already had his eye on Obstetrics and Gynaecology as the specialty that he would most like to pursue. They were, as it so happened, subjects that he was also particularly well-versed in as an undergraduate.

"David, have you ever heard of an arrhenoblastoma?" Linda wanted to know. She had been sitting at the kitchen table, picking the golden-brown skin off the cold turkey. It was quite delicious. The turkey had been a proper one, a sixteen-pound free-ranging bronze hen bought directly from a farmer in Kildare. David sat across from Linda and sipped on a glass of vintage port. Mother's milk, he thought to himself. This is what Christmas is all about.

"Yes, I think it is a rare type of ovarian tumour, and I think it is associated with the overproduction of androgens or male hormones. Why do you ask?"

"Because our GP, Martin Quinn, thought that there was a remote possibility of my having one and sent me to see this Professor Newman fellow. He, in turn, thinks that I should have a special X-Ray called a hysterosalpingogram or something like that."

David eyed his younger sister over the rim of his port glass before tossing the last of it back. She continued her turkey picking nonchalantly. He did not like what she had just so innocently told him. He did not like the sound of it one little bit. Like everyone else in the family, he loved Linda with a strong protective brotherly love. He had never heard of this Newman fellow – he must be from Surgeons or Trinity or one of those inferior medical schools. His gut feeling was that a salpingogram was far too invasive a procedure to be undertaken for far too little potential reward.

But he was not yet a doctor, and this, after all, was his lovely sister seeking his opinion. This is Indian Territory. What if he should try to dissuade her from proceeding, and it later turned out that she did, in fact, have an arrhenoblastoma, or for that matter, polycystic disease, or a more common ovarian cancer? Could he live with that? And in any case, should he, a medical undergraduate, be interfering in his senior colleague's medical decisions about his sister? In the end, David decided that he had no choice other than to kick for touch and play it safe.

A long period of silence passed between brother and sister. "I don't know what to say, Linda. You know, Jesus ----. At the end of the day, it has to be your decision. But remember that no operative procedure, however minor they may tell you it is, is ever totally risk-free. And in any case, why are they not doing hormonal assays first as a screening test?"

"Gee, David, thanks a bunch."

After this brief exchange with her brother, Linda decided not to further burden any other members of her family with her medical dilemmas. It was not fair on them, and in any case, it was Christmas and the season to be jolly. And besides, discussing her medical problems with others was a fruitless exercise because, as everyone said, at the end of the day, it was up to herself to decide the various merits and demerits of going ahead with the procedure or not.

"Hello, is that Dr. Newman's office?"

"Oh, yeah, hi. This is Linda Boyle here. You might not remember me, but I was in there to see Dr. Newman a week before Christmas?"

"Yeah, yeah, that's right, that's me. Listen, I have decided to go ahead with that tubal X-Ray thingy."

"Yeah, whatever, will you let Dr. Newman know, please?"

"Ok, that's fine. I will be listening out for you so. Thanks. Bye, bye, bye."

No going back now, she thought to herself, putting down the phone. The die is cast.

CHAPTER 4 - TOO PAINFUL FOR WORDS

Three doctors in the small Recovery Room now crowded around Linda Boyle. Consultant anaesthetist Dr. Walter Malone, Obstetrician Gynaecologist Dr. Peter Newman, and consultant cardiologist Dr. Michael Gaffney all wore worried faces. A deep sense of foreboding pervaded the space. Also in attendance at this critical time were Recovery Nurse Mary Gilles and Theatre Sister Mary McGonagall. These two members of the nursing staff should have otherwise been on their lunch break. But things were far too critical at this moment for anyone to even think of eating or being elsewhere. And besides, they were deeply upset by recent events inside the theatre and worried about the final outcome of those events.

The room was filled with tension, and the popping, sucking noise of the ventilator pumping air and oxygen in and out of Linda's lungs at a preset rate of ten inhalations per minute.

Since being wheeled out of the theatre a few minutes earlier, the anaesthetic gases had been withdrawn, and only oxygen was now being administered through the facemask at a high flow rate of eight litres per minute. A terrible but unspoken awareness filled the air. These professionals were only too painfully aware that, due to the prolonged period of cardiac arrest, the chances of at least some brain damages were high. The high rate of oxygen now being administered by Walter Malone was an attempt to overcome the effects of the possible brain damage by recent oxygen starvation. Linda remained hooked up to the ECG monitor and the Manley Ventilator. In addition, an IV drip had been established immediately after the cardiac arrest to provide a fast line of entry for any emergency medications that might be called for.

Cardiologist Michael Gaffney bent low over Linda's chest and listened to her heart with his high-tech stethoscope, moving the bell below her left breast. After a while, he straightened up and, looking at the monitor, gave his assessment:

"For what it's worth, lads, I can tell you her heart is fine anyway. The tracing is perfect, and all sounds are normal."

"Have you any opinion as to why she arrested, ah Michael?" Newman wanted to know.

"Not really, Peter, no. It could have been an egocentric reaction to the anaesthetics, or it could have been the procedure itself -- more likely the procedure itself, the contrast media hitting the diaphragm – vagal inhibition, you know yourselves."

Newman frowned and shook his head slowly. This was exactly what he did not want to hear.

"Anyway, lads, look, I'm sorry for your troubles, but there is not much more that I can do for you at this stage." The cardiologist straightened himself up and made to leave.

Newman caught him gently by the elbow and said, "Thanks, Michael. It was good of you to come up so quickly."

"Not a problem, lads. Let me know if I can do more." And with that, the cardiologist was out the door.

According to her chart, the anaesthetic gases at this stage had been withdrawn for over ten minutes. Therefore, by now, she should be showing plenty of signs of coming round from the anaesthetic. She should be opening and closing her eyes a bit, moving, and moaning a bit. After all, she had a rib or two fractured by the nurse during external cardiac message. She must be in pain. But she was not responding to anything.

"Linda, wake up. Can you hear me, Linda? Wake up!"

Walter Malone slapped his patient hard across the face with his open right hand, extreme anxiety in his voice as he urged her to come to. He had used excess force as if to deny the possibility that Linda was slipping from the anaesthetised state into unconsciousness, as if the only reason that she wasn't coming around from the anaesthetic was that she was not being stimulated rigorously enough. This, of course, was stupid thinking or not thinking at all, but then Malone was still not being rational. The Librium clouded his judgement badly.

Now he takes a pencil torch from the breast pocket of his green scrub suit, and, with a shaking left hand, prizes open her right eyelid and directs the tiny bright beam onto Linda's right pupil. Normally, this should cause the pupil to close down quickly, but Malone was not sure if her reaction was normal or not. If there was any constriction of her pupil, it was infinitesimal. More bad news. He moved the light beam on and off from the pupil, but there still seemed to be little movement. Her pupils were becoming fixed.

It was now almost fifteen minutes post-anaesthetics, and there were still no signs of returning consciousness. Linda's status was rapidly changing from that of being an anaesthetized patient to that of being a comatose patient. The hideous realization was slowly dawning on the doctors that the prolonged heart stoppage had obviously brought about a greater assault to Linda's brain than either of them had wanted to anticipate. They were now sailing into uncharted waters where their patient's ultimate destination was unknown, her prognosis utterly unpredictable. Anything from death to a full recovery and any of the numerous possibilities in between were all potential outcomes; it was anyone's guess, and only time would tell. This was a deeply unsatisfactory and worrying situation.

They couldn't take up any more time in the Recovery Room because the next patient for surgery had already been waiting for over an hour, and they were holding up the day's schedule. Linda and her accompanying medical paraphernalia were now wheeled into the awaiting elevator, and Dr. Malone pushed button number five for the Intensive Care Unit on the top floor of the hospital. Meanwhile, with a heavy heart, Peter

Newman went to find a quiet spot from where he could call Mary Boyle.

How was he going to tell a loving mother that her beautiful daughter was in a coma because she had a general anaesthetic? The general anaesthetic was administered to carry out a diagnostic procedure, not a curative or therapeutic one but a diagnostic one. How could he possibly explain how a beautiful and exceptionally talented and bright young woman's life now hung in the balance because of a clinical decision that he had earlier made about her, a clinical decision that now assumed the mantle of very poor judgment indeed?

It was this feature of this appalling tragedy, this utter catastrophe now apparently unfolding before him, that sickened Peter Newman the most; the fact that it happened during a diagnostic procedure that he had so strongly recommended. This feature of events made Newman feel particularly culpable and vulnerable to criticism, censure, or worse, from his peers. He may even face questions from The Medical Council.

He sat at a small side desk in the nurse's station, elbows on the desktop and head bent low into outstretched hands, face covered. Several nurses who were busy around him ignored him and went to and from about their business. Word had now spread around the entire hospital of the disastrous events down in theatre number two this morning.

If it had happened to anyone else other than Newman, some nurses at least might have come up to him and lent him a helping hand by giving him a word of comfort or commiseration. For most doctors and nurses lived by the 'There but for the grace of God go I' philosophy. Delight in a colleague's misfortune was rare indeed in medicine because always it could be your turn next, and everyone understood that.

But in the case of Newman, things were different. With his hot potato in the mouth phoney accent, he was never a man for whom sympathy would come easily. Nor, if the boot were on the other foot, would he be the first to comfort a colleague in a similar situation in which he now found himself.

It was one thing if things went wrong while someone was undergoing a life-saving operation under general anaesthetic. Newman, sitting their head in hands, agonised to himself. If, for example, Ms. Boyle had a cardiac arrest while undergoing an appendectomy, that would be awful of itself, but you could always say afterward that you were trying to save her life; appendicitis is a life-threatening condition. That would make the calamity that little bit more bearable, that little bit more explicable.

But in this case, there was no such comfort however small. No, none whatsoever. Newman tried hard to block these thoughts out of his mind but failed miserably. After all, and there was no good in his trying to deny this: he had talked his young patient into having this elective diagnostic procedure under general anaesthetic? He had told her that the risks were negligible – one in 100,000 was the figure he gave her. A figure he had pulled out of the air, that had no basis in science. She had tried to raise some objections about the risk/benefit ratio, but he had poo-pooed these objections.

To make matters even worse he had threatened her, he used the dreaded C word and backed her into a corner. This was medical bullying of the grossest sort. For her to be able to continue to argue that the procedure might be unnecessary or too risky she would have needed to have been much stronger and older. And now look at what's happened to her. She was now that statistic; she was now that mythical one in 100,000.

----

16 Ashgrove Lane, Rathfarnham, was a cut stone mews of generous proportions and considerable character. It started its life in the mid-nineteenth century as a coach house for the big house on Ashgrove Avenue. The big house had long been cannibalized and carved up into ghastly little bed-sits. Whatever claim it may once have had to Victorian elegance, these were now well and truly lost. The mews, however, retained its quiet appeal and authenticity.

A good fire of coal and beech logs blazed in the generous Wicklow granite fireplace. The coal smoke emitted a slightly tarry smell, but this was easily neutralized by the sweet-smelling logs. Orange flames licked their way enthusiastically towards the chimney opening, and the whole thing did much to dispel the gloom of this damp winter's evening.

It was coming up to half-past two in the afternoon, and Mary Boyle had just finished mixing brown flour with a sprinkle of bran, a teaspoon full of bread-soda, a pinch of salt, a pinch of caster sugar, one ounce of margarine, an egg, a carton of natural yogurt, and some fresh milk into a large earthenware mixing bowl. When ready, she turned the dough out onto the top of the pine kitchen table that had been dusted with white flour, there to knead the mix into submission and shape. She was expecting a phone call at any moment. Linda told her on the phone last evening that she expected to be discharged mid-afternoon.

David, Linda's medical student brother, was stretched out on the sofa next door in the sitting room, watching a repeat of the international rugby match between Ireland and Wales. Ireland was leading by a converted try.

Just as Mary was putting the loaded baking tray into the top oven and closing the Aga door, the phone on the wall started to ring.

"I'll get it!" Mary shouted in the direction of the living room while wiping the excess flour and dough from her hands in a tea towel and making her way toward the noisy phone. She picked up the receiver and put it to her ear.

"Hello?"

At first, there was silence, nothing. Mary thought that she could hear someone breathing on the other end of the line.

"Hello, is that Mrs. Boyle, please?"

"Yes, this is Mary Boyle speaking."

"Ah, yes, ah. This is Peter Newman on this end, consultant gynaecologist at St. Malachi's General. Listen, the news is not so good, I'm afraid, ah."

What was that? Oh my God, what did this man say? Make this just go away. This cannot be happening. Is this someone's idea of a joke? That's all right then. That's it. Make it a joke even if a sick one. Make it whatever you like but just do not allow it to be real.

It was as if Newman had punched her hard in the stomach. Her mouth filled up with sweet saliva, and she was becoming unsteady on her feet. Unsettled, she could fall.

"Is Linda all right?" Mary could hear herself ask.

She was rapidly becoming disembodied. She was now seeing herself standing there beside the wall, speaking into the phone and asking about her daughter. Two Mary Boyles were now in the kitchen. How could she be asking such a question? Why, of course, Linda was fine. Never felt better, in fact. What a silly question to ask!

"Well, ah, that's the point, actually. She is not that well. Do you see, during the procedure, toward the end of it actually, we were just finishing up when Linda had what we call a cardiac arrest, ah. Her heart stopped beating. It took over a minute to get it going again, and that's a long time, ah."

Here Newman told his first lie. Yes, it did take over a minute to get her heart going again; that was true, but that was after Malone had wasted the previous four precious minutes fluttering around. To tell the whole truth, mentioning these four minutes was essential, but Newman was, at least for the moment, withholding this information.

"When we tried to bring Linda around after the procedure," Newman droned on, "she failed to wake up, and now it seems she, ah, has lapsed into a coma."

Newman sounded detached and had about as much compassion and concern in his voice as one might expect from someone reading out the shipping forecast.

'Linda failed to wake up, did she? So, was that her fault then?'

But Mary was losing her ability to absorb the doctor's words and to make sense of them. The blazing fire was no longer confined to its solid housing of the Wicklow granite fireplace; instead, it moved in and out at will. The AGA, which for years had stood solidly anchored to the floor, now seemed to have become mobile and moved a bit to the left and then a good bit to the right.

"Sorry the news is not much better." Dr. Newman continued, "Prognosis is impossible at this stage—prolonged anoxia, oxygen starvation, depravation, brain cortex— complete recovery still a possibility, death a definite possibility, coma, persistent vegetative state, damaged neurotransmitters, circuit board without the wiring—too long in arrest. The longer the coma lasts, the worse the outlook—tissue ischemia, cardiac arrest, defibrillation, and resuscitation."

She was passing in and out of consciousness. She could hear no more. She must support herself on the heavy pine kitchen table. She slumped down onto one of the kitchen chairs drawn up to the table. The legs of the chair screeched against the tiled floor as she fought for equilibrium.

Hearing this, David wandered in from the sitting room to see how things were going. He found his mother seated and slumped across the kitchen table, phone still in her hand. He took the phone gently from her and put it to his ear. She moaned a bit but seemed to come around and to be recovering somewhat.

"Hello, this is David Boyle here. Listen, my mother has taken a bit of a turn while speaking to you. Can you tell me please what's going on?"

David, while expecting some sort of bad news, could not in his wildest imagination or worst possible nightmare have anticipated the response that came to his question.

"Yes, well, my name is Peter Newman, a gynaecologist. I oversee your sister Linda's care here in St. Malachi's Hospital. I am sorry if I upset your poor mother. Is she alright now?"

David glanced down at his mother. By now she was sitting up, holding a white handkerchief to her trembling lips. Stars flickered and moved about in the fire's flames as she looked at them through her tears. A few minutes ago, this dancing winter's fire was a thing of great warmth and comfort. But now it had suddenly turned into something cold and miserable. All joy and comfort had suddenly vanished. Sickness was everywhere and all pervasive. In the space of just a few seconds, Mary Boyle's life had changed utterly and forever. Devastation and utter misery, loss and profound sadness and pain—these horrible things now threatened and bullied her from all sides.

"She's fine now thanks. Can you tell me what the story is please?"

Newman now repeated for David what he had been trying to say to his mother a few minutes earlier. In a monotonous and somewhat disinterested voice, as though he was somehow removing himself from the situation, he told David how the news was grave. He related how Linda had had a cardiac arrest towards the end of the procedure carried out under general anaesthetic.

"I'm afraid that it took a long time for us to manage to get her heart going again. It took the best part of four minutes."

Newman once again retreated into lying and cover-up territory. What he had just said was not the whole truth. They did not resuscitate Linda in four minutes or in anything like four minutes. The fact of the matter was that well over three minutes elapsed before any attempt at resuscitation was commenced, and it was these three minutes that were critical.

"At first, we had hoped that this would not have had too serious consequences for Linda, but when we tried to bring her around from the anaesthetic, she failed to respond and slipped into a coma."

Newman droned along.

"Now, this would seem to indicate that there is at least a chance of some permanent brain damage, but it is too early yet for any meaningful prognosis, and only time will tell. In the meantime, I see little point in idle speculation."

Dr. Newman finished off by advising that the family should come into the hospital at once because the gravity of the situation was such as to make it impossible to predict what might happen next, and of course, there could be no guarantees at this stage either that Linda would even survive.

David replaced the receiver in its holder on the wall and sat down beside his still trembling mother at the large pine kitchen table. He had just heard the most shocking news of his lifetime. His lovely bright young sister, in the prime of her life and in the peak of good health, had just suffered a grave assault at the hands of the medical profession. They had cruelly and unmercifully struck her down for no good reason that David could think of other than for their own self-interests and self-aggrandizement. And just to think that this was the profession that he himself had designs on joining in just a few months' time!

Now it was David's turn to start shaking. How could this have happened? The surgeon was seeking one of the most esoteric gynaecological tumours in the textbooks. What was it called? An arrhenoblastoma? Wasn't that what Linda had asked him about just after Christmas? The chances of her having this as a cause for her facial hirsutism were about one in sixty thousand.

Why then did they risk giving his beautiful young sister a general anaesthetic and putting dye into her abdomen cavity when the chances of reward for this procedure were so low and the risks so relatively high? Was there not another way of diagnosing this androgen-producing tumour by carrying out some simple blood tests to ascertain hormone levels? But surgeons don't like blood tests, do they? No, they prefer cutting and tying and doing and writing up papers on rare tumours.

And now she was critically ill or at least her survival was in some considerable doubt. And what if she does in fact survive? What intellectual capacity will she be left with? What of her quality of life? And all that risk and danger and pain and uncertainty for what? The bastards. Fuck them anyway. If they had just left her alone, she would be fine right now.

And the arrogant sound of that stupid consultant fellow with his skin-deep put-on pretence at remorse and sorrow for what had transpired under his hands. These angry thoughts flew around David Boyle's mind while he sat there numbed and frozen beside his shocked mother as they stared into the blazing fire that no longer warmed them, that no longer cheered them.

The Offices of the Irish Revenue Commissioners are housed on various sites in and around Dublin Castle. Just off Dame Street in Dublin and established in 1204, Dublin Castle is one of the capital city's premier tourist attractions, and not without good reason. It is not a castle in the usual accepted meaning of that word, but it is a complex of buildings set out on one of the earliest sites of the city dating back to Viking times. Here you will find buildings like The Norman Tower dating from 1226 and The Chapel Royal built in 1814. The Offices of the Revenue Commissioners are contained within two buildings of this ancient compound. One is in the refurbished Ship Street Army Barracks dating from 1814. The second is housed in a recent purpose-built modern building.

Commissioner Joseph Boyle's office occupied 600 square feet of the second floor of the Ship Street Barracks, recently refurbished. A small, bald man, he was seated at his large Edwardian desk and was gazing out the window beside him to his right. He was having a mid-afternoon tea break. The room smelled of Yachtsman plug tobacco. Boyle was a pipe smoker who liked to cut his own plug tobacco from a block of pressed tobacco the size of a matchbox. He was well-dressed in a grey tweed jacket, matching charcoal grey slacks, brown handmade shoes from Tutty's of Naas, a white-striped shirt, and a green tweed tie. A folded white handkerchief protruded flamboyantly from his breast pocket.

On his desk were piles of biscuit-coloured folders held together with stout rubber bands, an elaborate EPNS ink holder and pen, three or four official seals, a nest of self-inking rubber stamps, a pipe rack holding three well-used straight plane meerschaum pipes, and two large black telephones. This was the desk of a top-ranking civil servant and a man of some importance in his early fifties.

Boyle let the in-house phone on his desk ring three times before picking it up, annoyed that his thoughts and his tea break had been interrupted. He had been wondering about buying that Hardy fly rod he had admired in Garnet and Keegan's shop window on his way to work this morning. At just £38.00, it looked like a real bargain and besides, his old split-cane rod had lost its springiness and outlived its usefulness. It was high time he treated himself to a new high-tech fly rod.

"Yes?"

This was as much as he could manage to say into the phone without sounding impolite.

"Sir, Ann at reception here. Sorry to disturb you. I have your wife on the other line. Would you like me to put her through?"

Boyle thought to himself that this was most unusual. Not that he ever asked her to or anything. In fact, to the best of his memory, they had never even discussed the matter. So, whatever it was that she wanted now, it must be pretty damn important. And then slowly he remembered Linda was in the hospital today. Some kind of 'women's problem' he understood. Remembering this suddenly, Joseph Boyle broke into a cold sweat, an odd kind of chill travelled down his spine. God do not let this be.

"Yes, Ann, put her through."

He could hear his wife Mary on the other end of the line but only just about. Her voice was weak and wavering, quick and urgent. And then the bombshell fell on his Edwardian desk, and his worst fears came crashing down around him. She had said it twice now. Linda is in a coma, and they must go into the hospital at once to see her. She will double park outside his office in exactly half an hour's time, and will he please be ready to jump in? And then the phone went dead.

Boyle did a quick tidying-up job on his desktop and finished off the end of his tea in one gulp, tossing it back. He selected one straight meerschaum pipe off the rack and pocketed it behind the white hanky in his breast pocket. He stood up and went to the closet to the left of the office door where he took out his hat, scarf, and gloves and donned these quite slowly. His heart was painful and heavy. Could this be really happening? Maybe it was just some kind of a mistake,

Boyle thought to himself hopefully. Linda had never been sick, a day in her life. She was a non-smoker. She had always watched her diet most vigilantly, taken lots of exercise, and generally looked after herself. Last summer she won her club's tennis tournament outright. And now she was in a coma. That sounded crazy. That could not be right.

Downstairs on Dame Street, a watery January evening sunlight struggled to function and was fading fast. People, mostly Christmas Sales shoppers up from the country, hurried by, laden down with their enormous paper shopping bags. They were oblivious to the turmoil, the pain, and stress that were going on inside Joseph Boyle's chest. They could not see it. He looked up and down the busy street for the double-parked blue Audi Coupe. She was late. He moved from foot to foot, trying to stay warm against this cold evening. Clapping his gloved hands together, he made a muffled sound like a pigeon's wing on take-off. Then he spotted the car coming along slowly, and he moved to the curbside. As she pulled in, he opened the passenger's door, jumped in beside her, and slammed the door shut again. All this was done at a rolling stop. They were off again and had merged into the main flow of traffic. Rush hour was still a long way off, and the traffic moved quite freely.

"What do we know?"

Joseph Boyle tried to sound as though his heart was not split in two as they drove across the Liffey via Capel Street Bridge and turned left for the hospital. Over the ten-minute journey, Mary did her best to recall everything that Peter Newman had told her but had to admit that she didn't take in half of it.

"The bottom line is that her heart stopped beating just when they were finishing the investigation, and it took them almost two minutes to get it going again."

"Yes, so what's the problem then?" Joseph was confused.

"The problem, love, would seem to be that her brain was starved of oxygen during those vital two minutes. That's the problem."

"Yes, but hold on, how big a problem can that be? Do you know what I mean?"

"I think he might have also said that she could yet come round and fully recover and that it's a waiting game that we would have to take by the hour."

The traffic was getting heavier; their progress slowed to a standstill. Joseph Boyle was now struck to his very soul as it began to sink in just how serious things really were for his beloved daughter.

"God Almighty, this is terrible."

Mary said nothing about the real possibility that Linda might not make it at all and that she might die. What was the point in over-worrying her husband at this stage?

They easily found car parking space outside St. Malachi's and pulled into the curb. Inside the grey and grim building, the hall porter in the shiny peaked cap and lighted cigarette in hand pointed towards the stairs and, without the tiniest hint of an apology, announced that the lift was out of order. Christmas carols were being played quietly over the public address system. The Intensive Care Unit was on the fifth floor. They tentatively started their climb. Mary wondered if she could in fact make it to the top. At this stage, she was beginning to feel the physical and emotional strain of the last hour or so.

On the landing of the third floor, she was so out of breath that she could go no further and must rest. Sitting on the cold stone steps, she asked her husband Joseph to please go on without her, and that she would follow in a little while. And there she sat, out of breath and feeling utterly dejected and wretched.

The Intensive Care Unit, or ICU, of St. Malachi's General Hospital was a busy place when Joseph Boyle finally reached the fifth floor and entered. That day a much-publicized head-on two-car crash at seventy miles per hour had occurred on the Naas dual carriageway and resulted in four fatalities and three critically injured—two men and a woman. All three were in this ward; two were unconscious and one semi-conscious and moaning. All had internal bleeding, internal organ displacement, and rib, pelvic, and spinal fractures. In addition

85

to these dreadful injuries, the woman had a collapsed lung or pneumothorax. All were on the 'critical' list.

In this ICU also was a fourteen-year-old girl admitted two days ago with meningococcal meningitis and septicaemia. She had been taken to her general practitioner the previous day but had at that time insufficient symptoms to make a diagnosis. She was unconscious and isolated inside an oxygen tent at the far end of the ward. Her parents, dressed in surgical gowns, peered in at her through the plastic covering. They looked sick with worry. The teenager was not expected to last another night. But where there was life there was hope, or so they had been told.

Linda's bed had been wheeled into a bay opposite the door as one entered this Intensive Care Unit. Behind her bed was a panel of facilities, including electrical sockets, a nurse call system, an angle-poise light, and an oxygen outlet. On the left-hand side of her bed, there was a drip stand holding two inverted-litre bottles of Lactated Ringers Solution. This was being fed into a vein deep in her left cubital fossa at the front of her elbow. On the other side of her bed hung a half-filled urinary bag, and into this was fed a clear plastic tube that emerged from under the blankets. This tube was full of gold-coloured urine. She was lying on the flat of her back.

Joseph Boyle saw all of this as he approached the foot of her bed. He was full of dread, fear, and foreboding. It was as much as he could do to bring himself to look at her. Tears welled up in his sad eyes as he looked around at the other patients and their plight. The ward was full of Christmas decorations—silver streamers, imitation holly, and shiny silver baubles. The faint sound of Christmas carol singing drifted in from the corridor outside.

'Joy to the world, the Lord is come.' What joy? What Lord?

Soon Mary was quietly at his side. Now together they stared in stunned and sickening silence at what, only a few hours earlier, was their gorgeous, healthy, bright, clever, and vivacious young daughter. And now look at her here lying unconscious on the flat of her back with tubes everywhere and a ventilator doing the breathing for her! How can this be right or what did she do to deserve to be in this state? What happened to her and why did it happen, and could it not have been avoided? Is she going to get better or is she going to deteriorate, and what are the chances of either of these two things happening and what was the more likely outcome expressed in simple percentages? Could she recover but incompletely and be left with some residual brain damage? Was she likely to be ever able to walk or talk again? Mary and Joseph Boyle had questions to ask, lots and lots of questions.

'Let every heart prepare Him room and Heaven and nature sing. And Heaven and nature sing,' – the carol singers insisted.

Sister Mary Assumpta was of the old school of nursing nuns. In her late fifties, she was assertive and authoritative and yet seemed to know her place in the pecking order at St. Malachi's Teaching Hospital. She could strike terror into the hearts of some patients and into the hearts of practically all those hospital staff under her charge. She adored God and hospital consultants in equal measure. A hospital consultant's word was never to be questioned, nor were their decisions and directives ever to be disputed. She had been in charge of this ICU as Ward Sister ever since it was first established in 1967, eight years previously.

A wisp of grey hair showed daringly in front of her forehead. This was her only concession to the wishes of Pope Paul VI who, towards the end of the Second Vatican Council in 1965, called for some relaxation in clerical garb. This lock of grey hair came from under her traditional nun's white headdress of coif and veil that framed her stern face, making it even sterner.

She wore a full-length white skirt with an elasticized waistband. Over her chest hung a large silver crucifix, and around her waist was tied an enormous, wooden rosary bead. These rattled as she walked across the ICU, and they were rattling now. She stopped beside the bed of the new admission up from theatre where Mary and Joseph Boyle were holding vigil, their shoulders gently shaking up and down silently weeping. The nun greeted them coldly and indifferently. She offered neither condolences nor any words of comfort. She did not introduce herself to them.

Mary believed it was time to start getting a few answers around here. The nun had a name tag pinned to her habit that declared her 'Staff Sister'. As soon as she had managed to compose herself somewhat, in whispered tones, Mary began to ask this tall and severe nun a few pertinent questions. But no sooner had she started than Sister Mary Assumpta held up her right-hand palm held outwards as if taking an oath on the bible. Her intention was though to stem the flow of questions.

"Excuse me, Sister. My name is Mary Boyle. This is my husband Joseph Boyle, and we are the parents of Linda, this young lady lying here in a coma," Mary said, pointing first to her husband and then to Linda.

"We need to know the answers to several questions, and we believe that we have a right to know these answers."

A definite testiness was only too obvious in Mary's voice, and the conversation now being conducted between these two women threatened to become less than civil. In the meantime, Joseph Boyle held his tongue. His turn would come later. For the moment, Mary seemed more than able to speak for the two of them.

"Yes, but the point about it is this, Mrs. Boyle—if you will just allow me for a second."

Sister Assumpta spoke with a soft North Kerry accent.

"The facts of the matter are that I only came on duty an hour ago, and I have not yet had a chance to be briefed about Linda. So, I do not have any useful information for you at this time, I'm afraid."

Mary calmed down a little bit on hearing this. Assumpta may be a sanctimonious pain in the neck, but if she has yet to be briefed on Linda's situation, then one had to give her the benefit of the doubt, at least for the moment anyway.

Just as she was thinking this, a tall thin bespectacled distinguished-looking man, dressed in a three-pieced pinstriped dark blue suit, stuck his head in the doorway and without as much as a glance in the direction of Mary and Joseph wiggled the index and middle fingers of his right outstretched hand while simultaneously jerking his head backward in a gesture that beckoned Sister Assumpta to come outside for a word with him. The nun bowed her head ever so slightly and, like a well-trained poodle, went immediately to her master's bidding. Her master on this occasion was Dr. Peter Newman.

Outside and well out of earshot of the Boyles, the Ward Sister and the Consultant Gynaecologist huddled and spoke in hushed tones.

"Listen, Mary, ah, briefly the situation with that Linda lady in there is that she was having a salpingogram under GA this morning when she arrested and it was a whore of a job to get her heart going again, and, ah. She almost certainly has some brain damage but how much is not my area of expertise, and we will be handing over her care to the Neurology fellows tomorrow. Is she showing any signs of responding at all yet, ah?"

Staff Nurse Sister Mary Assumpta explained to Peter Newman that she had not been on duty long enough to make a detailed assessment, but from what little she could gather, there was no change in Linda's situation one way or the other.

"Jesus!" This was Newman's only reply to the latest news.

Sister Mary looked pained. She would much prefer it if consultants in general, but Dr. Newman here in particular, would stop using foul language like 'whore of a job' and taking the Lord's name in vain in front of the nuns, as he had just now done. The nuns had often spoken among themselves about this unpleasantness but after much debate decided that there was not a great deal that they could do about it. Hospital Consultants were a law unto themselves. They were beyond reproach, the untouchables.

During this exchange between doctor and nurse outside in the corridor, Mary and Joseph were left inside the ICU looking helplessly at their stricken daughter struggling for her life in the bed before them. They each felt certain, in fact, they each took it for granted, that after their tête-à-tête outside in the corridor that Newman would return to the ICU and invite them into a room somewhere, sit them down, offer them a cup of tea, and give them a full explanation of what had happened, why and how it had happened, was there anything that could or should have been done to avoid its happening or was there anything that could or should have been done to get Linda's heart going sooner than they had.

Both Joseph and Mary Boyle had, independently of each other, drawn up a substantial mental list of some of the salient points that they would most like to have answers to right away. In addition to these, they would also like to know to what extent did the doctors think that Linda was brain-damaged, when might they know more definitively, and what, in broad terms, were the doctor's management or treatment plans for their daughter.

However, Peter Newman had no intention of sitting down or having cups of tea with Joseph and Mary in a quiet room somewhere, not this evening, not tomorrow, or not ever. Why should he? It had been a long old day. He was tired. Besides, he had not done anything wrong. He had nothing to hide. Let them go and talk to that gobshite Walter Malone. Maybe he could answer a few questions for them, the incompetent fool.

When he had finished his hurried and brief whispered conversation with the Staff Nurse, he turned on his well-polished heels and was about to take off when Mary spotted, through the opened ICU door, his retreating back. Incensed, she immediately gave chase. Where did he think he was going?

"Excuse me, please; excuse me, Doctor Newman, just a minute please!"

Mary shouted out at the top of her voice; her shrill words echoed around the fifth floor of St. Malachi's General Hospital.

Newman was rooted to the spot and pulled up like a Labrador on a choke chain. He would have loved to have kept going but this woman giving chase was too determined and too noisy. This is embarrassing. He turned to face her.

When she caught up with him, Mary Boyle was slightly out of breath and had to compose herself for a few seconds before she started to speak.

"Dr. Newman, do you not think that we, as Linda's parents, are entitled to at least a little common courtesy and to some preliminary explanations?"

Newman's dainty hands were going out in front of his gold watch-chain and tear-shaped fob, fingers spread out palms held supine. He shook his head slightly.

"But my dear Mrs. Boyle ah, I thought that I had already explained, in so far as I know anything, what had happened in theatre this morning. I thought I told you and your son David everything when I phoned you this afternoon. And beside this is no longer my bailiwick ah."

What was that? What was this horrible arrogant gentleman saying to her? What is a bailiwick? An area of responsibility or something like that was what it sounded like. Was he trying to say that he had no responsibility for the fact that Linda was now lying on the flat of her back in the Intensive Care Unit on a ventilator and obviously in a coma fighting for her life? This aloof consultant with his toffee accent seemed to be anxious to exonerate himself of responsibility, this, the very person who first suggested, no, who insisted actually, that Linda have this salpingogram under general anaesthesia. Mary Boyle began to see red. Who did he think he was anyway?

"Excuse me, Sir. What do you mean this is not your bailiwick or whatever you called it? Are you suggesting that you are not culpable for the state that our daughter is in right now?"

"Err, ah, hold on, Mrs. Boyle if you will, please -----"

But Mary ignored him and pressed ahead:

"Was it not you who insisted in your consultation with Linda that this special X-Ray under general anaesthesia was essential to rule out a rare but potentially cancerous ovarian tumour? And was it not you, Sir, who, just a few hours ago, presided over ---------"

Again, the hands went up defensively, and the head was shaking slowly.

"But my dear Mrs. Boyle ah."

If he says that just one more time, if this patronizing dandy refers to her one more time as 'my dear,' Mary will scream. But for the moment, she had better let him go on. She craved information, any information.

"When I say that this is no longer my bailiwick ah, by that I mean that this, Linda's situation in there, is outside my area of expertise. I am a consultant Obstetrician Gynaecologist ah, not a Neurologist."

"Yes, and so ----?"

"No, no, no, now please just hear me out. What she needs now is a Neurologist. To that end, therefore, I have already had a word with just such a specialist, Dr. Martin Mansfield, visiting Consultant Neurologist to this hospital and a man in whose opinion I have the height of respect ah. I have explained the situation to him, and he will be examining Linda in the morning."

"Why is he not in there right now? Why do we have to wait until the morning? Is this not an emergency?" Mary snapped.

"No, no, no, no, no. Just hold on a minute now, Mrs. Boyle, ah."

At least he has stopped calling her 'my dear.'

"No, no, this is a serious situation, but it is not an emergency in the sense that right now there is nothing urgent or curative that needs doing to her, ah. We are into a 'wait and see' situation here, seeing if and when she starts to show signs of coming round, starts to show signs of coming out of her coma."

Mary, now beginning to see the wider picture, visibly calmed down. Seeing this, Dr. Newman continued.

"And, by the way, I have not done anything wrong, you know, ah. I have not made any mistakes."

"I'm not too sure about that, Dr. Newman."

"That as maybe, Mrs. Boyle, but her heart stopped while she was under general anaesthesia. These things are rare, but unfortunately, they can happen even in the best institutions in the world. Will you excuse me now, please, ah?"

With these few terse words, Newman turned on his heels and walked away, leaving Mary Boyle seething with a sickening mixture of anger, frustration, grief, and guilt. She should have taken more interest and listened more carefully when Linda was telling her about having to go into the hospital for this test after Christmas. She could have stopped her, or at least advised that she get a second opinion about the necessity or otherwise of a salpingogram in Linda's situation. Of course, it was easy now to be wise after the event, but still, Mary felt miserably that she should have involved herself more in the early decision-making that had led to this catastrophe.

Her frustrations and anger were directed at Newman and his patronizing attitude. He never once said he was sorry, and he told her very little. Mary also got the distinct impression that he was hiding something on the one hand and attempting to distance himself from any blame on the other. With a heavy heart, she returned to her husband's side, where together they held silent vigil beside their critically wounded daughter for a further half an hour before facing the journey back to Rathfarnham and home across the dark winter city.

There were only four consultant neurologists in practice in Dublin at this time and six altogether in Ireland, serving a population of some three million people. These medical specialists dealt with diseases of the central nervous system, including common conditions like migraine headache, vertigo or Meniere's Syndrome, MS or multiple sclerosis, Parkinson's Disease, epilepsy, peripheral neuritis, cerebral palsy, brain tumours, and brain injury and damage, including the brain damage after anoxia or oxygen starvation.

Dr. Martin Mansfield was a consultant neurologist and, therefore, a member of this elite group of medical specialists. Public patients had to wait at least two years to get an appointment to see Mansfield. Two years was a long time if that patient was worried about epilepsy or Multiple Sclerosis but having only six specialists in this field for all of Ireland, that was how long it took.

Sister Mary Assumpta accompanied Dr. Mansfield to Linda Boyle's bedside. First, he checked for levels of unconsciousness by applying constant pressure with his thumb to the upper ridge of her eye socket just under her left eyebrow. This was a painful stimulus, and unless the level of unconsciousness was profound, the patient should grimace or moan or make some attempt to escape her tormentor. Linda

Boyd did none of these things. The pain clearly was not getting through to her.

Next, Dr. Mansfield repeated what his colleague, the anaesthetist, had tried the previous day down in the recovery room. He directed a strong light onto Linda's right pupil to see if it was capable of restricting. It didn't move at all. He saw with a heavy heart that Malone had noted in her chart eighteen hours previously that there was some reaction to light. Now there was none. Her condition was not getting any better; it could not even be described as 'stable'. Her condition was, in fact, deteriorating, as evidenced by fixed pupils and nonresponse to painful stimuli. This was not good. Whatever the effects of prolonged anoxia had on her brain cells yesterday in the theatre, it would appear to have been quite devastating. Could she recover from this? Could she come back?

With Sister Assumpta in attendance, Mansfield continued with his neurological assessment of his unconscious patient. He checked for spasticity or flexibility at elbows, wrists, knees, and ankles. Worryingly, there seemed to be a degree of spasticity at most of these joints. He lifted up her right knee by crooking his arm under her leg, and with a stainless steel and rubber patella hammer, he tapped the patella tendon below her right kneecap. Her leg jumped in an exaggerated knee-jerk reflex. This again was suggestive of brain damage, as the restraining influence of a healthy brain on this reaction seemed to be absent or at the least impaired.

After fifteen minutes, Dr. Mansfield had finished his careful neurological assessment of his patient. He now made detailed notes of his findings in her hospital chart hanging at the end of her bed. He knew that these notes were important; they would form a benchmark whereby further developments, good or bad, might be judged as a sign of deterioration, improvement, or stability. The assessment of a patient in a coma was all to do with physical signs like pupil reaction to light, reaction to painful stimuli, reflexes, and joint spasticity. It was by monitoring these that one could judge how things were going and speculate about the ultimate prospects of recovery.

Beyond that, in a situation like they were now in, there was not a great deal that the neurologist could do. The damage had already been inflicted. Neither medication nor any useful treatment existed that might make any difference. All one could do was play for time. Within a week or two, things might become a lot clearer. It was literally a waiting game at this stage. Before he left the ICU ward, Dr. Mansfield asked Sister Mary to organize that a nasogastric tube be inserted up Linda's right nostril and down into her stomach so she could be administered nutrition and hydration.

"Hello, is that you, Peter?"

Dr. Mansfield had found a house phone in the small office off the ICU and decided that it was time to let his colleague in on his findings of their shared patient.

"Yes, Martin, ah. Have you got any kind of good news for me, ah? And thanks very much for seeing her so quickly, by the way. Jesus, it's worrying, what?"

"Peter, it might be best if we discussed this over a cup of tea later this morning. How are you fixed later on?"

"I just have a D&C here to do now, and after that, ah, I should be okay for half an hour or so. How about the canteen at around eleven?"

"That's fine, thank you very much. I'll see you then."

Peter Newman replaced the black phone in its cradle and proceeded to the scrub room. He did not much like the tone of Mansfield's voice. There was nothing in it that would lift the enormous burden of guilt that he was feeling right now. And it hardly helped either that he hadn't got more than an hour's undisturbed sleep last night. Unwelcome reminders of the catastrophe kept invading his restless dreams.

Very few staff populated the hospital canteen when Drs. Mansfield and Newman took their cups of tea and plain biscuits to a quiet corner table under a tall window. The surgeon was dressed in a dark green scrub suit, over which he wore a starched white coat. On his head, he wore a dark green surgical cap, and around his neck hung a white surgical mask. After this discussion with his colleague, he would be returning to the theatre to perform a vaginal hysterectomy, his last major case for the day.

"Listen, Peter, I am not going to beat around the bush here. I know you well enough to know that you are a man who shoots from the hip and likes a bit of straight talking."

Dr. Newman nodded his head and encouraged his colleague to get on with it. He still did not like the sound of the neurologist's voice. It had a certain edge to it that suggested the news was going to be far from good.

"I have now made a fairly thorough neurological assessment of your patient up there in ICU, and I have to say straight off that it does not look good for her. She is profoundly unconscious and not responding in any way to painful stimuli."

Here the neurologist paused to take a sip of tea.

"Fucking hell, this is not what I want to hear."

"I know that, Peter. But you wouldn't thank me either if I tried to placate you, now, would you?"

"No, sorry, you're right. Go on."

"We know that people can make a complete recovery from a coma, even after many months. But in this case, it is the ancillary symptoms that I find the most worrying, those and the manner in which her brain was damaged in the first place. Can you tell me again and, in more detail, what happened in the OR yesterday?"

Martin Mansfield decided to give his colleague a small break from the bad news and allow him the momentary distraction of recalling the terrible events of the previous day in theatre number two. He observed the gynaecologist over the rim of his teacup, sipped on the weak brew, and nibbled on the plain biscuit.

"We were just finishing up after the salpingogram, which incidentally was normal to make matters even worse, when she arrested, ah. I do not know why she arrested, nor was Mick Gaffney able to throw much light on that question either, ah."

"Why she arrested hardly matters at this stage, does it?"

"No, I suppose not. But it may have been an esoteric reaction to the anaesthetics, or it may have been the radio-opaque dye entering her abdominal cavity via the fallopian tubes. For whatever reason anyway, her heart just stopped. But it was how that prick Malone reacted to this catastrophic event, or should I say how he failed to react, that was the crucial issue."

"Should this be reported to the Drug Advisory people, in case it was a drug reaction?"

"That's in hand."

Here Peter Newman paused and had a quick look around him before going on. Nobody was within earshot. He had no intention of trying to cover Malone's ass in front of his colleagues. He might have been a bit sparing with the truth when speaking to Linda's parents. But with fellow doctors— that's another question.

"Everybody in the theatre could see from the monitor that the patient had arrested. I mean, for God's sake, a dog with a mallet up its hole could see it, ah. The tracing was flat, and there was a continuous warning bleep coming from the fucking thing."

"So, if not arrest, what else could it have been?" Mansfield wanted to know.

"Oh indeed, that's the very point. What was Malone doing about it? He was doing shag all about it, that is what he was doing, ah. His first thought was that there was a mechanical failure of some kind or that the ECG leads to the monitor had been accidentally pulled out. He had us all lifting our feet to see if there were any leads under us. I mean—come on, for Christ's sake, ah!"

"Oh God! What did he do next, or need I ask?" Mansfield was finding this incredible.

"Then he went from bad to worse. He started checking the chest leads, listening to her heart and fiddling around trying to find a pulse, and all this time the patient was arrested!"

"What about the women?"

"Good point. If it were not for Ann Harris, Linda Boyle would be dead right now."

Martin Mansfield looked his colleague straight in the eyes and wondered to himself if it might not have been better if his patient were dead. However, he decided to spare Newman such morbid reflections for the moment.

"Without wasting another second, Ann and I acted together. She immediately started vigorous CPR while Malone, being the gobshite that he is, just looked on. I went for the crash cart. By the time I got the pads on, Ann's efforts were already starting to pay off, and there were signs on the monitor. Then with one blast of defib, and she was away for slates, ah."

"The question is, of course," Mansfield interjected, "how long do you think she was arrested for? I mean to say, that is the pivotal question, isn't it? For how long her brain was starved of oxygen?"

"Yes, I know that. Afterward, I asked everyone who was in the theatre that same question. Everyone, that is, except the anaesthetist Malone because he would claim that it was only a matter of seconds. But the rest of us knew only too well that, unfortunately, due largely to Malone's ineptitude, it was, in fact, a matter of minutes. The consensus actually was that the patient's heart had stopped for something just under four minutes, and I would go along with that estimation. We are not putting any of this in the record, by the way."

The neurologist emitted a long, low whistle before popping the last of the plain biscuits into his mouth.

"Four minutes, or even just less than four minutes, is a hell of a long time, Peter. If she comes back unscathed from this one, we will be in miracle territory. This is Padre Pio country."

Mansfield finished off the last of his tea and heaved a mighty sigh before proceeding further.

"Apart from her having absolute pain tolerance, three other things are quite worrying. Firstly, her pupils are dilated and fixed; there was no reaction to light, and that contrasts with what Malone thought he found yesterday when there was some movement."

"Sure, what would he know about it, ah?"

"Yeah, I take your point, but she may have deteriorated in the last twenty hours. Secondly, her patella reflexes are hyper, indicating a lack of brain modifying influences. And thirdly, there is early evidence of spasticity at her major joints."

"And the length of time she was arrested?"

"And as for the four minutes, or nearly four minutes— it doesn't really matter that much— she stayed in cardiac arrest, well, that is the most worrying of all. You already know this stuff, and I hardly need to remind you. But brain cells or neurons are exceedingly sophisticated structures that have a low tolerance for any insult such as prolonged oxygen starvation."

The canteen was getting busy, and both consultants had appointments to be elsewhere. Mansfield wanted to end this meeting.

"It is neurons alone that give us our senses – sight, hearing, taste, and touch, emotions, and so on. It is neurons that imbue us with intelligence; personality, love, spirituality, memory, appreciation, coordination, skills, dexterity, and you name it. Without neurons, we are nothing."

It was getting to a private and sensitive stage now. All the tables in their immediate vicinity were unoccupied. Across the canteen, Dr. Mansfield could see nurses Ann Harris and Theatre Sister Mary McGonagall. The women occasionally glanced in the direction of the two consultants. They could not hear what they were saying but were in no doubt as to what the subject was.

Mansfield continued.

"God gives us about one hundred billion neurons at birth. Age, wear and tear, smoking, alcohol abuse, and so on knock a lot of these out as we go through life. Thankfully that does not seem to matter that much, within reason, of course. Chronic alcoholics can destroy too many of their neurons and suffer from 'wet brain syndrome' and go mad. Neurons, unlike most other cells in the body, have no capacity to regenerate themselves. Once they are dead, they are dead, that's it, kaput."

Peter Newman knows this stuff already and wonders why Mansfield is rabbiting on like this. Mansfield senses that he may be irritating his colleague across the table from him, but he wants there to be no misunderstanding or ambiguity between them.

"Sorry if I seem to be going on a bit, but I just want that both of us are absolutely clear on what may be coming down in the case of this young woman."

"That's fine Martin. I'm with you, ah."

"I believe that during the almost four minutes of brain anoxia that she suffered, all, or at least most of her neurons were destroyed. Everything points that way — the pupils, the lack of response to pain, the hyper-reflexes, and the spasticity; all this points to virtual brain death."

"And the probable outcome, ah -----?" But he already knows the sickening answer that is coming.

"The most probable outcome is that Ms. Boyle will progress into what we call a Persistent Vegetative State or PVS for short."

"Jesus, that is the worst possible scenario, Martin."

"I know it is. I sincerely hope I am proved wrong by the way. But I think it would be less than honest of me if I were to try and gloss over things and not put you fully in the picture, Peter."

"You're right."

Newman now buries his face in his hands, his elbows on the canteen table. He is now badly shaken; his neurological colleague has just delivered him a heavyweight's body punch that sends him reeling. He knew things might be bad, like a coma for a few weeks and making an almost complete recovery. But PVS and making that gut-wrenching prognosis at this early stage! God Almighty!

Martin Mansfield reached across the table and tried to comfort his colleague by patting him lightly on the shoulder. Ann Harris and Mary McGonagall looked silently across at the doctors crouched over the table opposite them. They too now know that the news is devastating. Despite themselves, they cannot but feel sorry for Dr. Newman.

Eventually, Newman managed to compose himself sufficiently to carry on. He took off his spectacles and polished the glass with a corner of his scrub suit top.

"What should we tell her parents at this stage, do you think?"

"That's up to you, Peter."

"I know it's up to me, but what would you do?"

"I'd tell them as little as you possibly can, to be quite honest with you. Keep well out of their way."

"But that hardly seems fair, does it?"

"Fairness has nothing to do with it, Peter. You do not want them to get any hint that there was a cock-up in the theatre yesterday. They are going to sue anyway; we know that. They will sue you, Malone, and the hospital. People who are going to sue you must be looked upon as enemies, and only a fool talks to his enemies. How is your professional indemnity cover, by the way?"

"It's fine. I'm with The Medical Protection Society and was on to them this morning. I ran the thing by them, and they didn't seem to think that there would be a problem, ah."

"Did you tell them how bad it might be?"

"No, because quite honestly, ah, until just now, I had no idea that it was as serious as you have indicated. Are you going to tell the parents about the neurological situation?"

"You must be joking! No, no, no. I have just advised you to play dumb, so it wouldn't make sense for me to advise you that way and then for me to go and start talking to the relatives."

"There is another point too." Mansfield is now thinking out loud rather than addressing his troubled colleague directly.

"Before I left ICU just now, I asked Assumpta to organise a nasogastric tube. We need to start hydration and nutrition. With tube feeding, we can keep her alive almost indefinitely. This is what I would want to do, and I presume it is also what you would want?"

"What's the alternative, ah?"

"The alternative, Peter, is death by starvation. I, for one, believe that to be unethical and against our Catholic ethos here in this hospital. But we need to be careful here too."

"How do you mean careful, ah?"

"Tube feeding people in a vegetative state is becoming controversial, you know. We had that recent American case.

What was her name? Quinlan, wasn't it? Yes, that's it, Karen Ann Quinlan."

"No, no, no, Martin. We must feed her, for God's sake, and treat all that is treatable."

"I absolutely agree with you one hundred percent, Peter. Keeping her alive through nasogastric tube feeding, and when we must, the use of antibiotics is the ethical and morally correct thing to do. It is the Pro-life thing to do."

The conversation was drawing to a close. Both consultants have now been paged several times over the public address system and were urgently needed elsewhere in the hospital. Newman did not seem quite finished.

"I will not be saying this to many people, but I have to tell you, Martin. I feel utterly awful and profoundly guilty about what has happened to this lovely young healthy woman, ah. I might want to blame Walter Malone for his failure to get up off his arse and start resuscitation immediately. It is easy to blame others, but the fact of the matter is that it was my idea in the first place that she has a salpingogram."

"Oh, come on now, Peter, don't start beating yourself up over it."

"In fact, when she resisted the suggestion, I actually put pressure on her. The Medical Council is going to hear about this, ah. I am sick with worry that they could find me guilty of professional misconduct, ah, or something for carrying out a procedure under general anaesthesia that strictly speaking may not have been necessary."

Both men were standing up at this stage. They were needed elsewhere. Martin Mansfield gently prodded his right index finger into the lapel of Newman's white coat as he spoke: "Listen, Peter, this is bullshit, we will have no more of it. You are just upset for now. Believe me, I have been here before. This thing will settle down and eventually blow over. These things happen everywhere. How were you to know that she was going to arrest?"

They were now outside the canteen, about to go their separate ways. Mansfield needed to further reassure his colleague.

"Stop playing the blame game, Peter, like a good man. As for The Medical Council, forget them. No way can you be criticized for exercising your best clinical judgment. There is no question of any malpractice or professional misconduct, none at all. Do you hear me now? If you get any hassle from those quarters, please let me know immediately, and I will have a private word with the Chairman of the Fitness to Practise Committee. He is a good friend of mine, and good friends look after one another, alright?"

While imparting this final piece of information, Mansfield smiled and tapped the side of his nose three times in rapid succession, an international sign that says, *"let us keep this between ourselves shall we, we are in control of things around here."*

CHAPTER 5 – FROM COMA TO PVS

The spring of 1974 crept slowly into the large garden of 16 Ashgrove Lane, Rathfarnham, Dublin 14. The snowdrops arrived on time in the rock garden beside the clothesline. Their dark green, strap-shaped leaves and six-petal, milk-white flowers surprised Mary Boyle this morning as she hung out a small washing to dry. She hadn't thought of snowdrops, nor had she been looking out for them. It was the first day of February, the feast day of Saint Bridget. The snowdrops shimmered in the early spring sun. A hint of warmth hung in that sun, and from halfway up a mature silver birch, a blackbird sang out. His rich, liquid notes declared his presence and willingness to find a mate. His repertoire was long, varied, sweet, and impressive.

Mary thought to herself how this should be a time of hope, a time of lengthening days and the early stirrings of new beginnings—a feeling that the worst of winter was behind her. That was exactly how she would have felt every early spring when, first, the snowdrops surprised her as they shimmered under a watery spring sun. Where now was the joy in a blackbird declaring his presence from halfway up a mature birch tree? It was all gone, gone forever.

Since Linda was so cruelly and so needlessly smitten and struck down at the hands of the medical profession, everything had changed. Inside Mary's head, the same questions went around and around endlessly. Why did this happen or how did it happen had yet to be explained to her. Her daughter was deeply unconscious and on life support machinery, and, although nobody has said as much, it seemed to everyone concerned that the chances of her making any kind of meaningful recovery were fast fading.

So blighted has Mary Boyle's life now become that she can no longer enjoy the simple pleasures of a spring day. When she came back into the house with the dried washing, the phone on the wall was ringing. Mary lifted the receiver, and the ringing ceased.

"Hello, is that Mrs. Boyle?" the female caller with the soft Kerry accent wanted to know.

"Yes, this is Mary Boyle speaking."

"Ah, Mrs. Boyle, this is Sister Assumpta here at the hospital. Listen; there has been a small development here this morning. Linda opened her eyes for a few minutes."

"Oh God, sister, that sounds like it might be good news. Is it?"

Assumpta had to be guarded. She thought through her answer first.

"Now, of course, she hasn't spoken, and we have not been able to get through to her, but I thought that you should know that at least she has opened her eyes, and that has to be seen as some sort of development."

"Thanks for letting me know, Sister. Does this mean that she is coming out of her coma?" The urgency in Mary's voice was obvious.

"Well—let's just call it a development, shall we, for now anyway. Opening her eyes is one thing, regaining consciousness is another? Perhaps you should come in and see for yourself how she is doing."
"Fine, Sister, we will come in right away."

Mary thanked the nun again and replaced the receiver on the wall set. She was confused about the cryptic message she had just received from the hospital. That nun sounded guarded in the way she spoke. Something was not right. Yet the news that Linda has opened her eyes must be good news, surely? What did she mean by 'development'? Moreover, what was that about regaining consciousness being one thing and opening her eyes being another?

Was there some dark state in between the two that Mary had never heard about before? Perhaps Linda could lapse into some kind of state of suspended animation from which escape was uncertain. She badly needed to speak to that neurologist fellow; what was his name? Mansfield, wasn't it?

The moment Mary put down the phone, she picked it up again and dialled Dublin Castle and had a quick word with her husband, Joseph, to advise him that she would pick him up in forty-five minutes' time, and that he should be down at the door ready to jump into her car. She told him that Linda had opened her eyes, but that this might not be a very significant development.

Joseph and Mary arrived at the ICU, out of breath, having walked the nine flights of stairs up to the fifth floor. The lift had still not been fixed; this meant particular hardship for anyone wishing to visit the ICU and who was in any way infirm or disabled.

They observed their daughter stretched out on her back with her usual complement of attached tubes and machinery. There was the nasogastric feeding tube into her nose, IV ringer's lactate into a vein in her right arm, ECG leads from her chest to the overhead monitor, indwelling urinary catheter from under the bed covers to the plastic bag suspended from the mattress runners. Finally, there was the air hosing from her endotracheal tube running to the noisy Manley Ventilator.

They were one to each side of her head, both leaned over. Linda's eyes were wide open as if in fear or panic. They were almost unblinking. She seemed to stare directly at the ceiling, not shifting her gaze to the left or right as her parents looked down on her. Mary bent lower until her face was only inches away from her daughter's right ear.

"Can you hear me, love?" She whispered loudly into Linda's ear.

Nothing. No movement, no sign of recognition, no flicker of eyelids, or attempt to turn towards her mother's familiar voice. Nothing.

"Can you hear me, love?"

This time, Mary raised her voice so it could be heard all over the ICU while, at the same time, she gently shook Linda's right shoulder. Again, there was no reaction, none whatsoever.

"Shush, shush, please, Mrs. Boyle. You are in an ICU, for heaven's sake! What about the other patients, woman?"

Sister Mary Assumpta had unexpectedly materialized out of nowhere at the end of Linda's bed. This time, even the rattling of her wooden rosary beads failed to warn of her pending presence. She was just suddenly there and giving out, as she so often did.

"What about the other patients?" Mary snapped back, in no mood now for this nun's sanctimonious attitude.

"Mrs. Boyle, I will not be spoken to like that in my ICU. If you do not desist immediately, I shall have to ask you to leave."

Mary Boyle wondered if, in fact, this old holy so-and-so had the power to eject her from the ICU, given that her daughter is lying here in a critical state. She decided that this was not the right time to test her and that it might be best, for now anyway, to let things cool off a bit.

"Sister Assumpta, we would like to talk to the neurologist, Dr. Mansfield, about our daughter. We would like to know what went wrong in the theatre and why it went wrong. How long was our daughter's brain starved of oxygen, and what are the probable consequences of that?"

"We all have questions, Mrs. Boyle."
Mary ignored the nun's idiotic comment.

"We would also like to know what significance we should now attach to the fact that Linda has opened her eyes and how does this affect her overall outlook for the future?"

The nun's hands were going up slowly, palms facing outwards and head shaking from side to side in that, by now familiar, gesture that seemed to say, 'I do not want this conversation to continue.' She looked like a Blessed Virgin in a grotto.

"Mrs. Boyle, I can tell you this. It is not Dr. Mansfield's practice to talk to relatives of patients about their condition, treatment, management, or prognosis. These are matters between doctor and patient only and are therefore privileged and off-limits."

Mary was outraged at what she had just heard. What is this nun on about?

"With respect, Sister, that's nonsense. Linda is not a 'patient' in the ordinary sense of that word. Someone needs to speak on her behalf."

The nun, relenting a bit.

"Alright, I will have a word with him tomorrow and pass on to him your concerns. When I see you again then, I may be able to relate to you some of the key features of your daughter's case. Or we might be able to persuade the Senior Registrar, Dr. Patel, to speak to you. In the meantime, I bid you a good afternoon."

With these words, the gaunt figure of Sister Mary Assumpta turned ninety degrees and took her leave from the end of Linda Boyle's bed. Joseph and Mary were left none the wiser as to how come their once lovely and bright daughter had her eyes wide open now but yet was otherwise totally paralyzed, blind, speechless, and inaccessible to the outside world.

"I want you to think of the human brain as being like a giant printed circuit-board. It is, in fact, infinitely more intricate than any mere manmade piece of electronic equipment. It is far more technologically sophisticated than, say, the biggest computer in the world. So complex is the human brain that our present-day understanding of its workings is still, to be frank about it, quite primitive. The truth of the matter is that doctors and scientists still know very little about the human brain and how it functions."

Dr. Patel spoke like a man who was used to giving lectures. He was seated at a small table, in a grim consulting room, down the corridor from ICU. Placed on the table in front of him was a life-sized model of the human brain, and he used a yellow pencil in his right hand to point out the various features of anatomy as he spoke. Mary Boyle and her son David and daughter Margaret were all anxious to learn as much as possible.

Patel's boss, Dr. Martin Mansfield, had asked that he spend at least half an hour with the Boyles and explain to them the difference between coma and persistent vegetative state or PVS as it was known in short.

When so instructing Patel, Mansfield was careful to emphasize that on no account were Linda's relatives to be told anything about prognosis or the management strategy that the hospital had for Linda. These were internal matters and were strictly confidential. Neither, on any account, were they to be told how long Linda had been in a state of cardiac arrest and why it took so long to get her heart going again.

Only in his late twenties, Patel was Senior Registrar in neurology at St. Malachi's Hospital on the team headed up by consultant neurologist Dr. Martin Mansfield. To get to his present position, Patel had now got four years post-Internship under his belt, two of those years being spent at the Neurological Department of John Hopkins Hospital in Baltimore, Maryland, USA, one of the most prestigious medical research and development institutions in the world. The hospital's Board of Management thought Dr. Patel added considerably to their overall prestige. He was next in line for consultancy; being Indian was holding up his well-deserved promotion.

But the young doctor felt much aggrieved. It annoyed him quite intensely that his boss should have seen fit to instruct him to withhold any information and to in any way try to mislead these nice people. They were, after all, just the innocent victims of a surgical calamity. This was not how he had been taught to handle similar situations when in John Hopkins.

All his instincts and learning would drive him in the opposite direction and tell and share with the Boyles every bit of information that was available. Misleading people and attempting to cover-up never worked and was now rapidly going out of fashion. The fact that old Mansfield did not seem to have picked up on this latest trend of openness and honesty reflected the fact that he was deeply conservative and stuck in a time warp.

"When someone is in
apart from being totally para
neurological function, nor any
their environment. In plain
remember, nor have any thou
cannot communicate in any wa
swallow on their own, or fe
incontinent. They do retain
heartbeat, ability to breathe o
cycle. It is therefore inaccurate
'brain dead' since this part of
stays very much alive."

Dr. Patel tapped the br
of him with his yellow pencil b

"If properly hydrated
nasogastric tube and if properly
then people in PVS can live fo
full expected life span, in fac
frequent antibiotics. But still,
sort of good news. Has anyone

Margaret and her broth
stared in stunned silence and c
of the human brain on the tabl
Neurological Registrar. The sa
them concurrently. How coulc
live out one's full life expectanc

"So, if you imagine the brain as being like a giant circuit
board, then the connecting nerve cells, called neurons, are the
wiring on that circuit board. Now these neurons are extremely
delicate structures and are easily damaged. But worse than that,
unlike most other cells in the body, they have little or no
regenerative capacity. When they are gone, they are gone for
all time. When the brain is starved of oxygen for long enough,
the neurons can be permanently destroyed, leaving us with a
circuit board without any wiring. In that case, we are left only
with the brain stem down here."

Patel paused to make sure his message was getting
across. When he was satisfied that his little audience was
following what he was saying, he continued:

"By the way, interrupt me whenever you want to. We
know that Linda suffered a cardiac arrest while under general
anaesthesia two weeks ago. This lasted for a few minutes
during which time her delicate neurons would have been
starved of oxygen. This caused her to go into a coma, but what
the extent of this nerve damage was could only be determined
as the hours and days went by."

"Was there no scan or anything that might help make
an assessment?" David wanted to know.

"We have no CAT scanner in this hospital, David, and
in any case, she was not fit to move."

David nodded, allowing Patel to continue.

"When someone is
her procedure, they are in ;
cannot be reached by any (

Dr. Patel paused ag
table with his yellow penci

"Now, there is and
a coma where neuron da:
called the Persistent Veg
described only two years a,
is what happened to Lind:
has gone from being in a c
afraid, is not good news."

Mary Boyle was be
stomach again. Her lovel\
doctors gone and done to
happened to make it all gc
to be any good news out
litany of woes where thing
each passing day? Reachii
handkerchief and began
Margaret reached over fc
now she could cry; a few
much.

However, it was f
deliver the Boyle family s‹

no ideas, memory or awareness of self or surroundings, blind, deaf, incontinent, and mute and totally depending on others for everything, how could that be described as 'at least some sort of good news'?

"Is there any chance, however slim, that she might recover at least some brain function?" Margaret wanted to know.

"Margaret, we are talking of a rare condition when we speak of PVS, and therefore it is a condition about which not a great deal is known. There would not be more than, say, a few thousand people around the world at any given time in a persistent vegetative state. Therefore, to answer your question is not as simple as it might appear. The literature does contain a few reports of some people in PVS making a degree of recovery over a year or so, but they are the exceptions. It depends also to some extent on what caused the original assault on the brain cells. When PVS resulted from a non-traumatic injury, as for example in this case of cardio-respiratory arrest, only 15% of adults recovered some consciousness. The figures are disappointing, and the longer a patient is in PVS, the less the chances there are of any meaningful recovery. If no improvement is seen in the first twelve months, then it is unlikely that there ever will be any after that. One reported case only exists of a person being in PVS for three years and then recovering consciousness and awareness, but no movement, of course. But some say that that patient was a misdiagnosed PVS."

Now the room was filled by a sickly silence as the enormity and sheer horror of Linda's situation began, for the first time, to truly dawn on her mother, her brother, and sister. They suspected that things were bad but could have had no idea of just how bad. And it was to get even worse.

Dr. Patel continued, uncomfortable with the silence:
"Another thing about PVS is that it is a 'new condition,' making it even more difficult to study or fully understand. It is 'new' insofar as it is a product of modern technology and our better understanding of physiology. Fifty years ago, it did not exist because fifty years ago people who went into cardiac arrest died because cardiac resuscitation and defibrillation had yet to be invented. Improved antibiotics and a better understanding of nasogastric tube feeding have also contributed to the emergence of this condition."

"How can we be so sure that Linda has no awareness of herself or her environment?" Again, Margaret interjects.

Dr. Patel considers this for a few seconds before answering. The question, of course, was brilliant for its sheer insightfulness into the human dilemma that situations like PVS pose for those who must deal with it. Could Linda be aware, even at some superficial level, of the utter hopelessness of her situation where she was now trapped? If she could be so aware, then that would obviously make her life all but intolerable, and one would seriously need to question the ethics of prolonging it.

"To be quite honest with you, Margaret, that question poses even more uncomfortable possibilities than most of us would want to admit to. When we say of people in your sister's state of unconsciousness, that they have no awareness of self or environment, we are, in fact, making an assumption. I cannot, for example, point at any area on this model here on the table and say to you that here is the centre of consciousness and here the centre for awareness and here is where we have emotions. In our present state of knowledge, we simply do not know where in the brain these are located. But because the neuron destruction brought about by prolonged anoxia is universal, it is, one supposes anyway, safe to assume that it is total, and that consciousness and awareness are knocked out along with everything else."

Before this session ended, Linda's mother Mary had one final question:

"So where do we go from here, Dr. Patel?"

The Senior Registrar was now aware of his boss's instructions not to engage the family in the matter of long-term treatment plans for Linda. His own natural inclinations would be to involve the family in the decision-making process from the very start, but for the sake of a peaceful life, he decided to do as Mansfield had ordered and kick for touch:

"That is really a matter for the consultants like Dr. Martin Mansfield and Dr. Peter Newman to decide. For the moment at least, Linda will be hydrated and nourished, and her progress, if any, monitored. As already discussed, the eventual outcome of this is uncertain. I am sorry I cannot be more helpful. My contract with this hospital ends soon, and I will be leaving in three months' time. So, I am not going to be of much help to you, I'm afraid."

Mary thanked him anyway. He had been kind, honest, and for the most part sympathetic and at least tried to give them some kind of insight into what was going on and what they might expect the future to hold. That was more than any of his senior colleagues seemed prepared to do. They were better at fobbing people off and obfuscating matters. Mary still did not know the full story of what exactly happened in theatre that fateful day nor was she told the name of the anaesthetist involved.

"Thank you very much, Dr. Patel. We wish you well in your future career."

And with that, Mary gathered her few belongings before exiting the consulting room accompanied by her young adult son and daughter.

Spring continued to advance; the snowdrops and crocuses had come and gone, leaving only their spiky, arching green leaves behind to gather nourishment for their bulbs below the ground. Now it was the daffodil's turn to take centre stage, bobbing and weaving on the lawn's edge in the dappled shade of the horse chestnut, which was just now donning its leafy summer coat. The evenings had grown noticeably longer, a topic of conversation for everyone. St. Patrick's Day had passed a week ago, and for the first time in her fifty-five years of life, Mary Boyle hadn't gone to watch the lively parade across the city of Dublin. How could one possibly enjoy such festivities with their youngest daughter languishing in a seriously ill state in the Intensive Care Unit of St. Malachi's Hospital? The lengthening evenings, the daffodils in their dappled shade, and the awakening horse chestnut tree had all lost their ability to bring joy.

Around this time, Mary received a call from Sister Assumpta one day, informing her that they would be taking Linda out of bed for a while, and perhaps she would like to visit earlier than her usual time of three in the afternoon. The head of the ICU who called made it sound like a significant event, a milestone on Linda's supposed road to recovery, something not to be missed. Henceforth, when Mary's friends and relatives asked about Linda's condition, Mary could say that she was now sitting out of bed, and to those who were unaware, this might sound like progress. However, it was far from any real improvement.

"Good afternoon, Mrs. Boyle, a nice spring day, thank God," the porter with the shiny peaked cap greeted her cheerily as she entered the grim grey hospital.

"The lift is working again; you will be glad to hear. And about time too, I suppose you'd say."

Mary passed by the porter's desk, scarcely acknowledging the source of the warm greeting. 'That fellow is getting far too familiar of late,' she thought to herself. She entered the empty lift and pressed button number five for the Intensive Care Unit. Upstairs, she went past the statue of The Little Flower and on through the opened door into the ICU. Linda's bed was empty and made up with the top white sheet neatly turned back onto the green counterpane. Beside the bed, Mary was greeted with an appalling sight, the shock of which was to stay with her for her remaining days. At first, she thought it had to be someone else, some kind of mistake. But as she stood there, rooted to the ground in the middle of the ICU, it slowly dawned on her that this was her daughter, Linda, after all.

'Oh, sweet suffering Jesus! Is this the baby that she bore almost twenty-two years ago? Is this the young woman that she reared to become a bright, intelligent, vivacious, musical, athletic, and witty person? Was this the young woman that only recently was in the prime of her life with everything to look forward to? She went to the doctors with a minor skin problem and erratic menstrual periods, and this is what they did to her. She, who won medals playing the tin whistle and won cups playing tennis. She, who could entertain people for hours with her wit and her music. May God in heaven help us all, but would you just look at her now. Just look at what they have done to her. Look at her now, tied into that wing-backed armchair by a canvas strap.'

Horrified, Mary took it all in at a glance. Her daughter was dressed in a full-length short-sleeved white hospital gown. Her eyes were open and staring, yet not seeing. Her mouth was clenched into a sardonic leer. Her head was held backward, jerking and spastic. Both hands were held useless and claw-like under her chin; arms were fully flexed at the elbows. Both knees were bent in full flexion, her bare feet were somewhere under the chair out of sight. She was totally paralyzed and totally spastic; she was moribund and marooned in her own destitution. She made sporadic purposeless jerky movements. Occasionally she moaned loudly. She was tied into the wing-backed chair by a stout canvas ribbon. The ventilator was disconnected, and it appeared she could now breathe on her own. The nasogastric tube remained in situ, as did her urinary indwelling catheter tubing and bag, now half full of a yellow fluid.

Mary was appalled, shocked, and overwhelmed. Horrible and painful emotions flew through her brain. Pity, profound sadness, anger, pain, guilt, and revulsion were all mixed as if into one. As she approached her daughter, she noticed something quite extraordinary and totally unexpected. When Mary moved from left to right or right to left, Linda's eyes followed her every move. And yet, Dr. Patel had told them a week ago that Linda was blind. But if she was blind, how could she seem to follow people's movements as they approached her? No, she could not be blind. The doctor must be mistaken. However, if she followed her mother's movements with her eyes that was all she seemed to do. There was not a flicker of recognition or of acknowledgement on Linda's face. That it was her own mother who came into the room and who was now walking towards her did not register with her at all.

"How are you, my darling?"
Mary leaned down towards her daughter's right ear and spoke loudly. Again, there was not a glimmer of reaction to the familiar sound of her mother's voice. The jerky sporadic purposeless movements continued unabated, as did the groans and facial grimaces. Mary's heart sank lower. Her shock and distress at seeing the hopeless plight of her who was now 'sitting up' was unimaginably painful. She would not be able to stay long and in any case, what was the point?

Then suddenly something horrifying happened. Linda bent her head forwards until her chin and then her nose came in contact with her claw-like hands held uselessly under her chin. This sudden movement brought the nasogastric tube that emerged from her right nostril into a position where it now lay behind Linda's thumb and hooked index finger. With the tube thus anchored, she then quickly brought her head back again. By repeating this movement three times the entire length of the nasogastric tube was drawn up from her stomach, through her nose, and thrown out on the floor beside the wing-backed armchair.

"Nurse, Nurse! Nurse, please come quickly."

Mary shouted across to the next bed where a nurse was helping a patient take a sip of water. The terror and panic in her voice were obvious. The nurse looked across and saw the nasogastric tubing out on the floor.

"Don't worry about that, Mrs. Boyle. That's OK. It has happened a few times before. We will replace it when you have finished your little visit. We think the tube bothers her in some kind of way. But we can get it back in again. No problem."

The first floor of Ely House, the headquarters of The Order of the Knights of Saint Columbanus, near Saint Stephen's Green, Dublin, was reached by a Portland Stone cantilevered staircase. The sides of the balustrades of this great staircase were panelled with scenes of the labours of Hercules. Halfway up this stairway, on the half landing, was a massive stained glass Venetian window. The place reeked of opulence, power, and influence.

The Knights were engaged in many works of charity, mostly directed at young people from the poorer inner city. To their credit, they made little of their charitable deeds, and most of the time these went unnoticed by the broader community.

The Knights of Saint Columbanus had resonances with their medieval forbearers, The Knights Templar, and the Priory of Zion, whose task it was to suppress the secrets of The Holy Grail and the true family lineage arising from Jesus

Christ's marriage to Mary Magdalene. They were much given to ceremonial ritual, and they had secrets. Their membership was unknown and unpublished. What took place at any of their frequent meetings went unrecorded. When in positions of power, for example, in the judiciary, they never declared themselves as Knights but foraged away in the background surreptitiously.

As well as being clandestine in their good works, the Knights were open to male practising Catholics only. These could only be initiated into the Order on the recommendations of two existing members. On initiation, they were required to take certain oaths of allegiance to the Order, about which little was known to the outside world. At official meetings, Knights were required to wear ceremonial silk robes, the colour of which indicates their rank within the Order. They were heavily structured and intensely hierarchical. Knights were elected within their ranks to positions that carried anachronistic titles such as Supreme Knight and Supreme Advocate.

Three Knights of the Order of Saint Columbanus had just made their way up the Portland Stone steps to sit at the enormous boardroom table in the long reception hall on the first floor. At the far end of this room, there was a massive Adams fireplace of Carrara marble. A heavy brass plate surrounded the opening of the fireplace. Above the fireplace hung a portrait of the great Saint himself, Columbanus, going about his missionary work with zeal, book in hand.

The three men there were: Supreme Knight Walter Malone, Deputy Supreme Knight Peter Newman, and Supreme Chancellor Tomas O'Leary. Each man was dressed in a long silk ceremonial robe that reached almost to his black polished shoes under the table. The back of the robe bore a life-sized motif of the crucifix, the Order's logo. The Supreme Knight's robe was scarlet; that of Deputy Supreme Knight was purple, and the Supreme Chancellor's robe was black like a priest's garb. Together they made a colourful trio. They were formally and officially dressed for an assembly to be convened in half an hour's time. But what they wanted to discuss right now was private and just between the three of them.

The men kept their voices down as they huddled over the table. Supreme Knight Malone did most of the talking. It was a rule within the Knights that nobody was allowed to speak out of turn or interrupt another who had the floor. At the moment, that person is the Supreme Knight who was now on his feet.

"Brother Newman here will be only too familiar with a situation that we have going on in St. Malachi's at the minute. But I wanted to fill you in on it, Brother O'Leary, because we would appreciate your views."

Tomas O'Leary nodded across the table at the two doctors sitting on the opposite side from him. As a High Court judge, appointed by the State, O'Leary was often approached for advice or asked to discreetly intervene in certain delicate situations where he might have some power or influence.

Always within reason, of course, the honourable judge was willing to help out his Catholic brothers in Jesus Christ. That was why he joined the Knights in the first place — to uphold and promote the principles, ethics, ethos, and values of the Holy Roman Catholic Sea in an increasingly secular society that seemed increasingly hostile to Christian principles.

The Supreme Knight continued:
"The situation is this, and I have to say it is not good. About twelve weeks ago, while I was giving a general anaesthetic to a young lady — she is only twenty-two or three — she suffered a cardiac arrest. Her heart stopped suddenly for no good reason that any of us could figure out. Anyway, it took us a long time to get her going again, and she suffered quite extensive brain damage from the ensuing oxygen deprivation to the brain cells."

Nobody indicated they wished to speak so he continued:
"The situation at the minute is that she is now in a persistent vegetative state or PVS, and the chances of her coming back from this are remote indeed. She is breathing on her own, and we can keep her alive indefinitely by tube feeding, round the clock and excellent nursing, and the use of antibiotics as the need arises."

Again, he paused to allow for interruption, but there was no indication, so he continued.

"There are two problems that Brother Peter and I would appreciate your input into. The first concerns the patient's parents or her mother in any case. I have never met the lady, nor do I have any plans to meet her in the foreseeable future. But I am told that she keeps demanding answers to certain questions and seems not to appreciate our efforts in keeping her daughter alive. The first question is: are we as medics entitled to take charge of our patient's care or can relatives overrule our wishes? Secondly, are we right to keep her alive for as long as possible and using any means at our disposal? Remember now she is totally paralysed and has no cognitive function — no awareness, as far as we can judge, of self or of her environment."

Before answering him, the Supreme Chancellor drew himself up and straightened his back against the back of the oak Chippendale dining room chair. As the one answering, he was not required to stand up.

"I will answer your second question first, Brother."
Justice O'Leary cleared his throat.

"On the question of keeping her alive by any reasonable means, there is no ambiguity here whatsoever. It is your moral and ethical duty to do everything in your power to keep this young woman alive through hydration, nutrition, antibiotics, and excellent around-the-clock nursing care. That is your Christian and Catholic obligation before Christ. All life is sacred in the eyes of The Lord, and it is up to good Catholic doctors to bear witness to that sacredness by preserving life for as long as possible. That she has no cognition, no capacity, and no awareness of self or of her surroundings is beside the point."

Deputy Supreme Knight Peter Newman indicated he wanted to say something.

"Yes, Brother."

"Her prospects of recovery are about zero, I'm afraid."

"Alright, but that is not the point. There is no precedent in law where starving someone to death — the only alternative to what you are doing at the moment — was ever subsequently judged lawful. The tube feeding quite simply must go on indefinitely, and the antibiotics too, of course."

Here Supreme Chancellor Thomas O'Leary drew in his breath and looked at his fellow Knights across the table from him. The large room was quiet except for the odd crackle coming from the log fire blazing up the chimney beyond the Clarke's surround. That and the distant rumble of traffic going around St Stephen's Green down at the end of Hume Street filtered into the room.

"Now, turning to the first part of your question, about who are the rightful people to make decisions concerning your patient, the parents or the doctors."

The judge flicked his black Knight's robe further back on his shoulders before folding his arms on the polished mahogany table in front of him.

"From what you say, this young lady is severely mentally incapacitated, and therefore someone needs to act on her behalf and decide what's in her best interest short and long-term. In the absence of her being made a Ward of Court, and that's on the cards but I will return to that in a minute, in law it is her parent's and not the doctor's prerogative, as things stand, to make decisions on her behalf about her care and welfare."

Here the Supreme Knight made as though he wanted to say something but seemed to think better of it. The Chancellor continued.

"Now I do emphasise that that is in law. In practice, however, it is the doctors who take charge of things and who make decisions on behalf of their patients. Why? Well, just think about it. The parents are lay people. They are not in any position to make medical decisions. If they tried to take their daughter home and take things into their own hands, they could easily be unwittingly straying into criminality. No, you just keep going, Brothers. I do not think you have got anything to be afraid of. Just keep out of the parents' way. Tell them as little as possible and make your own decisions in line with Catholic ethos and sound moral ethics. If there are any new developments, I would be glad to hear about them and to assist in any way possible."

There now followed a respectful pause while the speaker gathered his thoughts.

"I just need to say a few words about Ward of Court. It may be very relevant later on."

The High Court judge pulled back the left sleeve of his dark blue pinstriped suit to check the face of his Rolex. They had ten minutes before the general fortnightly assembly.

"We are alright for time. I will be brief. You will need to think about the future just a little bit. The probability is that the parents will sue you, Walter, and you too, Peter, and they will sue the hospital. How or if you defend yourselves is for another day but for now you can reliably anticipate some legal activities down the road. If through this, your patient is awarded damages, then she will be automatically made a Ward of Court. In this event, it will then be the courts that will exercise parens patriae, and the natural parents will be subordinate to the courts. You will both be subordinate to the same court. When this happens, you might expect less hassle from the parents in terms of who calls the shots regarding your patient's care going into the future. But, by the same token, the balance of power will be very different. I will keep a watching brief in the background as events unfold. In the meantime, carry on the work of The Lord Jesus Christ."

The Supreme Knight leaned across to the Chancellor.

"Thank you so much, Sir. I am sure I speak for Brother Newman as well when I say that that kind of advice, coming from a man of your stature and influence, is most helpful and reassuring. We will be happy to keep you advised of any developments as they arise. In the meantime, thank you kindly, Your Honour, again."

A loud scratching sound of wood upon wood erupted as three heavy oak Chippendale dining room chairs were pushed back from the boardroom table in unison, and the three Knights stood up, bowed in each other's direction, left the room, and proceeded to the general fortnightly assembly across the hall, their colourful robes trailing in their wake.

Summer had come to 16 Ashgrove Lane, Rathfarnham. It was now almost seven months since Linda Boyle's catastrophic so-called minor operative procedure that had left her staring out from a non-functioning brain. Her mother, Mary Boyle, attended her hybrid tea roses with a heavy heart. A time was when spraying these roses against black spot used to give a quiet sense of purpose and achievement.

Before Linda's catastrophe, Mary used to love being out in the early morning sun in the middle of the summer with a small hand-held sprayer containing a dilute mixture of baking soda. She loved the sense of quiet satisfaction that came with giving the upper surface of each dark green leaf a light preventative spraying against the fungus. She used to love the warm caress of dappled sunbeams as they fell on her face and the sound of the blackbird or song thrush calling from the mature silver birch tree beside the clothesline.

But that was then, and this is now. Her daughter's grave and apparently irreparable brain damage hung heavily on her mind, such that it preoccupied her thoughts practically every minute of her walking day. And that thought blighted all pleasure and even turned the once joyous sound of birdsong into a kind of dirge and a lament. And worst still was the knowledge that she could have stopped this devastation from ever happening in the first place. Had she just listened to Linda as she nonchalantly told Mary of what Peter Newman intended doing to her and had she advised postponement of the procedure or of having a second opinion, then none of this might ever have happened. This thought alone was extremely painful and difficult to endure.

Burdened with these thoughts, Mary returned to the kitchen and put the kettle on the Aga. Margaret was next door doing the crosswords.

"How about a cup of tea in there, Margaret?"

"Yes, please. Dad is late, isn't he?"

"It's his evening for visiting, isn't it?"

"Oh yes, of course, I'd completely forgotten. They moved Linda a few days ago. What do you think of her new situation?"

Margaret abandoned her crosswords and returned to take her place at the kitchen table where her mother poured tea from a battered aluminium teapot.

"I think her new situation is an improvement. God, was I getting sick of that ICU and Sister Assumpta! She did her best, I suppose, but she wasn't easy. Anyway, there wasn't any more they could do for poor Linda up there, was there?"

"No, you're right. ICUs are not for Linda's situation. But I really like that sister what's-her-face —?"

"Concillio."

"Yes, thank you, Concillio. I think she's really nice. At least you can talk to her, and she will talk to you. I had an interesting conversation with her yesterday, but you might find it distressing."

"Margaret sweetie, I have found everything for the last seven months profoundly distressing, I'm getting used to 'distressing' at this stage. So please tell us what Sister Concillio had to say."

"Alright. We were talking about Linda's habit of pulling her nasogastric tube out almost every day."

"Yes, go on." Mary topped up her tea from the battered teapot.

"Well, Sister Concillio told me that Linda now only pulls her tube out when she is alone, and nobody is looking."

"Yes, so -----?"

"So therefore Mum, Linda may know when she's alone. To be able to know that she would need some hearing or sight or both. To avail of the opportunity, she would also need some reasoning powers and have intent."

"I see, so her brain damage may not be as total as Dr. Patel was suggesting."

"Yes, but to be fair to him, he was not adamant about anything. There is another distressing aspect to this though."

"Yes, go on Margaret please."

"If she has intent in pulling out her nasogastric tube every day, then what is that telling us?"

"I don't know, maybe the tube is uncomfortable in her nose or something."

"Yes, maybe. But Sister Concillio had another thought. Maybe Linda is trying to send a message that she does not want to be fed and that she wants to die. Is that not at least a possibility?"

"It is a possibility Margaret, of course, but to my mind it sounds fanciful. Do you know what I mean like? It sounds almost melodramatic. At least I hope that that's the case."

"So do I Mum because if Linda has enough cognition to be sending out messages, then she may have enough cognition to realise the situation in which she is trapped."

"I just don't want to think along those lines Margaret if you don't mind. Please."

Mary finished off the last of her tea with the cup shaking in her hand as she lifted it to her mouth. The conversation had clearly upset her, but Margaret wasn't finished.

"I asked Sister Concillio about some of the nurse's claims that Linda sometimes 'smiled' at them and seemed to recognise them."

"Margaret really, that's just a load of nonsense. In all the times that I've visited her, Linda never once gave me the smallest hint of recognition and I'm her mother for crying out loud."

"Yah Mum that would be Sister Concillio's opinion too. She thinks that Linda's so-called smile is no more than an involuntary grimace. But it's odd how people interpret things so very differently."

"People interpret things Margaret in ways that suit them. If you can ascribe cognition to Linda's 'behaviour' -- pulling out her feeding tube, smiling, whatever, then you can justify keeping her alive for as long as possible."

"That's right Mum. But the cruel thing about it is that if one suggests that she has some brain function then you are also suggesting that she may have insight into her horrible situation and that is unthinkable."

"It is indeed love and that is precisely why I do not agree with the carers. They mean well and they are very kind to Linda, but they are wrong in their interpretation of her actions, or at least I pray to God that they are wrong."

Sister Concillio gathered a group of six student nurses around Linda's bed for a clinical tutorial. She clapped her hands together once to get their attention.

"Ladies, please, listen up now, ladies. This is Linda Boyle here. Linda has suffered severe brain damage following a cardiac arrest while under general anaesthetic. Who can tell me, what the nursing priorities are in a situation like this?"

One of the students tentatively raised a hand.

"Would it be the prevention of decubitus ulcers, Sister?"

"It would indeed, Clare. Well done, spot on. Nursing standards are often judged on the presence or absence of these ulcers or so-called pressure sores. Now, what are the rules for preventing bedsores or decubitus ulcers in a bedridden patient? Anyone, come on?"

The student nurses answered in a random way, and Sister Concillio approved their answers:

"Frequent turning of the patient."

"Yes, good."

"Keeping the patient's bottom dry."

"Yes, absolutely essential and often neglected. That's why this patient wears Kango pads at all times and has an indwelling catheter."

"Sitting the patient out of bed."

"Yes, sometimes difficult but always worth it."

"Use of ripple mattress and sheepskin rug under the patient."

"Yes, very good girls. That's about it. There is a revolving bed being developed that may prove useful in the future, but for the moment, it's a bit experimental."

One of the student nurses had a question for her tutor and raised her hand politely.

"Yes, Anne, what is it?"

"Can Linda see or hear us? Does she know what's going on, Sister?"

"That's a good question and one that her carers are divided on. I do not think that she can see or hear, and I do not believe that she has any awareness of herself or of her surroundings. And I pray to God that I'm right in this."

Another hand was raised. Sister Concillio checked her watch; this tutorial should have been over ten minutes ago.

"Yes, Joan? Sorry, this will have to be the last question now."

"Can Linda move at all, Sister, and why is she lying on her side?"

"No, she can move nothing at all in her body except her eyeballs and her eyelids, and her diaphragm moves to let her breathe. But that's all. The rest of her is frozen solid. We have to nurse her on her side because her legs are contracted into the foetal position, and therefore, she cannot lie on her back."

And with that, the tutorial ended, and the little group dispersed.

Dr. Walter Malone needed another opinion. Linda's contracted limbs were causing severe nursing problems, inasmuch as she could not be nursed on her back and could only be turned from one side to the other. This limited nursing positions increased the danger of her developing pressure sores and ulcers and the complications that they gave rise to.

Malone arranged to meet orthopaedic surgeon Mr. Tom Tobin in the hospital canteen to discuss Linda Boyle's case.

"Tom, you will have heard about this tragic case that we have on our hands, this young lady who arrested while undergoing a salpingogram and who is now in a persistent vegetative state?"

"Yes, Walter. These things happen, unfortunately. I hear old Peter Newman is a bit cut up about it, especially since it was his idea that she underwent the op -----"

"Hold on now a minute, Tom. We are not here to discuss Peter Newman!"

Outrage showed all over Malone's face as he tried to cut his colleague short.

"Well, maybe we're not. But a salpingogram is becoming a very controversial procedure, you know."

Dressed in scrub-suit and white coat, Tobin was a small, neat man in his early forties. He was highly regarded as an orthopaedic surgeon and was single-handedly responsible for the introduction of safe hip replacement surgery into

Ireland on his return from America three years ago. He was generally regarded as a valuable asset to Saint Malachi's Hospital. He was considered by the hospital to be a 'good catch'. He had upped the profile of this institution quite considerably.

Malone viewed Tobin's recent remarks as simply unacceptable. What is the world coming to, he wondered to himself? You never criticise a colleague like that, not in front of a patient and not in front of a fellow doctor, never – it's a golden, unspoken rule.

"Well, Tom, I really cannot comment on the procedure itself or on its necessity or otherwise. It's inappropriate to do so, and in any case, what's done is done."

Malone struggled to hide his annoyance with his young colleague's suggestion of any impropriety on behalf of a senior consultant staff member. If he didn't need his help so badly right now, he would tell him to go and bugger off with himself. These young fellows coming up through the ranks these days, they did not seem to know where to get off. And what about respect?

Malone pressed on with difficulty:
"The point is this. Despite intensive physio, she has developed bad contractures of her joints, and this is a particular problem with her legs. She is now fully flexed and fixed at her hips and knees."

"Yes—so?"

God, this fellow is hard to take, Malone thought to himself. But he must press on:

"As a direct result of this," Dr. Malone went on to explain the obvious, "she can only be nursed in either her left or right lateral position. This situation does not give the nurses sufficient options to avoid decubitus ulcers. They have asked that I inquire into the feasibility of her having her legs straightened out surgically, and that is why I am talking to you now."

Mr. Tobin sipped from his mug of tea and observed his colleague sitting across from him at the canteen table. The place was full of hospital staff from all departments on a tea break, and there was a loud and general babble of conversation. This suited the two doctors. For the moment, what they were discussing was not for general distribution. The young orthopaedic surgeon did not like what his colleague had just suggested but was unsure as to how he might manage to get himself out of this unpleasant situation.

"Of course, it can be done, Walter. The question really is, though—should it be done? I mean to say, I can sever her flexor tendons at both hips and behind both knees and straighten her out. But it would go against my training, and it would go against my conscience as well to do this. Do you know what I mean?"

Malone knew what his colleague meant, alright, but was not prepared to concede.

"No, frankly, I do not know what you mean. We are trying to save a life here."

"Indeed, Walter. But what is the quality of that life?"

"That is not for us to judge. Surely, human life is human life and, as such, is sacrosanct."

"Well, that depends on one's perspective. In any case, I've another problem with your suggestion. Some critics could construe that kind of surgery as mutilation. It's a question of ethics, really. Is it ethical to deliberately destroy function? I know your ultimate goal is to reduce the risk of bedsores developing, and that might be laudable. But it seems to me to be a fairly massive price to pay for little gains. Putting it bluntly, Walter, if she develops bedsores—so what?"

Tom Tobin wanted to say an awful lot more to his colleague, but medical etiquette forbids it. Doctors, as a general rule, do not question each other's value judgments in matters of private morality. But if one were to judge by the extraordinary lengths that Malone seemed prepared to go to in order to just prevent pressure sores developing in his comatose patient, then his long-term plans for her became all too apparent.

It now occurred to the surgeon that the anaesthetist was going to keep her alive for as long as ever possible, and this was a strategy that found little favour with the younger man. His view would be that if someone were beyond medical help, had no prospects of ever recovering and were trying to die, then they should be allowed to do so with dignity. But Tom Tobin had no wish to go into that with his older colleague. It wouldn't change him anyway, even if he did. People of Malone's mindset never change. But that did not mean either that he was going to go along with this grotesque leg straightening business.

Walter Malone now knew that this meeting had been a big mistake. It should never have taken place. This fellow Tobin was not properly pro-life. He would let Ms. Boyle develop pressure sores and not give a fiddler's about her. Malone thought to himself: I should never have discussed this with him in the first place. I should have gone directly to Mr. Cribbin, who has done this kind of surgery on unconscious patients for me before.

With these thoughts running through his mind, Dr. Malone sprung abruptly to his feet and bade his colleague a curt good day. Tom Tobin was left sitting there with his empty mug in front of him and in little doubt as to Malone's annoyance with him for his refusal to row in with the anaesthetist's plans. But that was all right too. Each of us has to live with our own conscience.

Straightening out contracted limbs in a young woman in a persistent vegetative state, just so as she would be easier to

151

nurse, was not Tom Tobin's idea of good practice, and no amount of argument would convince him otherwise. Leave her alone and let nature take its course would be Tobin's philosophy.

Eventually, Dr. Mansfield persuaded orthopaedic surgeon Mr. Cribbin to carry out the major surgery required to straighten out Linda's legs so that she could be nursed in positions other than on her left or right-hand side. The operation took five hours in total to complete—two and a half hours per leg. It involved the severing of all the major flexor tendons at their point of insertion into the bone. The surgery was irreversible. In the extremely unlikely event of Linda regaining function of her muscles and limbs, then this surgery that Mr. Cribbin performed made it doubly impossible for her ever to walk again. The operation was then an unspoken acknowledgment of the hopelessness of her dreadful situation and a silent acknowledgment by her carers of her real prognosis. And yet, nobody talked about that.

The next surgery she was deemed to need was dental. During those periods when Linda appeared most agitated, she tended to bite her tongue or the inside of her cheek. This might happen as often as once a week and was most distressing for her loved ones to have to witness. The solution to this problem was simple but radical. By capping her back upper and lower teeth sufficiently, a situation was created whereby Linda was unable to close her mouth completely and bring her front teeth together. Thus, the problem of her tongue and inside cheek biting was solved.

Both of these operations, of course, required a general anaesthetic and a signed written consent from next of kin. In each case, Linda's mother, Mary Boyle, reluctantly performed this function. But she remained deeply unhappy about the situation insofar as she was never consulted about her feelings about Linda's long-term nursing management. What was the treatment plan, and what were the logistics behind that plan? Whatever decisions were made in this regard were made somewhere behind closed doors and without any input from Linda's family.

But, to judge by the aggressive nature of her management—the radical surgery required to straighten out her legs, the capping of her teeth to prevent her from biting her tongue and inside of her cheek, and the constant recurring use of antibiotics whenever Linda spiked a temperature—all of this strongly indicated that it was the carers' clear intention to keep Linda alive for as long as ever possible and by whatever means available and necessary.

CHAPTER 6 - SUE FOR DAMAGES

The summer of 1982 was a good summer by Irish standards. It was now over eight years since Linda Boyle slipped from a coma into a near persistent vegetative state (PVS). Her private ward was hot and oppressive. Against this, the single window, to the right of the door as one entered the room, was flung fully open to let in some fresh air. Traffic noises drifted in from the central city traffic far below. A car horn occasionally honked. A seagull occasionally cried. Otherwise, there was silence except for Linda Boyle's steady, quiet, rhythmic breathing, fourteen breaths per minute. She occasionally moaned or cried out as if in distress. She was now well past the point of no return. Nobody, not even the most optimistic of her carers, expected any recovery at this stage.

Nearly every day she managed to pull out her nasogastric tube, and so almost every day the nurses had to replace it with a new one. They did this against Linda's noisy protests and struggling. If on occasion her mother was present when the tube was being forcibly replaced, she could not bear to watch her unconscious daughter being so treated and had to leave the ward while this procedure was being carried out.

The whole business of having to routinely replace Linda's feeding tube up into her nose and down into her esophagus was most upsetting and distressful. It was distressing for those concerned, but not least, of course, for the patient herself. The nurses hated having to do it, Linda's mother could not bear to watch it being done, and clearly, the patient herself detested the ordeal. But they had to go on; it was doctor's orders.

If there was one thing the entire family was agreed on, it was about the quality of the nursing care their stricken loved one was receiving from the nursing staff of St. Malachi's General Hospital. Nothing seemed to be too much trouble for those fantastic women. With loving and gentle care, they turned Linda from one side onto the other every half hour for twenty-four hours a day and three hundred and sixty-five days a year. In this way, the danger of Linda developing potentially fatal pressure sores was minimized. That kind of devotion to duty was rare enough.

Relationships between the family members and the doctors making the decisions about Linda's care deteriorated with each passing year. Machiavellian communications were the norm and it drove Linda's family to distraction. All they wanted were some simple answers to some simple questions, but none, frustratingly, seemed to be forthcoming. Sometimes things deteriorated so much that the family were actually made to feel that they were somehow the ones to blame for Linda's desperate plight. Indeed, Joseph and Mary Boyle occasionally had to remind consultants like Newman that it was they, the doctors, who brought about Linda's downfall in the first place.

Of all these questions, it was the one about long-term treatment strategy that most deeply concerned Linda's family.

She had been in a near persistent vegetative state now for over eight years, long past the point where one could reasonably expect any improvement in her hopeless situation. It was clear to everyone that Linda was not going to improve. So, what then was the point of tube-feeding her, given that she seemed to find this so distressful and given that such treatment could in no way be described as curative or even palliative?

On one rare occasion, Joseph Boyle managed to catch up with consultant Peter Newman and put this very question to him. The only reason that this chance encounter occurred was that Newman had been called into the hospital during visiting hours to see a patient in the next ward from where Linda lay. Joseph could hear him pontificating next door and thought to seize on this rare chance to collar him. Normally, consultants involved in any way with Linda Boyle's care went out of their way, in a game of cat and mouse, to avoid any contact with members of the Boyle family. They were all, at least as far as the consultants were concerned, equally truculent and difficult.

"Excuse me, please! Just a minute of your time, if you please, Dr. Newman!"

Joseph Boyle was now in full chase after the consultant's retreating back. 'What an absurd way for grown-up adults to communicate with each other,' he thought as he ran. But by now Joseph Boyle was used to this kind of bizarre behaviour from consultants and was prepared to do whatever it took to have a word with this aloof doctor.

Newman muttered under his breath,
'Fuck it, I'm caught rightly now.'

With that, he pulled up sharply and, turning clockwise
on his heels a full ninety degrees, he faced his tormentor. On
his face, he had switched on a broad smile that bore as much
sincerity as that worn by the tailor's dummies in Cleary's shop
window.

"Yes, sir, and what can I do for you today, ah?"

Joseph Boyle was momentarily thrown by the
supercilious attitude of the consultant. It took him a few
seconds to regain his composure before he could go on:

"Dr. Newman, it is well over a year now since any
member of my family has had a chance to talk to you. We want
you to know that the longer that this goes on, the unhappier
we are becoming."

Joseph waved his hand back towards Linda's private
room to indicate that it was her ongoing care that he was
referring to.

"Excuse me, Mr. Boyle," Newman interjected sharply.

"What exactly do you mean by 'this' when you say: the
longer that this goes on for, ah? Does 'this' mean the excellent
care and attention that Linda has been receiving from those
terrific and dedicated nurses down through the years? There is
nothing that any one of those dedicated nurses would not do

to try and help Linda. Is that what you mean by 'this' when you say the unhappier the family is becoming, ah?"

Joseph was beginning to feel the same exasperation every time he spoke to Newman. The man captured the high moral ground from which he browbeat and bullied anyone who dared question his authority or decisions. Any rational discussion with someone like this was nearly impossible. Nor was Newman finished yet.

"You do realize, don't you, that your daughter requires the attention of two fully qualified nurses around the clock, seven days a week? You do realize also that she needs to be turned in her bed every half hour to prevent her developing bedsores. In over eight years, she has remained totally free of these life-threatening skin lesions; that, in itself, testifies to the quality of her care. Her nasogastric tube needs constant replacing because she keeps pulling it out. She needs a daily bed bath, and her bowels need to be evacuated manually every four days. Now, what is it exactly, Mr. Boyle, that the family is complaining about?"

Dr. Newman was now well up on the high moral ground. Joseph Boyle, on the other hand, only had one chance to get his message across. He had tried and failed before, and he would probably fail again, for the contest was an unequal one.

"You yourself, Doctor, have repeatedly said over the past couple of years that Linda's chances of making any kind of recovery were zero. If there is no chance of her making any kind of recovery from here on in, then we wonder what exactly is the point of keeping Linda alive with forced feeding and frequent courses of antibiotics."

"What are you getting at, Mr. Boyle?"

"We are concerned about her dignity, her autonomy, and her right under the Irish Constitution to bodily integrity. We, the family, knew Linda well before she was put into a PVS by the medical profession. We are absolutely convinced beyond a shadow of a doubt that, were she to be given a choice, it would not be her wish that she be kept alive indefinitely like this."

Again, Joseph Boyle indicated with an outstretched arm Linda's ward down the corridor. He was glad that he was able to put in that bit about it being the medical profession's fault that Linda was the way she was today. It was extraordinary how the doctors in charge of Linda's care seemed to conveniently forget this central fact.

Now Dr. Peter Newman's hackles were well and truly up. Who the hell did this layperson think he was? The notion of him criticizing this hospital and its medical and nursing staff after their efforts to keep his daughter alive and as comfortable as possible over the last eight years! This was simply intolerable.

Newman glared at Joseph Boyle. Joseph held his ground and glared back at the doctor. Visitors passed up and down and noticed the pair of them.

"And what, Mr. Boyle, are you suggesting we should do? Or could it be that you have a better plan for your daughter that may not have occurred to us doctors?"

Newman made no effort to disguise his absolute contempt for lay interference in what he clearly saw as a medical matter alone. His condescending sarcasm in his last remark made this crystal clear.

"What I am suggesting, Dr. Newman, is that in the first instance, we, the family of Linda Boyle, be afforded an opportunity to sit down with you and the other doctors and nurses involved in her care, and that we discuss Linda's ongoing care plan in a calm and mature fashion. Again and again, we have asked for such a meeting, but again and again, it has been refused or falsely promised. Whichever, it has never happened."

Joseph Boyle paused for a second to ensure that his message was striking home. It is often difficult to tell one way or another. The doctor's face had little expression other than one of annoyance and irritation.

Boyle pressed ahead for his final salvo.

"But it seems to me, Dr. Newman, as it seems to the entire family, that this requested meeting is, for whatever reason, never going to happen. In its absence, therefore, standing out in this hospital corridor, I can tell you what way Linda's mother, sister, brother, and I are thinking. We believe that your treatment of Linda, while well-meaning, is nonetheless utterly futile. We believe that Linda wants to die, is trying to die, and that you and the nurses are preventing her from doing so. This treatment that you are giving her—tube feeding and antibiotics—robs her of her autonomy, strips her of her dignity, and is probably a violation of her Constitutional right to bodily integrity. We would like to see a treatment plan in place that at the very least envisaged the discontinuation of antibiotics and ultimately the discontinuation of nutrition and hydration via her feeding tube."

Joseph now knew there would be no turning back. At long last, it was out in the open. And not a bad thing either. At least now the nurses and the medical staff caring for Linda would know where the family stood on the matter. Whether they would act on it was another matter, of course. But at least now they had the information, and that could hardly be a bad thing.

Dr. Peter Newman moved back to let people pass. He rested his bottom against a windowsill and, with folded arms, glared at Joseph Boyle, who stood two feet away from him. Both men were of about equal height and age. This interminable argument needed to be settled once and for all.

The doctor took a quick glance over his left shoulder to make sure that there was nobody within earshot. Joseph Boyle couldn't decide if this gesture was genuine or just for effect, but he thought it more likely to be for effect.

"Listen, Mr. Boyle," Newman began, "I want you to know that what you and the family are suggesting, most particularly the discontinuation of the feeding tube, cannot happen, must not happen, and will not happen. We don't do euthanasia here, is that clear? What you and your family are suggesting is, in our opinion, immoral, unethical, and frankly illegal. There is not the slightest chance in hell that any member of the caring staff in there ----" Newman pointed a finger in the direction of Linda's ward, "—would allow her to suffer a treatable illness and not be treated. And as for denying her food and water, well, I mean to say, you wouldn't do that to a dog, now would you? Such an act would constitute a deliberate attack on Linda's life and would be tantamount to euthanasia and murder. And I hardly need to remind you that euthanasia is a crime under the law of the land and a grave mortal sin under the laws of our Church. In short, Mr. Boyle, what you are suggesting is utterly and absolutely out of the question, and I would thank you never to even mention them again. Good evening to you, sir."

With these final and emphatic words, Newman hauled himself off the windowsill and proceeded to walk down the corridor. Throwing caution to the wind and quite indifferent to the fact that he would be overheard by lots of people passing up and down the corridor, Joseph Boyle tried one final salvo:

"Withholding treatment and allowing someone to die is NOT euthanasia. Doctors in Ireland do it all the time. It involves an act of omission, not one of commission."

These words had the effect of stopping Newman in his tracks. He pulled up sharply. Turning around, he pointed his right index finger straight at Boyle's face and said:

"If you think that I am going to spend any more time philosophizing with a man who wants to see his daughter dead, then you're mistaken. Life is precious, and it must be preserved at any cost, and that, sir, is the bottom line and the end of the story. I hope I make myself clear."

With this, Dr. Newman finally made a hasty retreat down the corridor, determined that this time he would keep going even if Mr. Boyle should try to further pursue him. He didn't. Instead, Joseph Boyle felt drained and defeated. Argument, appeal, or persuasion was clearly not going to work. There simply would have to be another way. It might be time to think of the law. Certainly, they needed a solicitor's opinion.

***

It was mid-summer, and the evenings were at their longest. Soon the days would be shortening, and the long, slow countdown to autumn and winter would begin yet again. In the shaded garden of number 16 Ashgrove Lane, the tea roses were in full bloom, white and scarlet. Using sharp secateurs, Joseph

Boyle cut a bunch of these roses and arranged them in a narrow-necked Waterford crystal vase he had set centre stage on the pine kitchen table. Then he took up his place by the unlit fire, where he began to fill his straight-stemmed meerschaum pipe with Yachtsman plug tobacco. This ritual, cutting and rubbing plug tobacco, and then expertly filling it into the bowl of his pipe, had been a lifelong habit for Joseph Boyle. He was well-practiced. While doing so, he reflected on the wholly unsatisfactory and petulant exchange he had had yesterday with Peter Newman. Mary was ironing a few of his shirts next door in the sitting room. Joseph shouted through the half-opened door:

"I happened to run into Newman yesterday when I was visiting Linda."

"Oh?"

"Yes, I wasn't going to tell you at first because it was an unsatisfactory encounter. But on reflection, I suppose you had better know."

Mary Boyle emerged from the living room holding two freshly ironed shirts out in front of her. She laid them gently over the stainless-steel lid of the Aga's simmering plate. Leaning back against the cooker, arms folded in front of her slim waist, she turned to face her husband.

"You're damn right I had better know. It doesn't matter how unsatisfactory the meeting was; I need to know everything possible about what's going on in the minds of those making decisions on our daughter's behalf. I thought that we had agreed on that years ago. You know, like share and share alike. So come on, spit it out, and do not spare me any gory details."

Somewhat chastened by her gentle rebuke, Joseph Boyle lit his freshly filled pipe and embarked on a five-minute monologue, puffing away as he did so. He told his wife, Mary, how he had met Peter Newman yesterday in the hospital by pure chance. He related how he first expressed, on behalf of the family, their dissatisfaction with the ongoing situation regarding Linda's care and how Newman misinterpreted his comments, as always, and took offense at this. He told her how he had held his ground and again expressed dissatisfaction at the fact that the family was never consulted about their feelings toward Linda's ongoing care.

"Then, toward the end of this tetchy encounter, I made it clear to Newman that it was the wishes of this family that Linda is not given any further antibiotics if she springs a fever. I expressed this as a minimum but suggested that discontinuing nutrition and hydration at a later date might also be considered."

"And how did he react to that, or need I ask?"

"Predictably, I suppose is the short answer. He completely ruled out stopping the antibiotics, saying it would be unethical and immoral not to treat treatable illness. And as for discontinuing the tube feeding, he said that you wouldn't do that to a dog. Then, just as he was taking his leave of me, I pointed out to him that withholding treatment was not euthanasia and that doctors do that kind of thing all the time."

"Good on you, Joseph, that's telling them."

"Yea, you might think so, but I came away from my encounter with Newman yesterday absolutely certain about one thing, and that was that as long as he and those other fellows, what's their names? Walter Malone and that neurologist chap Martin Mansfield, as long as those doctors were in charge, there would be no change in their thinking, and our daughter will be kept alive for as long as is ever possible. I even brought in the matter of Linda's constitutional rights and her right to dignity. But I might as well have saved my breath."

"No? Well then, it may be time that we started to rattle a few birds' cages."

Mary left the warmth of the Aga and moved around the pine table, with freshly cut roses on it, to join her husband beside the unlit fire.

"The time might have come when we should start talking to some good lawyers. What do you think?"

"At first, I did not want to sue; I just hate the notion of suing doctors."

Mary looked disapprovingly at her husband. Sometimes he was difficult to fathom. He continued:

"But given the situation that we now find ourselves in and the intractable nature of her carers, I believe now that we have no choice but to proceed." Joseph's pipe had gone out.

"Yes, love, I agree. But will you stick with that now and not go changing your mind again?"

Joseph decides to ignore the gentle barb and continues.

"For one thing, it will force the doctors to tell us exactly what happened in the theatre all those years ago. Also, it will get poor Linda a lump sum of money. Not that any money could ever even begin to compensate her. And lastly, this will make her a Ward of Court, and as such, her care will not be up to the doctors, but it would be a matter for the courts to decide. What do you think?"

"I agree with everything you are saying there, Joseph. The time for legal action has sadly come. Who will we use? Brogan, I suppose?"

Tom Brogan's solicitor's practice was located in a terraced Victorian house on the South Circular Road. A heavy-set, stocky man in his late fifties, he had long been a friend and solicitor to the Boyles. He greeted his clients warmly but formally, shaking each by the hand as they entered his large office.

"Mary, Joseph, how good to see you. Now, please take a seat and make yourselves comfortable. Before we begin, would anyone like a cup of tea or maybe coffee?"

Both politely declined.

"Alright then, let's get straight to the point." Now, the solicitor was all business. "I am, of course, aware of the tragedy that befell your lovely daughter. How many years ago was it? Six or seven years ago, I suppose?"

The solicitor leaned back in his high-backed leatherette office chair and swung to and fro a little.

"It was eight and a half years ago, actually," Mary quietly interjected.

"Eight and a half years ago! Oh my God, where does the time go? Anyway, I know about the broad outline of the case, but what I need from you now are some more details of what exactly happened. As far as you are aware, what were the immediate and long-term effects of that? And was there any negligence or breach of duty of care as far as we can tell?"

"By the way, Tom, it was never our intention at first to sue anyone," Joseph explained, almost apologetically, before continuing, "I personally loathe the whole concept of suing people."

The solicitor raised his hand. This kind of talk raised his hackles. With impatience evident on his face, he interjected, "Listen, Joe, sorry, but everyone says that."

"Well, maybe they do. But as time went by and the consultants continued to refuse to meet with us and continued to exclude us from decision-making regarding Linda's care, it became clearer that they were, in fact, hiding something. It was this feeling that there was some kind of cover-up taking place, more than anything else, that drove us to contemplate these proceedings."

Mary nodded in agreement with her husband, and he continued.

Brogan decided to hear him out.

"We felt that we owed it to Linda to get to the whole truth about exactly what happened, and suing for negligence was the best way to achieve that. The money doesn't actually matter that much, although the proceedings will probably result in Linda being made a Ward of Court, and that might help."

The solicitor nodded in their direction, tapping on the desk lightly with his pen. He needed to caution these gentle people against any false expectations.

"All of that is correct, except I would caution you against any assumptions. We will seek full Discovery, of course, including Discovery of her hospital charts, records, and operation theatre notes."

This news clearly pleased the Boyles, and spotting this, the solicitor wanted to instil some more caution:

"Yes, but hold on a sec. Because they may have been anticipating legal action down the road, these notes and records might tell us very little. I just don't want the pair of you expecting great revelations through the Courts because that may not happen; in fact, it seldom does."

"But surely they will have written notes about what took place," Mary sounded incredulous.

"Yes, of course, but written up by the very people with the most to hide. They may be truthful insofar as they go, but it is only in evidence during the hearing that something closer to the truth might eventually emerge. And that will only happen if they contest our claims. I am just trying to keep your expectations realistic, that's all."

"Alright, Tom, that's fair enough, I suppose. What about the Ward of Court thing?" Joseph sounded resigned.

"What you say about settlement and Wards of Court is correct, I think."

"Regarding the settlement figure itself," the solicitor continued, "you might want to give it some more thought. I will be having a word with a good Senior Counsel in the next few days, and he will be able to further guide us when we meet. In the meantime, though, you might remember that damages come in under three headings thus:"

Brogan held up three fingers of his left hand one at a time.

"(a) Pain and suffering to date.

(b) Pain and suffering into the future.

(c) Special Damages."

"As for that last one, Special Damages, these include losses and/or expenses arising from the incident to date and into the future. They will include things like Linda's loss of earnings to date and into the future, her medical and travel expenses, and so on. I will need to ask you to gather up invoices, receipts, and documentation that can support all of these claims."

"We anticipated most of those, Tom, and we have it in hand."

"Good man, Joseph. They didn't make you a Revenue Commissioner for nothing, did they?"

Solicitor Brogan surveyed his clients across the desk from him for a few seconds before continuing. Despite his efforts to introduce a bit of levity, his clients looked worried.

"I know, Mary and Joseph, that you will say that no amount of money will repay Linda for the appalling hurt done to her. This is always the case in Personal Injury Claims. But nowhere could it be truer than in this truly shocking case. The law too recognizes that compensation can never restore a person to their pre-accident state. But it is the best that we can do. It is no more than a gesture and a recognition that damage has been done."

The meeting lasted another forty-five minutes. Tom Brogan asked the couple about the chronology of the various events. What happened to Linda while under anaesthesia and how the tragic events unfolded afterward? Mary did most of the talking, with Joseph interjecting every now and again with some little forgotten detail or other. Brogan took notes throughout.

Finally, he summed up as follows:
"Alright then, I think that's about it for the moment. How quickly we can move on from here will depend on how quickly the hospital and the two named defendants respond to our demand for disclosure of hospital records or Discovery as we call it. That sometimes can take months, but you may be assured that I will be doing everything in my power to move things along as quickly as is possible."

"Can you give us an idea of the timescale and so on?" Mary looked anxious.

"These will be High Court proceedings, of course, and I will be issuing the Plenary Summons and the Statement of Claim. What happens then is that the Defendants will raise Notices for Particulars. This will be their request for more information arising from what we allege against them in our Statement of Claim. We then reply to these. All this formal correspondence is designed to narrow down the scope of our claim so that at the end of the day, we have a good idea of what we have to prove in order to win."

Suspecting that his clients are losing interest, he ploughs ahead.

"After that," he continued, heaving a sigh, "we will be given a date for hearing, but just off the top of my head, I would not expect this to be much before the end of next year or maybe well into the following year."

"God, it's very slow, isn't it?" There was exasperation in Joseph's voice.

"Didn't Shakespeare talk about 'the law's delays?'" Mary interjected, trying to defuse things a bit.

"Generally speaking, Discovery can take up to a year and a half, and there is a two-year waiting list after that. The

Courts need to appoint more Judges. It's as simple as that. I will be arranging for you to meet with Senior Counsel before that, of course."

With these words, Tom Brogan was on his feet and shook the hand first of Mary and then Joseph Boyle. At the same time, he assured them that all would be well and advised that they not worry about it unduly. Joseph and Mary Boyle left the solicitor's office, quietly reassured.

"That went well, I thought," Joseph said to his wife as he turned the car and headed in the direction of home.

"Ah, it was alright. But I'm very disappointed to think that we still may not get the answers. You know, what's the point if we don't get answers?"

The Round Hall of the Four Courts on the Liffey's North quays was an awesome and even frightening place for people who had never been there before. Joseph and Mary Boyle had never been there before, and they now sat huddled together, waiting for their solicitor to come and rescue them. Their seat, made of stone, was just to the left as they entered through the massive entranceway. The Round Hall was 64 feet in diameter and was roofed with a massive dome that was a prominent part of Dublin's skyline. Inside, sixteen Corinthian columns supported this roof, and between these were empty niches that once housed statues of famous lawyers. These were largely destroyed during the Irish Civil War of 1922. The battle to oust the anti-treaty forces caused much damage throughout the building.

The floor of The Round Hall was tiled in concentric circles of alternating black and white, triangular-shaped stone tiles. Across this floor, High Court judges frequently passed and re-passed, preceded by their stick-carrying tipstaff. Some people knew what was expected of them and bowed low, as tradition dictated, when they saw this procession pass. Others, not knowing about this protocol, simply ignored it.

All the while, there was this terrific hubbub of conversation going on as people – junior and senior Counsels, solicitors, and their clients, the Plaintiffs and Defendants, trainee barristers known as Devils, newspaper reporters, witnesses and jurors, Apprentices and Law Clerks, convicted criminals in chains and their warders – moved in and out of this dance as if they were partaking in some ghoulish ballet. All sound was greatly magnified by the tiled floor below and the massive, domed roof high above the gathered throng. Mary and Joseph Boyle did not know this yet, but it was in this space, not in the adjoining courtrooms, but right here in this Round Hall, that the majority of legal cases in Ireland were settled between opposing legal teams.

Eventually, they saw him approach them from the direction of the Law Library. Their solicitor, Tom Brogan, was weighed down by masses of legal files. These he barely managed to accommodate under his right arm, holding them against his ample belly.

"Good morning, Joseph, and good morning, Mary. Excuse me if I can't shake hands with you, but I don't want to drop these files. Follow me, please. We are in consultation room eleven, I think."

And with that, he turned on his heels, and they were off—all three of them, into the ghoulish ballet and across the 64-foot diameter of The Round Hall of the Four Courts. Up the three steps at the far side, bear left, and a quick right, right, and a quick left again, passing men and women dressed in long black and intimidating legal garb. Wigs with ringlets. This was opera.

"Good morning, Tom."
"Good morning, Catherine."
"Oh, Tom, just a quick word in your shell-like, please!"

The solicitor excused himself from his clients and went into a whispered conclave with the Junior Counsel named Catherine. The exchange lasted just over one minute.

"I'll look after that for you, Catherine, love. Don't give it another thought." The overweight solicitor half-turned back to the lady barrister and stuck his left thumb up in the air.

"That will be alright now!" he cried back to her.

They were off again. Led by their solicitor with the massive pile of legal files under his right arm, closely followed by Mary and then Joseph Boyle, the little procession entered the hallway in front of the Law Library where there were eight open consultation booths, each one occupied by barristers, solicitors, and their clients in murmured consultation, among mountains of documents and files teetering precariously. Turn right at the entrance to the Law Library, speed down the corridor. More wigs and gowns flash by.

"Morning, Tom. Must have a word with you sometime. There have been developments, but I must fly. Catch up with you later." Turn left and then a quick right past the stationery and newspaper shop and down the passage with numbered doors to the consultation rooms proper.

Tom Brogan flung open the door to number eleven and stepped back to allow his clients into the tiny room before entering himself. The room contained one large old-fashioned radiator against the right-hand sidewall. Directly opposite the door was a large window looking out onto a courtyard. The room was almost entirely occupied by a heavy oblong oak table and four dining room style chairs.

"Make yourselves comfortable," the solicitor said while dumping down his heavy load of files and records onto the centre of the table.

"If you will excuse me now, please, for about five minutes, and I'll go off and try and find Mr. Lavelle, our Senior

Counsel. We have a Junior as well, but she can't make it this morning. It doesn't matter; she is not needed at this stage."

And with that, he was gone.

Neither Joseph nor Mary Boyle was sure what their solicitor meant by his parting remark about the Junior being 'not needed' at this stage, but they decided to leave it. The Boyles were becoming reconciled to the fact that a great number of things that went on in this legal world were incomprehensible to the vast majority of laypeople. They sat there patiently and silently. Joseph regretted now that he hadn't brought an Irish Times along with him. He could at least be doing the crossword. Almost three-quarters of an hour had passed when there was a quick rap tap on the door, and without waiting for a response from within, it was opened, and Mr. Lavelle entered the room, followed by the solicitor, Mr. Tom Brogan.

"Sorry to have kept you waiting like this. These barristers can sometimes be hard to track down."

Tom Brogan winked at his clients, signalling he wasn't entirely serious. He introduced the Senior Counsel to them as David Lavelle. After exchanging handshakes, they all took their seats.

David Lavelle cut an impressive figure. Dressed for court, he wore an open-fronted, full-length black silk gown with elbow-length sleeves. Beneath this, he sported the customary black embroidered morning coat and dark grey striped trousers. His shirt was brilliantly white with a raised wing collar, and around his neck, he wore the traditional white tabs. Gold cufflinks and a gold Cartier watch with a bracelet completed the ensemble. Mary Boyle, sitting across from him, estimated his age to be in the mid-fifties. He had a full head of dark hair, greying at the temples. Resting on the table in front of him was his short horsehair wig with tassels, an icon of the judicial system. His hands were folded on the table as he surveyed the room, ensuring everyone was ready.

Lavelle's voice was soft, carrying an acquired accent— a peculiar blend of Oxford and Dublin:

"Alright then, I'll get straight to the point. Tom has briefed me on the details of this unfortunate case. I've also gone through the medical records and reports. From what I gather, your daughter Linda has been grievously harmed by the medical profession, and I can't discern any valid reason for it. Her hospital notes are notably sparse and lack detail, especially the post-operative notes."

The barrister's tone was measured. Mary and Joseph Boyle leaned in, trying to catch every word. Sensing their difficulty, David Lavelle raised his voice slightly.

Joseph interjected, "But the post-op notes are pivotal."

"I'm aware, Mr. Boyle. However, they merely state that Linda had a cardiac arrest towards the end of her

179

hysterosalpingogram procedure and that she was immediately resuscitated. Crucially, these notes don't specify times. We need to know the exact moments Linda's heart stopped and when it resumed. Without this vital information, these notes are practically useless. The author likely anticipated these records might be used against him in the future and thus was scant on details. But this tactic can backfire, making it seem as though there's a cover-up."

Lavelle paused, ensuring everyone was following. They were.

"Regarding the matter of consent, Tom, do you have a copy of the Consent Form Linda signed before the operation?"

"It should be in your brief, but I'll check," Tom replied, thinking, 'these Senior Counsels really should come with assistants.'

Tom began rifling through his extensive files. Joseph observed the dynamic between the solicitor and barrister, intrigued by the peculiar relationship. Solicitors chose and engaged barristers, yet in client consultations, it seemed the solicitor danced to the barrister's tune.

After two minutes of fruitless searching, David Lavelle glanced at his gold Cartier watch, noting he had another consultation in just over twenty minutes.

"No need to continue, Tom. We know it's there somewhere. Let's move on."

Tom ceased his search, and the Senior Counsel continued:
"I've reviewed the hospital consent form Linda signed, and it's woefully inadequate—a generic consent form, really. It vaguely mentions that surgical procedures carry inherent risks, specifying haemorrhage and postoperative infection. This form could be used for anything from toenail removal to major brain surgery."

"Linda probably didn't even read it," Mary suggested.

"You might be right, Mrs. Boyle. But here's the crux: the consent form made no mention of the potential, however slight, of a cardiac arrest, nor the possibility of a coma or a persistent vegetative state. There's no written evidence that Linda was informed of these risks. This omission significantly weakens the defence's case. If she had been informed, she might have declined the procedure and would be in good health today."

Mary Boyle felt a pang of guilt at Lavelle's words. She regretted not questioning the medical staff more thoroughly about the risks of general anaesthesia and the hysterosalpingogram. Why hadn't she accompanied Linda to the hospital that fateful January afternoon over nine years ago? They could have reviewed the consent form together, asking pertinent questions. She felt she had failed her twenty-two-year-old daughter, who had to make these decisions alone. The weight of the consequences bore down on her. Reaching into her handbag for a tissue, her eyes welled up with tears of pain and guilt.

David Lavelle was conscious of time constraints. He needed to get this meeting over with and rush off to the next consultation. Sitting up erect, he straightened himself against the back of the dining room chair, which creaked slightly under the strain.

"And then, of course, there's the whole vexed question as to the need for Linda having a hysterosalpingogram in the first place. We have identified an expert witness in the UK, Professor Tim Weighbridge. Is that his name, Tom?"

The solicitor nodded his head three times quickly.

"He's a heavy hitter. He's the past President of the Royal College of Obstetrics and Gynaecology in London, and they don't come weightier than that, let me tell you. He's prepared to come over to Dublin and give evidence on our behalf. He's prepared to swear under oath that a hysterosalpingogram was not indicated if you suspect a hormone-producing tumour, as outlined in the correspondence between Newman and the GP — whatever his name is. Professor Weighbridge will say that in circumstances like this, what you need first is a simple blood test to determine certain hormonal levels. It's as simple as that. Linda's disastrous operation, from which she has suffered so grievously, was unnecessary. She didn't need a hysterosalpingogram. End of story."

A pause now while Lavelle looked around the table.

Joseph and Mary were clearly traumatised by these latest revelations. The Senior Counsel appeared not to notice.

"I'm not supposed to say things like this, and normally I wouldn't. However, I think that I might make an exception here. The case against these defendants is, in my view, as watertight as they get. In fact, the probability is that the insurers will not contest it on the grounds of costs and potential damage to their client's professional reputations. They simply cannot win this case, and running it would only make an already bad situation worse."

Consulting room number eleven suddenly filled with a stunned and sickening silence. Joseph and Mary's thoughts concurred. How could people calling themselves doctors do this to an innocent young woman in the prime of her life, whose only crime was to place her trust in them?

David Lavelle broke the uneasy silence. His watch told him that he only had a few minutes left. He had to move on.

"And finally, there's the question of any settlement figure. On Linda's behalf, we have to try and decide what kind of sum of money would go some way towards compensating her for the terrible hurt done to her. She will never come out of this persistent vegetative state. In practical terms, her life is over. So, how can you compensate anyone for that? You can't, is the answer. So, don't look at this in terms of compensation in the conventional sense. Look at it more as a token of liability from those responsible for Linda's terrible predicament. With that in mind, I am suggesting a bottom-line figure of one million pounds plus costs. But you two can think about it. Nothing needs to be set in stone at this stage. Now, do you have any questions? I'm under a bit of pressure elsewhere, I'm afraid. Sorry about that."

Mary Boyle raised her left hand.

"Yes, Mrs. Boyle?"

"You said that the probability was that the other side would not contest it. Does that mean that we may never even get into court?"

"I'm sorry, Mrs. Boyle, but I am needed in court right now."

Lavelle glanced at his watch again.

"Tom, you can take that one. I'll see you again before the date of the hearing. In the meantime, keep well and don't worry. We will get through this together."

David Lavelle stood up, shook hands warmly with everyone in the room, grabbed his short horsehair wig off the oak table, and was out the door in a flash.

Tom Brogan coughed quietly to himself before addressing Mary Boyle's question:

"It very much depends on a number of factors, Mary. A settlement offer, out of court, can be made without their having to admit any negligence. If that's the line they take, then there's precious little that we can do about it, except, of course, refuse their offer. Nevertheless, the offer could be such that you would be ill-advised not to take it. At the end of the day, you two are in control here. I am here to take your instructions. By refusing, let's say, a very generous offer, you run the risk of getting less through the courts. Worse than that, when in court, they can always just accept liability, and the case still would not run. Now, I did warn you about this possibility, and I must say, after what we have just heard from Mr Lavelle, my 'possibility' has moved up to be a 'probability'."

Mary and Joseph looked each other straight in the eye for a second before Joseph spoke. What they had just heard was not what they wanted to hear.

"I appreciate what you've just said, Tom, but you must look at it from Mary's and my perspective. The prime reason, the only reason if you like, for us bringing this action against Newman, Malone, and the hospital was to get the full story behind what exactly happened to our daughter. We wanted the full story, and we wanted to hear those bastards admit that they were negligent, if you'll pardon my French. The issue as to the size of the settlement was and is of secondary importance, if you follow."

Brogan held his right hand out across the oak table, palm held forward, three feet away from Joseph's face.

"Joseph, Joseph, look, believe me. I know exactly where you and Mary are coming from. However, this matter is outside of our control. If they come out waving the white flag, then there is not one thing that we can do about it."

"But isn't agreeing to a settlement acknowledging guilt?" Joseph wanted to know.

"Yes, in a kind of way. However, I know that was not what you were hoping for. I am sorry. There are other avenues open to you afterward, and we can discuss those later. In the meantime, I believe we should get on with this action for damages for Linda and get it behind us."

"Other avenues, what avenues?" Mary Boyle wanted to know.

"Well, like making a formal complaint to the Medical Council. This would at least have the effect of ventilating the issues," Tom replied, more in hope than in expectation. They had all been here before. The Boyles were not interested in the Medical Council idea, and Tom knew he was wasting his time.

"Now, before we go for a well-deserved cup of coffee downstairs," Tom continued, "I do need to say a few words about Ward of Court."

Joseph and Mary Boyle leaned forward in their seats with their elbows on the table, arms crossed.

"Immediately after this settlement, we will need to apply for Linda to be made a Ward of Court. This is only a matter of form, and it is not something that should bother you unduly.

Very briefly, we will need the following:

(a) Written opinion from two psychiatrists testifying as to Linda's mental incapacity. We can start looking for that now, actually.

(b) Nominate a Petitioner to bring the case to the High Court. The petitioner can be either of you. You can decide later.

(c) A Committee needs to be formed to control the assets of the Ward. A committee can be just one person and is usually, though not necessarily, the Petitioner.

(d) The Petitioner has to swear an affidavit. I will look after that when the time comes.

And that's about it, really. Is there anything else we need to discuss?"

Mary and Joseph remained silent. They had had enough of this legal stuff for one day. They needed to go home now and give themselves time to absorb it.

"That cup of coffee downstairs, Tom, sounds like one of your better ideas recently," Mary managed to quip, lightening the gloomy mood that enveloped the room.

They stood up in unison. The solicitor scooped up the voluminous files off the oak table and grappled them to his chest with his right arm before opening the door and leading the way. The trio retraced their steps past the stationery and newspaper shop, through the swinging doors, and down the corridor to pass in front of the Law Library. Straight across and through more swinging doors they went. Mary could now smell coffee brewing somewhere. A sharp right before the Dining-hall, and they proceeded down the stone steps.

"Good afternoon, Tom!"

"Afternoon, Bryan. Oh, Bryan, that reminds me, come here a sec."

The two solicitors went into a huddle. Wigs and gowns flew past them, male and female. Mary thought to herself that nothing looked quite so absurd as a blond horsehair wig sitting on top of a pretty brunette's head. What did she think they were doing? Mary wanted to know from Joseph, but Joseph hadn't noticed.

A large central-hanging Waterford crystal chandelier lit the first-floor boardroom of Ely House. It was left on all day, winter and summer. The Knights of Columbanus liked to show it off. The thing was worth thousands, and it showed just how opulent the Knights really were. They liked to flaunt it.

At the polished mahogany table under this chandelier, three robed men sat in deep conversation. The portrait of the great saint himself, book in hand, looked down on them from above the white marble Adams fireplace. Although it was the month of August and still quite warm outside, there was a small log fire glowing within the fireplace. The Knights liked the look of it.

Seated at this table were: Supreme Knight Thomas O'Leary, a High Court judge. Sitting across from him were Supreme Secretary Dr. Peter Newman and Supreme Warden Dr. Walter Malone. O'Leary was talking now.

"Brothers, it's quite a while now since we first discussed this sad case. Would you believe it's over nine years ago? God Almighty, where does the time go at all? Anyway, I believe that there have been some developments that you would like to discuss with me. However, just before we go into details, it would be reMiss, of me if I did not offer you my heartfelt congratulations. That this young woman should still be alive after all these years bears witness to the loving care and attention that you, the doctors, and of course the nursing staff under your direction, and the sisters have been giving her. In keeping this woman alive, you are being truly pro-life and respectful. You are doing God's holy work, and you must be commended for that."

Both doctors sitting across from Thomas O'Leary inclined their heads ever so slightly in his direction as if taking a modest bow. They knew, of course, all three men in that room knew, that if it were not for the same two doctors who were now being praised for keeping her alive, Linda Boyle would be walking around leading a normal, healthy, and happy life and not be imprisoned for all time in a persistent vegetative state.

Supreme Secretary Dr. Peter Newman raised his right index finger, indicating that he wanted to speak.

"As anticipated a long time ago, the family has commenced legal proceedings against the two of us and, of course, against the hospital. Why it took them so long to do this, I do not know. Both Brother Malone and I are naturally worried about this because it seems to us it will be difficult to defend our position."

"I can actually help you there," the Supreme Knight interjected, standing up and walking over to the log fire. He bent down and, using a spill made of newspaper, lit a filter-tipped cigarette. The doctors turned their heads in the judge's direction. With his back to the fireplace, he drew on his cigarette, inhaling deeply before speaking again.

"I have actually had a look at the papers lodged in court a few days ago. You will be hearing about this too in the near future, so I am not really disclosing any secrets here. I only had a quick peek, but two things struck me immediately. Firstly, the consent form as signed by Ms. Boyle does not refer to cardiac arrest or coma. And secondly, they have located a world authority that is prepared to give evidence in court to the effect that her operation was unnecessary in the first place."

High Court Judge O'Leary, cigarette in hand, returned to his seat at the table.

"Gentlemen, let's cut straight to the quick here; this is a case that you simply cannot win. Now, your own Senior Counsel may advise you otherwise. I do not know who he or she is, nor do I want to know. I am sure that your solicitors would only choose the best. However, barristers can sometimes have their own agenda. They might be trying to make a name for themselves by going into court. They might be looking to drag things out to justify higher costs. They might be looking to get their name in the papers. Who knows? Just take my advice, will you? It is given to you as a fellow Knight before God. Do not let this thing go inside the doors of any courtroom."

The Supreme Knight leaned over the mahogany table and stubbed out his cigarette in the large cut-glass ashtray.

While doing so, he looked each doctor in turn straight in the eye to ensure that he had gotten his message across.

"And here is another point that we need to bear in mind," the Supreme Knight said, warming to his subject. He was on his feet again, standing with his back to the fire and the portrait of St. Columbanus. "Let's get some coffee and biscuits up here, shall we?"

With that, Thomas O'Leary pressed the ivory button on the brass plate to the left of the Adams fireplace.

"We do not want this thing to get into the papers or the media at all if possible. Let's keep it as nice and quiet as we can. And one way to do that is to accept liability and settle out of court, nice and low-keyed like that. This is absolutely essential at this time, and I will tell you why."

There was a knock on the door.
"Come in!"

A middle-aged woman with a blue scarf around her head entered the room, carrying a heavy silver tray laden with coffee cups and saucers, a pot of freshly brewed coffee, and a plate of Kimberley biscuits. It rattled as she struggled under its weight and placed it down on the mahogany table between the Knights.

"Thanks, Mary."

Nobody spoke until Mary left. Then the Supreme Knight continued.

"As you will be only too well aware, over the last five years or so, The Knights, working as individuals in their own rights and by infiltrating various organizations like The Society for the Protection of Unborn Children, the Pro-life Amendment Campaign, The Guild of Catholic Doctors, various pro-life groups of doctors, nurses, educationalists, politicians, lawyers, and so on, have been doing trojan work in trying to persuade the various governments to hold a referendum on the question of abortion. And now, at long last, after many broken promises and much bungling on behalf of the politicians, it looks as though the referendum is going to be held, and a date has been fixed for next March."

"If successful, and indications at the moment are that it will be successful, then a clause will be inserted into the Irish Constitution whereby abortion can never be legalized in Ireland without the consent of the people. When that happens, Ireland will be seen to the rest of the world as a shining beacon of light guiding people towards the way of absolute respect for all human life from the moment of conception."

The Supreme Warden settled the cups onto the saucers and poured out the coffee.

"So, what's this got to do with your case, you may well ask? It has everything to do with your case in this sense. Suppose word was to get out that a hospital and two doctors were being sued for malpractice over a young woman who is in a persistent vegetative state. And suppose some bright young journalist was to get their hands on this story and blow it up out of all proportion, do a bleeding hearts job on it about force-feeding and not allowing someone to die and that kind of nonsense. The public debate that might follow such exposure could do untold damage to the 'Pro-life' image. Or at best, it would introduce yet another complication that might deter people from coming out and voting on the Pro-life side. We do not need any more complications in our efforts to save the baby inside its mother's womb and keep the evil that abortion surely is out of this country for all time."

Supreme Secretary Dr. Peter Newman felt it might be time to speak up.

"All right, Your Honour, I think we understand what you're saying. Your advice seems to be to settle this matter out of court as quietly and quickly as possible because it's a case we cannot win, and we don't want to stir up any issues in the Pro-Life debate. That's fine, thank you. We'll do just that. At the end of the day, it's only money, and not even our own at that. We're covered by The Medical Protection Society, which has promised to support us."

Dr. Walter Malone, finishing his coffee, asked, "And what about this Ward of Court matter?"

"I can help you there as well," the Supreme Knight interjected. "This is now a certainty. She's going to receive a settlement of God only knows how many hundreds of thousands of pounds. Because she lacks capacity, she'll have to be made a Ward of Court. We might as well accept this as a given. In this scenario, the courts will assume the role of Loco Parentis. This significantly changes things and impacts the autonomy you caregivers have had. We'll address those challenges when they arise. Just keep me informed, will you?"

"There's something you should know, Tom," Peter Newman began, breaking the usual formality. The Supreme Knight turned his attention to Newman. "I had an encounter with Mr. Boyle last year in the hospital. It was more of a heated exchange than a conversation. During it, he mentioned a few concerning things. He said that, in the long run, the family wishes to let Linda pass away by discontinuing the tube feeding. He also mentioned Linda's potential constitutional right to bodily integrity and her right to refuse medication."

The room grew silent, interrupted only by the clinking of cups. The Supreme Knight looked troubled.

"It seems Mr. Boyle has been seeking advice," he mused. The smile he wore earlier had vanished. He saw an anti-life agenda taking shape. He approached the fire, lit another cigarette, and took a deep drag.

"Brothers, I foresee a sinister plan here. First, they sue, they win, and she becomes a Ward of Court. Then they might petition the High Court to discontinue her tube feeding. Depending on the judge, they could rule in favour of letting your patient pass away. An appeal to the Supreme Court might not change the outcome. We don't have enough Knights within the judiciary to prevent this. It's concerning."

He exhaled a smoke ring and continued, "Perhaps it would be best to speak with the family directly, be transparent, and urge them not to pursue this anti-life path. Could you propose an out-of-court settlement now to prevent this from reaching court? Keeping it out of court entirely might be the best pro-life strategy."

Walter Malone, the anaesthetist, and Supreme Warden, signalled his intent to speak. "We'll try to guide this family towards the righteous path. But honestly, I believe there's too much resentment and antagonism between us now to reverse course. And our insurers might not support payment offers without prejudice just to appease the family."

"Yes, you're probably right. We should aim to keep it out of court as long as possible. It's counterproductive to secure a constitutional change that protects the unborn while opening the door to euthanasia. These are troubling times. Let's conclude for now."

The Supreme Warden and Supreme Secretary nodded in agreement, pushed back their chairs, expressed their gratitude to the Supreme Knight, and, gathering their robes, respectfully exited the room walking backward.

CHAPTER 7 - SETTLEMENT ON A WARD OF COURT

In the autumn of 1984, soft, wet winds fell against the golden, frail leaves of the horse-chestnut tree in the back garden of 16 Ashgrove Lane. The weight of the rainwater broke the leaves' tentative hold, and they slipped away one by one, tumbling and spiralling down to the grass below. They landed gently with a damp rustling noise. In their thousands, they formed a russet rug, spreading from the base of the tree across the lawn and onto the rose bed. The evenings were drawing in. The swallows and swifts had returned to Africa. From the birch tree, a robin tried to bring some late autumn cheer. Pale golden sunlight filtered into the garden between the showers, and the air was laden with the sweet smells of gentle decay and turf smoke.

Mary Boyle was out in the fuel shed, bent over gathering an armload of turf. She placed the first sod across the fingertips of her upturned right hand. The second sod she placed across her palm, the third across her wrist. She continued this way until the last sods of turf reached the bend of her elbow. On top of this, she built a second row, then a third, and finally a fourth. When she straightened up, she held eighteen dark brown sods of machine-cut turf in the crook of her right arm. She brought these into the kitchen and dropped them gently into the empty sally basket beside the granite fireplace.

The pain from the loss of a daughter still lingered. Had Linda died ten years ago, Mary thought, the pain might not have been quite so acute. Linda would be dead and buried, and Mary could visit her graveside and pray for her eternal rest. But Linda hadn't died; she wasn't buried. She lay on a hospital bed in a pungent ward, alone except for her caretakers. She stared into space, moaning. Watching her was agonizing, and Mary's pain was chronic and unremitting.

Joseph Boyle sat silently before his daughter. She was propped up, half-sitting and half-suspended, in her high-backed winged armchair. Her head bowed forward, chin resting on her chest, her body rocking slightly. She resembled a puppet resting between engagements, a rag doll. He gazed at what remained of his once beautiful daughter, a vibrant, talented, and endlessly entertaining young woman filled with tin whistle playing, storytelling, and always laughter.

Then, slowly, Linda began lifting her head, blinking a few times before looking her father straight in the face. Shuffling her body, she sat upright. Her once lifeless hands, held under her chin, now animated. The sardonic leer and clenched mouth relaxed into a broad smile. She said, "Oh, Daddy, how wonderful, you've come to see me. I love you. Thank you for being so kind. Daddy, my tin whistle is in the locker here beside me. Can you get it for me, please?"

Moving slowly, Joseph Boyle stood and walked to the other side of Linda's bed. Bending low, he retrieved a much-used brass D whistle with a green plastic mouthpiece. Returning to his chair, he handed the whistle to his daughter. Linda smiled at her father, and placing the whistle to her lips, she covered the six holes with the ring, middle, and index fingers of both hands, left over right. Joseph said, "Can you play 'The Foxhunter's Reel' for me, darling?"

Linda began to play 'The Foxhunter'. The tune, with its five turns, was fast, free-flowing, and sweet, evoking the sounds of the chase, galloping horses, baying hounds, and the huntsman's horn. But as she neared the end, the sound began to fade, though her fingers continued their dance. Too soon, Joseph's vision of his vibrant daughter began to fade, and she reverted to her previous state. The brass whistle crashed to the floor, and the beautiful moment was lost forever.

The phone rang on the wall beside the kitchen table. Picking it up, Mary said, "Hello".

"Ah, hello. Is that Mrs. Boyle? Yes? Hello, Mary. Tom Brogan here. Listen, I've got some news for you. We've been given a date for our High Court hearing. Do you have a diary there with you? Alright, we're scheduled for Tuesday, November 22nd. I hope that's okay with Joe and yourself."

"Tom, that's very short notice after waiting so long."

"Ah, it's okay. It gives us just over three weeks to prepare. I'll notify our witnesses and Senior Counsel immediately. Also, it might be a good idea to book a consultation room for the duration of the trial. We've been allotted three days. We won't know the trial judge until the day itself."

"That's important, isn't it?"

"Yes, pivotal actually, but out of our hands. Listen, I won't say more over the phone. I'll contact you closer to the date. In the meantime, don't worry about anything."

"Alright, Tom. Thank you. I've marked it in my diary and will tell Joseph this evening. Goodbye for now."

Mary returned the telephone to its cradle on the wall and began lighting the fire.

The morning of Tuesday, November 22nd, 1984, was a wet and windy one. Winter had arrived in Dublin. Outside the Four Courts, the Liffey was at its highest. The tide was in. Its waters were brown and grey, choppy, and threatening. Seagulls circled high overhead, shrieking loudly, or they rested themselves on the balustrades of Father Matthew Street Bridge, pointing their grey and white bodies eastwards and towards the river's estuary. The wind threatened to dislodge them from their precarious perches.

The big clock in the Round Hall of the Four Courts told them that it was half-past nine in the morning. It would be another half hour before the courts proper opened for business but already the place was hopping. Two young men with their heads bowed low and with long, scruffy, unwashed hair were handcuffed and chained, each to their own personal prison warder in dark blue uniform. They scurried across the great hall, wasting no time. Clusters of cloaked and wigged barristers were scattered around the place, like jackdaws on a field of stubbles. Each of them was clutching legal documents of varying thickness. A loud, excited babble of conversation drifted up to the massive dome one hundred feet above their heads. An occasional guffaw broke out, but generally, the place was sombre and respectful. Joseph and Mary found a hard seat along the wall to the left of the entrance and sat in silence, waiting for their solicitor to show up.

Fifteen minutes later, Tom Brogan made his breathless entrance into the Round Hall and soon located his seated clients beside an empty statue niche. "Sorry Mary, sorry Joseph. Jaysus, the traffic out there is just unreal. Listen, please don't get up." He gently pressed on Mary's right shoulder as she attempted to rise. "You just sit there and relax for a few more minutes while I go off and organise a meeting room and see if I can locate Mr Lavelle." And with that, their solicitor was gone, weaving, and ducking through the rapidly growing crowd.

Tom Brogan looked into consulting room number eight. It was unoccupied, thanks be to goodness, he thought to himself. He left his pile of papers on the oak table to indicate that the room was now booked and went off to see if he could find Lavelle. Just outside the Law Library, he caught up with him in conversation with the Crier. The solicitor stood off to one side, waiting for his Senior Counsel and the Crier to finish their conversation. In one minute, they were shaking hands and parting.

"Good morning, David. And how are we fixed?" "Good morning, Tom. We are fixed grandly, thank you. I'm all set anyway. Can give this matter as long as it takes. Have we got a consulting room?" "Yes. I have grabbed room eight," Tom said, pointing back down the corridor from where he had just emerged.

Now the solicitor could relax a bit. On the day of a hearing, it could often be quite tricky to bring the pieces together—a consulting room, clients, expert witnesses, Junior Counsel, documentation, and most of all, pinning down your Senior Counsel who may often have several cases going on during the same morning. But not this morning, of course, Brogan reminded himself. This morning we are looking at a case with a value of up to one million pounds hanging over it. This was the biggest personal injury case that either David Lavelle or Tom Brogan had ever been involved in. And what made it even sweeter still was the fact that it probably would not even be contested—a 'shoo-in' as they say. And they did not get much better than that.

"I'll see you in there in fifteen minutes, David. Is that alright?"

"That's fine with me, Tom."

And with that, the Senior Council turned on his shiny patent leather heels and, head down, scurried off with himself, black silk robe trailing in his wake.

By ten past ten, everyone was assembled and seated in consulting room number eight. Mary and Joseph Boyle sat on the left-hand side as one entered the tiny room. On the right-hand side of the table and seated on her own was Junior Council Catherine Mullins, wig and brief out on the table in front of her. Seated at the top of the table with his back to the tall window was Senior Counsel David Lavelle, and opposite him, with his back to the door, was seated Solicitor Tom Brogan.

"Alright then, I think I'll kick off proceedings if everyone is ready."

Senior Counsel cleared his throat and proceeded, all business.

"First off, I have just been at List Call Over, and the news is good. The judge appointed to hear our case this morning is the Honourable Mr Justice Patrick O'Flynn."

"Ah, Santa Clause himself, is it?" Brogan could not contain himself.

"Well, I wouldn't quite go that far, Tom. But last year, the same Mr Justice O'Flynn made the biggest personal injuries award ever in the history of the State. The other side will be only all too well aware of this fact, and it will act as yet another deterrent for them wanting this case to go into the Courtroom."

"How are we for witnesses, Tom?"

Senior Counsel enquired of the solicitor seated opposite him at the far end of the table. "All ship shape and ready to go. The actuary and the two medical men are on standby, and all three can be here, if necessary, within the hour. I met Professor Tim Weighbridge in the Round Hall about twenty minutes ago. He had just taxied in from the airport. I sent him downstairs and told him to have a hearty Irish breakfast for himself. He cuts an impressive figure, I can tell you, wonderful Oxford accent and deep booming voice. He looks like a lad that has just come out of the House of Lords."

David Lavelle allowed himself a wry smile down the table at his colleague. Things were looking up. "I think that's about it for now. Am I forgetting anything, Tom?" "No, I don't think so. But I would just like to remind Mary and Joseph here that this is often just a long waiting game and to ask that they be patient with us. People sometimes come to court thinking that it's going to be all action and drama like it is in Hollywood movies. But in real life, it's not like that, I'm afraid." "Alright then, I'll go off now and test the waters to see what the mood and sentiment is like in the other camp. Excuse me for a few minutes. I will be back as soon as I can." And with that, Senior Counsel was up and gone.

David Lavelle was out of the room now for a good half hour. Joseph Boyle and his solicitor Tom Brogan tried to make small talk about the upcoming Five Nations Cup, but Joseph was finding it hard to concentrate. He was extremely anxious, not so much about the size of the settlement but more so because he had to rub shoulders out in The Round Hall with his long-term adversaries and enemies, and Joseph hated that kind of human conflict. It was at odds with his nature.

Mary Boyle warmed to the Junior Counsel, Catherine Mullins, sitting across from her. The young barrister was at once fascinated and appalled by the details about Linda Boyle's terrible plight. She had studied the pleadings lodged in the court in minute detail, but they could only tell her so much. It wasn't until she had a chance to converse with the victim's mother that, now for the first time, Mullins was getting any real sense of the horrors that this family had been through over the last twelve years or so. And even still, there was no end in sight since nobody could say when, or if, Linda would be allowed to die. It had to be the nightmare to end all nightmares.

Just then, the door opened, and Mr. Lavelle entered and took his seat at the head of the table. All heads turned his way.

"Well, as expected, the news is good and bad. First, I'll give you the good news. They want this thing settled out of court. Or to be more accurate, their clients want this thing settled without going before the bench. Their legal team seems quite bullish, but the doctors, their insurers, and the carers— most particularly the doctors—are deeply determined to stay out of court. I'd hate for them to be my clients!"

"Not very subtle then, David, are they?"
"Tom, they're about as subtle as a baboon's arse, if you'll excuse the expression, Mary."

But Mary and Joseph Boyle ignored their lawyer's moment of levity. They both shared the same thoughts. Senior Counsel had just said that this was good news, that the defendants' refusal to go into court was 'good news'. Had they not emphasized at their first meeting with David Lavelle that their primary reason for taking this case to the High Court was to expose the doctors and force them to reveal the whole story behind Linda's catastrophic accident, and to hear them admit their own culpability in these disastrous events?

Moreover, they needed to hear an apology, if the doctors were even capable of one, something Mary doubted. And now it was clear they weren't even going to court, and their Counsel was calling this 'good news'. Not for the first time, Mary and Joseph Boyle wondered if barristers ever truly listened to their clients.

"So far, and I would emphasise 'so far', their offer of settlement is derisory. I put it right up to them that we wanted one million and that we were not interested in one penny less. My God, they nearly had a canary. I thought that their senior was going to go into a state of apoplexy at the suggestion. You'd imagine that he was being asked to pay it out of his own pocket. Anyway, after much toing and froing between their clients and insurers, they came back with an offer of settlement. I am not going to upset you by telling you what that figure was because, quite honestly, it was way off the mark, and of course, they know that all too well. The figure that they suggested as settlement would be more appropriate for a fractured ankle than a persistent vegetative state."

"So, where do we go from here?"

Tom Brogan wanted to know, although he already knew the answer.

"That's simple, Tom. I made it absolutely crystal clear to them that their offer was so far off the mark that it did not even represent a starting point. Therefore, I told them that, sooner than wasting any more time, I would see them in court in half an hour. What I suggest we do now is we go into court number three as a full team, including, of course, the good Professor, and we simply sit in there until the case starts. Or else they can come up with a realistic offer. I believe that they will see the light and choose the latter. I believe that those funky doctors do not want to face the music and will agree to anything to avoid the truth coming out."

Tom Brogan looked across the table at his colleague seated with his back to the tall window. He had to admire this no-nonsense approach. "That should make the other side appreciate just how serious we are taking things," he thought to himself.

With that, they all stood up and gathered their goods and chattels, wigs, briefs, records, and briefcases. The Solicitor and Junior Council between them carried the heavy records and led the way, turning right outside the consulting-room door. They were closely followed by Mary, and then Joseph Boyle, and Senior Council David Lavelle brought up the rear of the little procession. On past the paper shop they went, turning left through the next swinging doors and then right down the long corridor that brought them out in front of the Law Library. Here they turned left again and passed through the open consulting booths occupied by solicitors, barristers, and their anxious-looking clients. And then it was straight ahead, turning right and then left, and now they could hear the hubbub coming from the great Round Hall. Into this, the procession made its grand entrance via the three steps downwards. As they entered the Round Hall, they were watched closely by a small group of worried-looking people, huddled together like pheasant chicks under a warming lamp, at the far side of this massive hall.

The place was crowded. Mary reckoned that there must have been well over one hundred people standing, talking to each other, or standing reading the newspaper or looking around as if waiting to meet someone. She stole a glance across at the defendant's camp. She recognised the gaunt figure of Sister Mary Assumpta and wondered what she was doing in this case and decided that she was probably representing the hospital.

With Assumpta were two other ladies who Mary took to be theatre staff. Then, of course, there was the dapper figure of Peter Newman and another gentleman stood right next to him who Mary did not recognise. Could this be the Scarlet Pimpernel himself, the slippery eel of an anaesthetist, Dr. Walter Malone? Could this be the doctor who was in theatre throughout the entire debacle and who would know exactly what happened to Linda on that fateful day? The same professional who never ever even once had the courtesy or the common decency and good manners to have as much as a word with Joseph or Mary?

Because had he and his colleague Newman there been possessed of even the smallest amount of common courtesy, then the likelihood would be that none of them would be in the Four Courts today. Mary looked away in disgust. Joseph saw none of them; his gaze was fixed on his black shining shoes. He could not bring himself to meet their eyes.

Tom Brogan quickly located Professor Tim Weighbridge, briefcase in hand, standing with his back to one of the empty niches. He asked that the rest wait a second while he went over to his expert witness.

"Well, Professor, did you have a good breakfast?"

"Yes, I did rather," Weighbridge replied in his best Oxford accent, putting emphasis on the word 'rather'.

"We are now going into court number three over there if you don't mind joining us, please."

Brogan pointed across the Round Hall to court number three and, asking the rest of the party to follow him, led the way into the empty courtroom.

Inside, he took up his position on the solicitor's bench, immediately underneath the Judge's rostrum, and sat facing out onto the body of the court. David Lavelle and his junior, Catherine Mullins, donned their wigs before taking up their positions on the barrister's bench, facing Tom Brogan, who was now busy organizing the impressive pile of legal documentation before him. Mary and Joseph Boyle, along with Professor Tim Weighbridge, seated themselves in a row at the back of the court.

Both Mary and Joseph agreed with each other afterward that the whole atmosphere of the place was most intimidating. The Judge's tipstaff entered the room through a door to the left of the judge's bench and walked down the four steps until he was abreast with David Lavelle. Bending forward, the tipstaff had a word in the barrister's ear that nobody else in the courtroom could hear. He was inquiring if the case was likely to go on or if it was more likely to be settled outside. The judge wanted to know this.

The two barristers were deep in whispered conversation. The solicitor continued to rummage through the files. Mary and Joseph exchanged occasional observations with each other, and the expert witness kept his own counsel. Time passed. They had now been in that courtroom for almost half an hour, and still, there was no sign of the other side appearing. But then suddenly, the door at the back of the courtroom squeaked open, and the Senior Counsel, who earlier Mary had noticed talking outside with Newman and that other creep, came into the courtroom and went right up to Mr. Lavelle. After a brief whispered conversation, both men left the courtroom, to be quickly followed by Tom Brogan and Catherine Mullins. Negotiations had re-started, or so it would appear. The Boyles and the expert witness from the UK sat on in the empty courtroom, not knowing really what was going on.

Over three-quarters of an hour passed before Catherine Mullins came in and told the little group huddled in the back of the otherwise empty courtroom what was happening.

"Professor, you are free to go now for a while if you wish. We will see you back here after lunch at two o'clock, please. But the case is not going on for this morning, and that's the only certainty that I have for now. Mary and Joseph, Tom is outside, and he will escort you back to the consultation room. All right, everybody? Goodbye for now, Professor; see you this afternoon."

Outside in the Round Hall, Mary and Joseph Boyle noticed that David Lavelle and the senior from the other side were deep in conversation. The two doctors, the nun, and the nurse stood bunched together off to one side. Each of them looked pale, drawn, and anxious. Mary found it difficult not to feel just a little bit sorry for the lot of them, though God only knows they brought this down on top of themselves. Both groups exchanged cold glances before Mary and Joseph moved away to follow their solicitor.

Back in consulting room number eight, Joseph Boyle took out a crooked meerschaum pipe from his breast pocket and reached for his tobacco pouch in the pocket of his tweed jacket.

"Does anyone mind if I smoke?"
Mary considered the room far too small for pipe smoking but decided not to say anything. God knows they

were going through enough right now without her making it
any worse for anybody, she thought to herself.

"No, Joe, smoke away. Sure, we can always open the
window if things get too bad. Isn't that right, Mary?" The
solicitor was in jovial form.

Joseph Boyle slowly, skilfully, and lovingly filled the
bowl of his well-used meerschaum with Yachtsman flake
tobacco while his solicitor spoke:

"Listen, folks, things are looking up. About ten
minutes ago, they offered three hundred grand plus costs.
Now, I know, I know, that's an awfully long way back from
our bottom line. But still, by the same token, it is an awfully lot
better than what they were going on about this morning before
we went into court. I believe that at least now they are
beginning to take us seriously."

Joseph lit his pipe using three Maguire and Patterson
safety matches in succession before he got the thing going
properly. Soon the little room was full of sweet-smelling
Yachtsman tobacco smoke. Neither Joseph nor Mary made
any response to what the solicitor had just said. They felt the
same way about things. What did it matter to their lovely
daughter Linda right now whether she got one hundred
thousand or five hundred thousand pounds? Would any of this
lessen their pain and sorrow by one single iota? Would it bring
back Linda from the depths of her persistent vegetative state?

Would it stop her moaning and stop her pain? Would it reduce the number of times she screamed and whipped out her nasogastric feeding tube and flung it on the hospital floor?

The three people in that smoke-filled room knew the answers to these questions all too well. In fact, Joseph and Mary felt that there was something quite distasteful about what was going on—something disrespectful and even insulting to the memory of Linda and how she once used to be. The suggestion, however oblique, that money could in any way assuage the dreadful hurt done to her was, quite frankly, outrageous. They just wanted this thing to be over and done with so they could get out of this hideous place and go home. They sat in silence for a while.

After some time, Senior Counsel put his head into the consulting room and suggested that everyone go to lunch. He told them that negotiations were going on apace. Tom Brogan escorted his clients to a pub across the street, where he ordered minestrone soup and chicken sandwiches for three. They ate in silence. His clients had no appetite for neither food nor conversation.

By this time, Mary knew her way around the Four Courts fairly well. At one stage in the afternoon, she left the consulting room to escape the smoke from her husband's pipe and to stretch her legs. Just outside the Law Library, she spotted Professor Tim Weighbridge wandering around aimlessly and, like her, just killing time.

215

"Good afternoon, Professor," Mary greeted the big Englishman cordially.

"Isn't all this hanging about exceedingly tedious?"

"Yes, indeed, Mrs. Boyle, I should say. Tedious it certainly is."

"Tell me, Doctor; do you think that there is any chance at all that this case will run?"

The Professor eyed Mary up and down for a second before speaking. He was unsure about protocol in a situation like this. But hesitating for a second, he realized that they were on the same side of the fence and that talking to this pleasant woman could not possibly do any harm.

"I have just been speaking to your lawyer chappy, and he advised that I wait another hour. Then, unless I hear from them in the meantime, I am free to leave. It looks as though my trip to Ireland, while pleasant, may also have been futile. But then that is the nature of this business."

The Professor shrugged his broad shoulders in resignation.

"It's such a pity. I would have dearly loved to hear your evidence given in open court and with Dr. Newman there in person to hear it. He has not ever admitted any wrongdoing in this catastrophe, nor of course has he ever apologized. All of which only serves to make the pain worse, of course."

The Professor looked Mary straight in the eyes and was immediately filled with a sense of sadness for Linda's mother and for what she must have gone through at the hands of his colleagues in the medical profession.

"If you have a couple of minutes, Mrs. Boyle, I do not mind telling you what I gleaned from going through Linda's medical records. I mean to say you are fully entitled to this information, and in any case, it is in writing in your lawyer's records. Can we sit over there, out of the way, while we talk?"

Weighbridge indicated some empty chairs in an alcove, and the pair grabbed these before anyone else could. Empty chairs in this place were hard to come by.

"All right then. I'll start at the beginning, and please interrupt me anytime you like. The General Practitioner— sorry, I am no good at remembering names, but you will know who I'm talking about ----"

"Quinn, Martin Quinn was his name," Mary interjected quickly.

"Ah yes, Martin Quinn, that's the chappy. In some ways, your daughter Linda was unlucky that she went to this particular GP. Not that he was bad or anything, but he was too careful and too clever by far. Do you see, given Linda's symptoms of scanty menstrual periods and facial hirsutism, most GPs, certainly in the UK, and I can't imagine that it would be that different in Ireland, would just kick for touch and treat her conservatively. Very, very few GPs would think like Dr. Quinn did of the possibility that all her symptoms were arising from a rare type of ovarian tumour called an arrhenoblastoma. Most GPs would never even have heard of them, never mind thinking of them as a diagnosis. But Quinn mentioned arrhenoblastoma in his referral letter to Newman, and once that hare was raised, it had to be chased down. And so started a terrible chain of events that led inexorably to Linda's disaster. To be absolutely fair about it, Quinn did not mention a salpingogram in his referral letter. That was entirely Newman's inspiration."

The Professor paused here to see if Mary followed what he had been saying. She did.

"So there, if you like, was piece of bad luck number one. Going to Quinn who, in turn, decided to refer to Newman. Newman's subsequent disastrous decision to press ahead with a salpingogram, when hormonal assays by way of a blood analysis would have been the appropriate course, was of course poor Linda's second piece of dreadful bad luck. That was a clinically incorrect decision, even if it never had the catastrophic outcome that we now know it did have. And now, of course, Newman does not want to have himself exposed in open court, and I'm being sent home. It is frightfully unfair, really."

Mary felt the professor's words were strangely comforting and confirmed what she had long suspected. She wondered if he might have any insight as to what happened in the operating room.

"That's interesting, Professor. Would you have any theories about what happened during the procedure?"

"Now, as to what actually happened in theatre that day, we will never really know. Many people arrest while under anaesthesia, are resuscitated quickly, and come out the other end unscathed. So, what was that fellow up to? The hospital notes tell us nothing, and the chances are that if put in a witness box, that anaesthetist would tell you nothing useful either. I'm sorry, Mrs. Boyle, but that is just how it is."

"But Professor, it is hardly your fault that things should be the way they are. And apart from that, I must say that I found what you have just said useful and interesting. You are the first professional ever to help me put the whole calamity into some kind of perspective. Do you know that you have told me more just now than any of the doctors charged with Linda's care have ever told me in the past ten years? Thank you very much indeed."

"It's my pleasure, Mrs. Boyle. Heaven knows it's the least that any of us could do."

With that, they stood up, shook hands, and were about to bid each other farewell. The Professor had a final thought.

"Mary — you don't mind that I should use your first name, do you?"

"Of course not."

"It is absolutely none of my business, of course, and you can tell me so if you wish. But I was just wondering if you had any thoughts about Linda's future. I mean to say they could carry on with the tube feeding for years and years. But I just wondered if that was what your daughter would want to have done to her where she compos mentis?"

"Yes, of course, and thank you for asking. Linda's future is of considerable concern to my husband and me. But the subject has always been something of a no-go area with her carers, the doctors, nuns, and nurses. They refuse to even discuss any alternative to their regime of tube feeding and antibiotics whenever they seem to be needed."

Professor Tim Weighbridge searched in the breast pocket of his dark blue pinstriped waistcoat and brought out a business card and handed it to Mary Boyle.

"Listen, Mary, I would like you and your husband to feel free to contact me anytime in the future if you thought that it might be of any help. Today shall change a lot of things. Linda will almost certainly be awarded a settlement. Therefore, she will need to be made a Ward of Court. Therefore, those with the ultimate say in her management will no longer be her carers, but henceforth the courts will have the final say. We have a similar case in the USA just now, and it would be worth keeping an eye on that."

With this, Weighbridge bowed ever so slightly in Mary's direction, turned, and was off with himself. Mary watched his departing back blend into the madding crowd outside of the Law Library.

She was now very glad that she stopped to talk to the Professor. Little did she think that he would have been so incredibly forthcoming? English men, she had always thought, tended to be a bit guarded and cold. But this kind gentleman showed none of that stiff upper lip old nonsense that many of his compatriots were so renowned for. Instead, he was warm, kind, concerned, and clearly prepared to help further if asked to.

Mary returned to consulting room number eight with much to think about. With her husband and solicitor, they sat in there for the rest of the afternoon. Occasionally Brogan made the long journey up to the Round Hall to see how things were going. The other side had not taken a consulting room, so negotiations were conducted across the black and white stone-tiled floor of the Round Hall.

David Lavelle knew in his heart that those two doctors had absolutely no intention of allowing this case to run. It was written all over their faces. And besides, did that fellow, what's his name — Newman was it; did he really want to go into an open court and hear a world authority declare that the operation that he was performing on Linda Boyle when she arrested was an unnecessary and an inappropriate procedure? Did he really want to hear that? You must be joking.

And as for that other fellow Walter Malone the gasser! Did he really want to hear it said in open court by a colleague that he was a recovering alcoholic taking benzodiazepine 10mg three times a day? Did he want to have the real story of what happened on that fateful day back in January 1973 brought out in open court? Again, you must be joking. Not a chance! No, no, no, no. Lavelle had been here before many is the time. This was just a waiting game. Wait, wait, and then wait some more. Then every so often simply bluff and say that you are going to bring your clients into court. This usually had the effect of the other side upping the ante. It was like a game of poker and a cattle market rolled into one. At another level, it was horse-trading, but unlike in Ballinasloe, this horse trading was being conducted by people with wigs and gowns, law degrees, and privilege. The stakes were high, the rewards for the winners colossal.

By mid-afternoon, the offer from the other side had gone up to £500,000. Even at this figure, this was the biggest

personal injuries award that either Tom Brogan or David
Lavelle had ever been involved in. Both men stood to do well
from their involvement in this lucrative case. But they could do
even better. Just hold their nerve. Word had gone around the
Round Hall, and those in the inner circles knew that something
big was happening. The press and media had been tipped off
and were buzzing around like bees at a honey jar. This was grist
to Lavelle's mill. About the last thing that the other side needed
right then was for this story to break and for those involved to
be named. Now the figure had gone up to £650,000. Word was
sent to Tim Weighbridge that he was free to leave and return
to the UK whenever he could get a flight. This case was now
definitely not going to go into court. Settlement was, in fact,
near. The pressure was on, and everyone was getting tired.

It was just after 7.30 pm when David Lavelle returned
to consulting room number eight for the last time. It had
suddenly turned dark outside, and there was a gale blowing.
When David Lavelle and his junior, Catherine Mullins, came
into the smoke-filled consulting room, they looked tired and
bedraggled. It had been a long old day of tough negotiations.
Yes, it had been productive but tough.

David Lavelle, with his back to the tall window
opposite the door, had the floor:

"Their final offer was £725,000.00. Now that is still a
long way back from the one million that we said was our
bottom line. And when I say, 'their final offer,' I am not saying

that we could not milk them for more. I mean to say they are as vulnerable as a stray kitten and have loads of crap that they would like to hide. But still, you know it's up to you really. You have the final say. Would you like us to leave you alone for a while so you can mull it over between yourselves? Or alternatively, I can go back and tell the other side that you want to sleep on it? That should give them a good night's rest!"

Mary Boyle was now feeling slightly nauseated. She was tired, hungry, and now slightly sick. She really had had quite enough of this humiliation. How can she make these lawyers appreciate her position and that of her husband Joseph? Haggling over a settlement figure that, in fact, would not make the slightest difference to their grievously wounded daughter was, in some way that she could not quite explain to these people, disrespectful towards her daughter Linda. Money at this stage was no good, and to suggest otherwise, however indirectly you may be doing that, was totally missing the point and was disrespectful in the extreme. This simply had to stop. Without even looking at her husband first to see how he was reacting, Mary decided for herself that it is about time that she asserted herself and ended this circus.

With barely disguised anger in her voice, Mary said:

"We accept their final offer on behalf of our daughter Linda. We appreciate the efforts of our legal team, Tom Brogan, David Lavelle, and you, Ms. Mullins. Thank you all for your help. We would now like this matter to be brought to a close as expediently as possible if you please. We understand that there will be the matter of making Linda a Ward of Court soon, but that is for another day."

Everyone in that little room could feel the barely concealed frustration behind Mary's words. A long period of silence followed. This was broken at last by her solicitor:

"Alright, Mary, I think that makes your position very clear. Are you alright with that, Joe?"
Joseph Boyle nodded consent.

The solicitor spoke again:
"Right, so. It would appear as if we are in agreement then. All we need do now is inform the other side. They'll be fairly relieved, I'd say."

"We need to meet here again tomorrow morning," Catherine Mullins was speaking.

"Round Hall, about ten to ten, please. We will then need to go into court before the Judge and advise him that a settlement has been reached. This is only a matter of form, and there is nothing in it to worry you. Be advised, though, that the other side will also be in court at the same time. I know that some people might find this upsetting, but it should be over in a matter of minutes. Just ride it out. Immediately following this, the other side should leave; of course, they do not have to leave, but I think they will, and we will go straight on to applying to have Linda made a Ward of Court. How are we fixed there, Tom?" Junior Counsel asked the solicitor.

"Everything is in order, I think, Catherine. I have the written opinion of two Consultant Psychiatrists confirming Linda's mental incapacity. You, Joseph, have agreed to act as Petitioner and Committee, and we have your affidavit. So---"

Tom Brogan looked across at Senior Counsel for confirmation that what he had just said was correct and sufficient.

David Lavelle nodded twice in the solicitor's direction.

"Good. That should do it then. All here tomorrow before ten, if you please."

Catherine Mullins wished everyone a good evening, and the meeting broke up. The legal team crossed the street for a drink before heading home. Joseph and Mary Boyle returned to their black Morris Minor, only to find two separate parking tickets tucked under the windshield wipers and fluttering in the winter breeze.

At ten o'clock on the dot, The Honourable Mr. Justice Patrick O'Flynn swept into Courtroom Number 3, entering through a door to the right behind his bench and ten feet above the main body of the court. He moved swiftly and silently towards his tall chair, which his tipstaff now held back in readiness to receive his considerable weight. Bewigged and gowned in the manner of the judiciary, O'Flynn cut something of a comical figure, the quintessential High Court judge making his grand entrance.

"All rise!"

The Court Clarke shouted out in a good clear Clare accent. Everyone shuffled to their feet obediently and quickly --- barristers, senior and juniors, solicitors, Petitioners, Plaintiffs, Defendants, witnesses, potential jurors, Stenographer, Registrar, press people, and lookers-on. As soon as they had risen to their feet, they were seated again, and David Lavelle was immediately on his feet facing the Bench:

"Your Honour, I represent the Plaintiffs in Linda Boyle -v- Newman, Malone and St. Malachi's Hospital."

Mr. Justice O'Flynn donned his reading glasses and surveyed the ledger in front of him for a few seconds. Then, lifting his head and peering over the rim of his reading glasses, he surveyed the large attendance before him.

"I understand, Mr. Lavelle, that this matter has been agreed and settled. That is indeed good news. However, I am needed elsewhere right now and would ask that you return before me in, let's say, one hour's time. Is that alright with you, Mr. Lavelle?"

"That's fine, My Lord. Thank you."

Seated at the back of the courtroom, Joseph and Mary Boyle had to strain their ears to follow what was going on. Spotting them there from across the room, Tom Brogan nodded in their direction while holding up his right thumb, indicating that all was well and that they only needed to hang on for a little while.

"All rise!"

Mr. Justice O'Flynn was on his feet and turning to exit the court. The assembled crowd rose in unison to honour his departing back.

Now a queue of bewigged barristers formed along the left-hand side of the Courtroom. Each in turn approached the bench with some kind of request of The Registrar, and each was dealt with in muttered voices and brief exchanges. Mary and Joseph did not know what was going on, other than that it had nothing to do with them and that they must wait their turn. Within thirty-five minutes, everything seemed to have been dealt with, and the court was cleared of everyone except for the Plaintiffs and Defendants in Linda Boyle –v—The State, plus a few press people.

"All rise!"

At midday on the dot, Mr. Justice O'Flynn returned to court number 3 to the flurry of people scrambling to their feet. The case was entering its final stage.

Having listened to the terms of settlement, the Judge made an order awarding costs to the Plaintiff. They then moved seamlessly on to the matter of the application to make Linda Boyle a Ward of Court.

Mr. Lavelle was on his feet again:

"My Lord, I have in my possession here the documentation required to make Linda Boyle a Ward of Court. We have nominated her father, Mr. Joseph Boyle, as Committee and Petitioner. If it pleases Your Lordship, I can pass these papers up to the bench."

"Yes, I will take them, but I cannot rule on this today, as I am sure you will appreciate. This is a matter for the President of the High Court, or his nominee, and I am neither. Rest assured, though, Mr. Lavelle, the matter will get my urgent attention, and be advised also that I will revert in a day or two at the most. I cannot envisage any difficulties."

"Thank you, My Lord."

Mr. Lavelle now sat down and turned around to see if his clients, Joseph and Mary Boyle, at the back of the Court seemed to understand what had transpired that morning. They seemed happy enough under the circumstances. The other side had long left court. It was all over and time to go home.

A cool north-westerly early summer breeze blew down from the Maumturks Mountain in Connemara, and on across the choppy dark waters of Lough Corrib below. It was the end of May 1987. The mayfly was up, and every available boat and their gillies were out on the water.

The gillie manned the outboard motor and tied on flies for Mary and Joseph Boyle. It was his job also to bring and hold his boat over the shallow waters towards the shore, the favoured haunts of the elusive brown trout. Both anglers were using long dapping poles from which they 'dapped' a single mayfly on or close to the water's surface. The gillie had caught the mayflies earlier that morning as they clung to bushes on one of the lake's many islands. He kept them in a ventilated wooden box and tied them on live as required.

All was silent except for the lapping of the water against the boat's bow and the breeze through the bushes on the nearby island. Talking was not encouraged. Any noise could frighten away the fish. While dapping the mayfly, one only spoke when necessary. The fishing was slow this morning, and neither angler had had a rise. They each sat astride one of the boat's two wooden seats, their backs to the wind. Mary Boyle was looking forward to her lunch, as she ate little of the greasy breakfast that the B&B had on offer this morning. She concentrated hard on keeping the fly on or close to the water's surface. Her husband Joseph had asked the gillie to take over from him while he filled his pipe from a round tin of

Yachtsman's flake tobacco and sat there in utter contentment, smoking, and musing.

Lunchtime arrived, and the gillie lifted anchor, started up the outboard motor, and steered his boat towards the nearest island. When they were safely up on dry land, the gillie got his storm kettle going, using small pieces of dried driftwood for fuel. He had the water boiling within a few minutes, and soon cups of strong tea were being passed around, together with chicken and ham sandwiches and potato salad.

After lunch, the gillie went gathering fresh mayflies clinging to the gorse bushes, leaving Mary and Joseph alone, each seated on a large boulder.

"Joe, I never told you about that day in court, almost two and a half years ago now when I spoke to that Englishman. Oh, what was his name? Weighbridge, wasn't that it? Tim Weighbridge?"

The gillie's storm kettle was on the ground between them, still smouldering and emitting a sweet-smelling blue smoke. Joseph had opened a bottle of stout for himself and was lighting his pipe, struggling against the strong breeze to do so. Mary looked across at him before proceeding.

"At one point in the afternoon, to stretch my legs and to get away from your smoking, I took a stroll around the place.

Outside the Law Library, who should I run into but the bold professor from England, and he looked as lost as myself."

"A nice sort of gentleman, I always thought."

"Yes, but wait till I tell you. Just to pass the time, I struck up a bit of a conversation with him. You know, about the case and all that and how it was such a pity if he were not allowed on to give evidence and so on."

Joseph's pipe was now going well at this stage as he looked across at his wife and waited for her to continue.

"We sat down and talked for a few minutes. He said that in his view, the GP Martin Quinn was as much to blame for the whole debacle as anyone else. If he hadn't tried to be so smart and come up with his fancy diagnosis, then he never would have referred Linda to Newman. Had he not done that, Linda would be walking around today in the fullness of her health. It's amazing the difference that one doctor's decision can make!"

Joseph was not sure what the point of this observation was but decided, uneasily, to hold his peace.

"Then he went on to confirm what we already had suspected for quite some time. You know that the investigation that Newman was performing on our daughter was unnecessary and inappropriate. There was nothing new here, but it was nice to have it confirmed by an outsider."

Mary paused to take a sip of strong tea.

"Finally, then----" she said, drawing in a deep breath, "he asked about our feelings towards Linda's continued medical care -- the tube feeding and the antibiotics and so on, saying that there was a similar case in America that we should be watching. He gave me his card and invited me to stay in touch if I wished."

Joseph Boyle looked at his wife, primly seated on the smooth boulder. The gillie's storm kettle had stopped smoking and would appear to have gone out completely.

"He would have been referring to the Karen Ann Quinlan case, of course. She died of pneumonia a couple of years back."

"That's right," Mary continued, "but her parents did not ask that the tube feeding be stopped; they asked only that the ventilator be switched off. And when the New Jersey Supreme Court granted this, and they switched off the ventilator, she lived on for years after that, much to everyone's surprise."

"Linda does not have a ventilator. So, if we were going to court, we would be asking that they discontinue antibiotics and nutrition and hydration as well. Linda's case goes far beyond the Quinlan one," Joseph observed, doubt written all over his face.

"That's right, Joseph. Linda's case would go far beyond the Quinlan case, as it happens. The New Jersey Supreme Court ruling in the Karen Ann Quinlan case does not offer Linda any legal precedent."

Joseph Boyle stood up and looked out over the choppy waters of Lough Corrib. From this vantage point, he could count four other clinker-built wooden fishing boats manned by two anglers each, straddling a centre seat, with a gillie in the stern directing operations. Their voices carried easily across the water. Nobody seemed to be catching anything. Boyle was deep in thought. He spoke with his back to Mary.

"Do you know something, Mary? I have to admit that I have been thinking about this now for some time, and I have not always been as forthright with you on the subject as I should have been."

He turned to face his wife.

"Lately, I have started coming around to the view that discontinuing nutrition and hydration is not right. We could ask, through the courts, that they discontinue antibiotics and other life-saving interventions. But stopping food and water— well, I don't know. Even if Linda seems to reject this way of being fed, just discontinuing it like that seems not right somehow."

Joseph paused, shielded his eyes with his hands to look out over the water again, before continuing.

"She would be dead within ten days, and we cannot be sure that she would not suffer horribly. Withholding medical treatment is one thing, but discontinuing an established treatment is another matter entirely."

"We have been over this a hundred times before, sweetie. I thought we had it sorted out between us."

"Yes, I know, dear. But food and water are not medical treatments; they are basic human necessities to stay alive. As she is now, Linda is not dying. In order for her to die, her nutrition and hydration would need to be withdrawn. And that, to me, sounds horribly like euthanasia."

Mary found her husband's words exasperating in the extreme. Why did he have to go on like this? They had been over this territory many times before. One day Joseph seemed to be saying one thing, and the next day he seemed to be saying the exact opposite. She was finding it hard to control her anger right now. This was causing a serious rift between them at a time when they most needed unanimity in their approach to their daughter's future care.

"Listen, Joe, I wish that for just once in your life you would focus on this serious question. You owe it to Linda to focus on it. She is the one who is suffering and who needs us to be clear-headed for her. You are her Committee as a Ward of Court, and you are her father. Together we can help her, but to do so, you need to be absolutely clear and absolutely focused. Just focus on these few facts, will you, for the love of Christ!"

Mary turned towards her husband and held up one finger at a time until all five fingers were in the air. A confrontation had started, and Joseph Boyle hated confrontation.

"One. Linda does not seem to like what is being done to her. Okay, fact number one – does not like her treatment. Fact number two --she is suffering. Fact number three -- she has no dignity. Fact number four -- her human rights are being violated. And fact number five -- what's being done to her is utterly futile medical treatment."

Now Mary stood there with all five fingers pointing skywards, anger written all over her face.

"She is not dying, you're right. She is not allowed to die. What's being done to her, therefore, simply must stop. Just keep it nice and simple like that, will you, for the love of Christ?"

Joseph Boyle hated to see his wife upset like this. It was most unlike her to swear like that too. They came away on this fishing trip to the West of Ireland together to relax and get away from the grind and pain of visiting Linda in the hospital most days and seeing the sheer hopelessness of her situation and the futility of her suffering. And now here they were arguing about her again.

Joseph now began to feel a familiar pain welling up deep inside his chest somewhere. It was tight and gripping and restricting. He had had this before, but this time it was different. Before, when he exerted himself, for example, in walking up a hill on a frosty day or doing a bit of light digging in the garden, he would get this constricting pain in his chest. A year ago, he had spoken to his own GP about it. A touch of angina pectoris, he said. Just take it easy and cut down on the old pipe smoking, he advised.

But now, this was different. For one thing, it had come on unheralded by physical exertion. And, for another thing, this was much, much worse than anything he had experienced before. It felt as if his chest walls and rib cage were being squeezed between a rock and an oncoming steamroller. The choking pain travelled down his left arm and into his jaw. His wife, Mary, had turned away from him and was speaking with her back to him. He couldn't really hear her.

"I am utterly sick and tired of these do-gooders telling the rest of us what's best for our daughter. How can they possibly know when they have never been in the situation themselves? The do-gooders do not have to witness a feeding tube being forced up their daughter's nose every day. Do-gooders do not have to witness enemas and digital extractions being administered to their unconscious daughter in order that she can keep her bowels empty. Do-gooders don't have to listen to her screams of pain or see her looks of sheer terror as her carers approach her bed. And, above everything else----"

Mary turned to face her husband to drive home her final point, but he was not there. Jesus, where had Joseph gone?

And then she spotted him in a crumpled heap beside the storm kettle. On the ground, his purple, upside-down face was turned towards her, eyes open, fixed, and staring. His mouth was held ajar, meerschaum pipe still in his left hand, still alight.

As the gillie was returning with his box of mayflies, he could see Joseph crumpling up slowly. First, falling to his knees and holding that position for a few seconds while clasping his chest. Then he saw him going the rest of the way, ending up on the flat of his back.

The gillie knelt beside the stricken man. He then looked for a pulse and, finding none, looked up at Mary, who stood at a distance with her hand held up to her face. The gillie shook his head slowly and looked out over the water as if seeking help. One of the other fishing parties had spotted what was going on and was now speeding towards the island. But for Joseph Boyle, it was almost certainly too late.

CHAPTER 8 - DECISION TIME AT LAST

When the fishing boat arrived, about three minutes after Joseph Boyle collapsed on the island in the middle of Lough Corrib, it delivered two young male anglers in their mid-thirties. One of these young men knelt on the ground at Joseph Boyle's right-hand side and felt for a pulse below the man's thumb on his right wrist. He shook his head slowly. Next, he opened the dead man's snap buckles in front of his fly-fishing vest and lifted his underlying woollen sweater and checked shirt. Then, placing his right ear just under Joseph's left nipple, the young man listened for a heartbeat. He found none. Then he placed the heel of his left hand over Joseph's lower sternum and placed his right hand on top of this and, stretching himself upwards and straightening out his arms, the young man brought his weight and considerable strength to bear on Joseph Boyle's chest. This moved the dead man's sternum and chest wall backward towards his heart by a good six inches. Joseph Boyle was not a big, strong man. His ribs could be heard to crack under the strain.

Through her tears, Mary Boyle could just about make out what was happening and quickly moved over to the young man kneeling beside her dead husband. He looked up at her. She was tapping him on the shoulder and slowly shaking her head. Clearly, she did not want any heroics. The young man understood immediately and agreed. Without a defibrillator, efforts at external cardiac massage at this late stage were futile. They were also dangerous because Joseph might well have already suffered fairly extensive brain damage and was better off dead.

Now the little group of two young men, two gillies, and Mary Boyle gathered respectfully around the body of Joseph Boyle, heads bowed, each uttering a silent prayer. The man who had only minutes earlier attempted resuscitation introduced himself to Mary, saying that he was a General Practitioner from Athlone. He also said that, in his view, there was no need to call the Garda or a coroner or any other authority for that matter. Since he had seen what had happened and given Joe's history of angina pectoris, there should be no need to fuss. He would be more than happy to issue the death certificate at a later time. Mary thanked him.

Using the oars from one of the boats, along with several four-foot lengths of blue nylon rope, and working quickly together, the two gillies fashioned a workable litter. They placed it under the body of Joseph Boyle before the four men, one at each corner, lifted him and placed him gently across one of the centre seats of the boat. Then they released the oars. Mary covered his face and shoulders with a sweater that she had been carrying in case the weather turned chilly.

And that was how Joseph Boyle's funeral started from an island in the middle of the Corrib at the end of May three years ago, where he had been out dapping the mayfly in time-honoured fashion when he was struck down by a heart attack leading to cardiac arrest. They said at his funeral that maybe at seventy-three he was a bit young to die, but equally, everyone had to agree, as they toasted him after the burial, that it was not a bad way to go.

Mary never told anyone that Joseph and she had been arguing about Linda when he collapsed and died on that island in the middle of Lough Corrib in the West of Ireland. Nothing would be served by such disclosure. Some things are sooner not said. But she remained conscious of the nature of the argument, and it was to do with whether or not to ask, through the Irish courts, that Linda's tube feeding be discontinued. On this issue, her late husband found it difficult to reach a conclusion. One day he seemed in favour, and another day he seemed to change his mind, and it was this kind of vacillating that Mary found so infuriating.

Since then, through sorrow and grief and through not a little guilt and out of respect for the memory of her late husband and taking his wishes expressed minutes before his death, Mary considered it only respectful to his memory that she does not pursue the matter of Linda's care for at least three years. Those three years had now passed, and Linda's continued distress seemed, if anything, to be worse with each passing year. It was time to revisit the case. Next Sunday after lunch might be as good a time as any to discuss it again with David, now a qualified doctor studying OBGYN, and her daughter Margaret.

It was mid-summer; the sun was struggling to break through the thick clouds from time to time. The family gathered in the back garden of number 16 Ashgrove Lane for a late Sunday lunch alfresco. It was quite warm and close. Roast leg of lamb with mint jelly, mange tout peas, and new potatoes were being served, and David Boyle was doing the carving at the head of the table while his sister Margaret and mother Mary looked on approvingly. Mary poured everyone a glass of Chilean Cabernet Shiraz while Margaret spooned out the buttered new potatoes covered in parsley and chopped mint.

David, addressing no one in particular, asked, "Has anyone been following the Tony Bland case?"

"No, who's Tony Bland?" This was news to Mary.

"Tony Bland is the young man who was caught up in the Hillsborough soccer disaster last year. Remember? The poor fellow was crushed in the crowd and could not breathe for almost ten minutes."

"Oh God yes," Mary now recalled. "There was an iconic photograph of him being crushed against a chain-linked fence. It was horrible."

"That's right, Mum. He was held that way by the weight of the crowd behind him for over ten minutes, and nobody could do a thing to help him. As I say, he couldn't breathe. Later, they resuscitated him, but he never regained consciousness and is now, just like Linda, in a persistent vegetative state. He too can breathe on his own and is being tube-fed. The parents are unhappy with the situation."

"The parents are what?"
"They're unhappy with the situation."

"No, no David. I heard you the first time. What I'm getting at is how could they be unhappy already after only a year or so? They should try living in our situation. How long is it now? Just over sixteen years, is it?" Mary was aghast at what David had just said.

"But still----" David continued while carving off three thin slices of rare leg of lamb onto each plate before he passed them down the table.

"This opens up the whole question of the ethics, the morality, and the legal implications of keeping a person in PVS alive indefinitely. God knows this is a subject that needs more discussion!" Margaret now joined in, relaxing a bit.

"Indeed."

"I read a statement from a spokeswoman for SPUC (the Society for the Protection of Unborn Children) commenting on that same Tony Bland case. It was her contention that food and water were not 'medical treatments' and therefore could never be discontinued. To do so, again in her opinion, would be tantamount to murder or euthanasia, and therefore their withdrawal could never and must never be made legal."

"Listen Margaret, you know, and I know that that simply is not true." Mary had heard this argument before many times, and she now felt exasperated.

"It is all very well and fine for these bible-thumping fundamentalists to be holding forth and telling the rest of us how we should feel and how we should behave. Would that SPUC spokeswoman feel the same way if she had to endure the stress and pain of seeing her daughter being tube-fed while in a vegetative state for the past sixteen years?"

"I know Mum, I know. Take it easy. You know full well that David and I are one hundred percent behind you in this. You have our total support. You know that."

"I do know that love and thank you. And thank you too, David. I don't know how I would cope without the pair of you. Honestly, I don't. But just let me finish the point there."
"Yeh, sorry, go on."

"Of course, I accept that food and water or nutrition and hydration are not of themselves 'medical treatments.' But I believe that it is the manner by which they are administered that is relative here. For example, a few months ago, as you know, Linda had her nasogastric tube taken out and replaced by a gastrostomy tube. This was done without discussion with any of us and without our permission, but then what else is new?"

"Yeh well, what else is new is right?" There was sarcasm in Margaret's voice.

"Yes, yes, but that aside----" Mary continued, "Putting the gastrostomy tube into position from outside here," Mary pointed to her stomach, "and directly into her stomach required that Linda have a general anaesthetic and a surgical operation. This is clearly 'medical treatment.' Therefore, logically, for Linda to receive or maintain regular hydration and nutrition, she requires 'medical treatment.' It is not the food itself but the manner by which it is administered that fulfils the criteria of 'medical treatment.' Putting food down a nasogastric tube or into a gastrostomy tube is, at least in my view and in the view of most people that I have spoken to, medical treatment."

"To be quite honest with the two of you ---" Mary paused for a sip of wine.

"I think this aspect of the debate, while important, is something of a red herring. It takes us away from the central issues. It has long been my view that the most important aspects are to do with Linda's rights to dignity and to bodily integrity and not having to undergo treatments that are utterly futile. When a treatment fails to serve any useful purpose, then its continued use seems perverse. Or put another way, must

Linda lose her rights and her autonomy just because she has no mental capacity?"

"I don't think so." David had now joined them at the table.

He finished off the last of his lamb and mange tout and emptied his glass of Cabernet Shiraz before addressing his mother again.

"Alright Mum. You know that no matter what, Margaret and I are fully supportive of what you want to do, and we will support you all the way. What next?"

"We also realize that Dad, God rest his soul, was ambivalent about letting Linda die by discontinuing her tube feeding," Margaret added. "But now that he is dead David, we can move together on this."

"I have an old friend, as you know, in the Cistercians — Fr. Tom Lucy, Professor of Moral Theology, Maynooth College. Tom and I were brought up together in the same Tipperary village and have known each other all our lives. Before I move on this, I would just like to have a word with Tom and to hear his views, as a Moral Theologian."

"On the morality of letting Linda die by discontinuing her nutrition and hydration?"

"Yes, exactly. It is not that I would necessarily be swayed by his views. It is just that I think such views would be helpful and maybe even comforting if they happen to concur with my own."

"Alright, let's go and see the reverend gentleman then."

Fr. Tom Lucy's office was at the end of a long, high-ceilinged passageway on the ground floor of the main building of Maynooth College, known as the Pugin Buildings. As David and his mother, Mary Boyle, walked along this austere and grim corridor, a thousand eyes seemed to follow their every step. Large oak-framed pictures, holding the photographs of young priests who were graduates of the college, lined the walls on both sides. Each picture represented a year's graduation class, with one hundred or more faces on each frame. Their eyes appeared to track mother and son as they made their way toward Tom Lucy's office.

The Professor of Moral Theology stood up behind his desk the moment Mary and David entered his spacious office. Mary noticed the tall, cheerful-looking man dressed in clerical attire. He warmly greeted his guests, directed them to comfortable seats, and asked if they would like some refreshments. The scent of old leather bindings and pipe tobacco filled the room. Behind Fr. Tom's desk hung a large crucifix, the only wall hanging indicating that this room was deep within a venerable seminary.

They declined the light refreshments and were eager to keep the visit short and to the point.

"So, Mary, I know what brings you here. How terribly sad this whole situation is, and what an awful loss and waste of a beautiful young life!"

"Thanks, Tom, it's good of you to say so." Mary was anxious to get to the point and minimize pleasantries.

"Linda's family, including myself, have long been wondering about the appropriateness of subjecting Linda to indefinite tube feeding and courses of antibiotics."

"Yes, the doctors seem very determined to continue, don't they?"

"The doctors and caregivers simply refuse to discuss the matter with us, but from our limited discussions, we know that their intention is to continue giving Linda antibiotics whenever she has a temperature spike and to maintain forced feeding indefinitely."

"Do you think she suffers, Mary?" The priest inquired.

"We believe that she may be suffering, and we believe that this futile treatment has gone on long enough, and it should be stopped to allow her to pass peacefully," David added.

"And you want my opinion on the morality of discontinuing the antibiotics and tube feeding?"

"Yes, please."

Fr. Tom Lucy observed David and Mary Boyle across his desk for a few moments, noting their fatigue and anxiety. Then, as if he had made up his mind, he leaned back in his tall office chair, rocked for a second, and leaned forward again.

"The antibiotics are not a problem," he began.

"Because they are medicines?" Mary interjected.

"Yes, they are medical treatments, and there is no obligation to continue them if they cannot achieve anything beyond a short-term reprieve. Withholding them is neither unethical nor immoral, nor has it ever been."

Once again, the priest paused for thought.

"That's the first thing. Now, hydration and nutrition pose a different issue. In my opinion, if these were being given to a competent person using a cup and spoon, then withholding them would certainly be immoral and unethical."

"So, there's a distinction here?" David asked.

"Yes, indeed, David. No right-minded person would withhold nutrition and hydration from someone capable of receiving them in the usual way. However, in Linda's situation, it's not the same. Her nutrition and hydration are administered through a tube surgically inserted into her stomach. This makes it a medical treatment, at least in my understanding."

"And withholding medical treatments is acceptable?"

"That's right. Withholding a medical treatment that is futile is acceptable. That has always been the case."

David appeared puzzled.

"But it's keeping Linda alive. How can we call that futile?"

"David, if a treatment has no prospect of improving a person's condition, then it has no benefit and can be considered futile."

Fr. Lucy leaned back in his chair and continued, "The treatment is essentially just prolonging or postponing Linda's inevitable passing. In my view, it's pointless and futile."

"Do we have any references to support this?" Mary inquired.

"Yes, indeed we do. The Vatican's Declaration on Euthanasia from 1980, for starters." The priest reached across his desk, picked up a pamphlet, and turned to a marked page.

"It says here, and I'll quote: 'By euthanasia, it is understood an action or an omission which, by itself or by intention, causes death in order to eliminate suffering.'"

"Now, Mary and David, I see you're frowning and confused over there, and who could blame you? Vatican Declarations, typically written in multiple languages and often by committees, aren't known for their clarity. But the key word here is 'intention'. This touches on Thomas Aquinas's principle of Double Effect. In essence, it states that an action's morality is determined by intention, not the outcome."

"Yeah, I've heard of this principle before. It's rather unusual," Mary remarked, feeling perplexed.

"Well, whether it's odd or not, the Church frequently applies the Principle of Double Effect in debates like euthanasia and abortion. In cases like ectopic pregnancy, where the foetus is developing outside of the womb, a surgeon can operate to save the mother's life, even if it results in the foetus's destruction. This isn't considered an abortion because the primary intention isn't to terminate the pregnancy but to save the mother. It's not an exception to the ban on abortion. Semantics come into play here."

"So, if I understand correctly," David cautiously added, "In Linda's case, discontinuing her tube feeding wouldn't be considered euthanasia because the primary intention isn't to end her life but to stop a medical treatment with no benefit other than prolonging her suffering?"

"That's exactly it, David. You've grasped it perfectly."
"And does that declaration mention anything about PVS?" Mary inquired.

"No, the closest I could find was the assertion that withholding useless treatments isn't the same as suicide; instead, it should be seen as an acceptance of the human condition or a desire to avoid disproportionate medical procedures. Mary and David, this closely aligns with Linda's situation. There's a disproportion between her treatment and the expected outcome."

The priest stood up and walked around his desk, leaning back against it with folded arms as he continued to speak softly.

"To put it simply, the Church strongly opposes euthanasia and doesn't condone it under any circumstances. Euthanasia means intentional killing to end a patient's life and relieve suffering, akin to lethal injections in executions. The Catholic Church unequivocally forbids that."

"So, if I understand correctly," Mary began to see the distinction, "medical treatments can be withdrawn or withheld even if it indirectly causes death. This isn't considered euthanasia and is permissible according to the Church?"
"That's right, Mary. That's how I understand it."

Mary wasn't sure if she grasped all the details, but what mattered was that this expert in Moral Theology was indicating that, in his opinion, discontinuing Linda's tube feeding would align with Catholic Church teaching, which was reassuring for her.

She thanked her old friend warmly before David and she took their leave, requesting that Tom Lucy keep in touch and perhaps join them for Sunday lunch soon. The priest promised he would.

Linda lay awake, motionless on her left side, having been turned by the nurses. As they turned her, one of them whispered something in her ear, but she couldn't understand the words. The language spoken by the nurses and others who came into the room was incomprehensible to her. Despite this, the nurses were kind to her. Her eyes were open, and she blinked as she looked out into the ward, with the wall behind her. In another hour, she would be turned onto her back to face the ceiling above her, and in yet another hour, the night shift would turn her onto her right side to face the wall. During those times, she might become less wakeful and drift in and out of sleep. She preferred the nights because that's when she could see, though everything appeared in a single, nameless colour.

Linda could only move her eyeballs and eyelids; the rest of her body felt like wood, immobile and rigid. She felt like she was trapped within a tree, unable to move her mouth, jaw, neck, limbs, or toes. Breathing was possible; she could hear the air entering her lungs, splitting into two streams as it reached her bronchi, and then spreading throughout her alveoli, where oxygen was exchanged with red blood cells.

Visitors came into her room, walking across the floor above her head and sitting in chairs that hung down into the room at the end of her bed. They always spoke in that strange language before falling silent, just sitting and looking at her. She wondered who they were.

Taste was a distant memory, but smell remained. The nurses inserted a tube into her nose, which she removed most days, resulting in their loud and incomprehensible protests. Twice a day, they pumped a colourless and foul-smelling concoction through the tube. It was a miserable existence, and Linda wondered if it would ever end.

Margaret had entered 16 Ashgrove Lane using the key she had since leaving home five years ago to get married. She eagerly awaited her mother, Mary, and brother, David Boyle's return from Maynooth. She wanted to know how their meeting with the Moral Theologian had gone and how he had reacted to the suggestion of discontinuing Linda's tube feeding. While she waited, she found some of her mother's blouses drying on the clothesline and decided to iron them to occupy her mind.

After about half an hour, Margaret heard the sound of gravel crunching as the car pulled up outside and the doors slammed shut, signalling her mother and brother's return.

"I have freshly brewed coffee, Mum. Would you like a cup, David?" Margaret called out from near the Aga.

They gladly accepted the offer of refreshments after their long journey back from Kildare. The three of them then sat around the pine kitchen table, sipping their hot drinks.

"Well, Mum, I'm dying to know," Margaret said, eager for an update.

"There's not much to tell, really, Margaret," Mary began.

"Tell us, how did you get on with the Reverend Doctor? Did he nearly blow a gasket when you told him what was on your mind?" Margaret inquired.

"No, actually, Margaret, it was a calm, reflective, and reasoned discussion. No big deal, no agonizing. You know, just a matter of fact," Mary replied.

"Great, that makes a nice change," Margaret said.

"At the end of it, Father Lucy concluded that the antibiotics and the tube feeding were futile 'medical treatments' that imparted no benefits to Linda other than prolonging her dying and postponing her death," David added.

"That's the bottom line. He said that and a lot more besides," Mary said.

"Some of it was kind of convoluted, and at times, I sort of lost him. But the gist of the thing was this: If Linda had the competence to do so, she could refuse medical treatment, even if such refusal were to bring about her certain death. A document called—oh, what was it, Mum? The Vatican, how's your father—?"

"The Vatican Declaration on Euthanasia, David."

"Yeah, thanks, that's it. In this, the Church says that the discontinuation of medical treatments is not akin to suicide or in any way immoral. Equally, we can refuse treatments on her behalf and petition the Courts that they be discontinued?"

"And that would not be seen by the Church as mercy killing or euthanasia?" Margaret was amazed at their frankness.

"No, and Tom explained it. Euthanasia is any direct and intentional act specifically designed to end a person's life, such as giving a person a lethal injection. He cited the execution of prisoners by lethal injection in the US. If you did that to a very ill person, that would be mercy killing or euthanasia, and a wrong thing to do in the eyes of the Catholic Church. But stopping futile treatments, even where the inevitable consequences of doing so were to bring about death, that is not apparently a direct attack on a life and consequently not wrong?"

Mary stirred in half a teaspoonful of brown sugar into her coffee and awaited her daughter's response.

"By the Holy Mum, that sounds like good news. I mean to say it's nice to think that if we are going down this road, we won't have to contend with the wrath of the Catholic Church on top of everything else," Margaret said.

"Also, it gives us ammunition against the so-called 'Pro-life' people," David added. "If we can argue that discontinuing tube feeding is in line with Vatican guidelines as outlined in their Declaration thingy."

"Yes, it's good news. It is, of course, only the interpretation of one Moral Theologian, but it is what he called 'the dominant theological position'. Wasn't that it, David?" David gave three little nods in his mother's direction.

Mary continued, "To be quite honest with you, though, I have to say that I found Tom's opinion quite surprising. I mean to say, removing the gastrostomy tube will bring about Linda's death. I wouldn't dream of questioning a learned Moral Theologian, but I would have thought that an act that brings about death, irrespective of motivation or intention, was tantamount to killing, tantamount to euthanasia."

David had been sipping his coffee and listening with interest. But now he thought he needed to interject. His mother was making things complicated yet again.

"Mother, for God's sake, don't start introducing complications again. I mean, we've been to Maynooth this afternoon. We've spoken to a world authority on Moral Theology, and it's his view that discontinuing Linda's present and futile regime of medical treatment would not be morally wrong."

Margaret nodded across the table at her brother and spoke, "Yes, Mum. You're always preaching about keeping it simple. So how about practicing what you preach? Keep it simple."

All three fell silent, realizing that unity of purpose and keeping their philosophy as simple as possible was essential.

Mary brought her empty cup to the sink.

"You are both right. We will keep it nice and simple, as you say," Mary agreed.

It had been almost six years since Tom Brogan acted in a professional capacity for Mary Boyle. Now they were sitting across the solicitor's desk facing each other. David had come too, as always, lending his mother support during these difficult meetings. His mother was about to embark on a course that, if successful, would bring about the death of his sister. And, whereas they had discussed among themselves as a family the implications of what they were proposing, this was the first time that they had aired the idea outside of the immediate family setting other than with their friend Nurse Catherine Rooney and Fr. Tom Lucy.

Brogan was speaking:

"Let me just be clear in my mind here Mary what it is that you are proposing. You, in your capacity as Committee to Linda and in your capacity as Linda's mother seek to petition the Courts to issue an Order allowing for the discontinuation of Linda's tube feeding and for the discontinuation of other medications. Is that it?"

"That's correct Tom, in a nutshell – yes."
"Yes, but what if Linda was in pain or appeared distressed as a result of having her nutrition and hydration suddenly withdrawn. What then?"

Mary looked over to see how David was reacting to what appeared to be the solicitor's reservations. She was beginning to wonder if this lawyer had the bottle for what was being discussed. The last thing she needed right now was a reluctant petitioner. She needed to get this straight right from the beginning.

"Tom, are you alright with this?"
"No, no, hold on Mary."
"Because if you have any moral qualms or if you are not comfortable with what's being proposed here then please say so right now before we start going down this road. We can always go elsewhere you know?"

The solicitor's hands went up palms held outwards head cocked off slightly to one side. The body language said, 'take it easy that was not what I meant at all'.

"No, no, no Mary. Sorry now, take it easy. That is not what I was getting at. And let me say at this juncture that I am not just behind you on this quest. I am in fact right up beside you shoulder to shoulder and you may rest assured that, whatever way it goes, you will have my one hundred percent support from beginning to end."

"Alright Tom, but sorry, that was not the impression you were giving a second ago."

"Will you listen Mary in heaven's name. You know that I know the pain and suffering that you and your late husband Joseph went through. I know that your lovely daughter Linda has been stripped of every shred of dignity that she ever possessed. I know that her 'treatment' is utterly futile and perverse. And I feel strongly that she is being denied her constitutional rights to privacy and to bodily integrity. So come on now, never doubt my absolute agreement with you and the family with this application."

"Alright Tom, that's good to hear and thank you. But I think you will understand the absolute necessity that we are all singing from the same hymnal here before we start. The task ahead is difficult enough God knows without our having to carry any dead weight with us like reluctant litigants."

The solicitor nodded in agreement and Mary continued:

"You were asking there about the discontinuing of Linda's medications in the context of her being in pain or in some other distress resulting from the sudden withdrawal of her food and water. We have been thinking about that too. Linda has an old friend Catherine Rooney who is now an Intensive Care nurse, and she has been enormously supportive and helpful. She believes that we should ask the Courts to allow for the discontinuation of the tube feeding and medications except those needed to sedate or to relieve pain or the so-called palliative medicines. Will that cause a problem do you think?"

The solicitor paused for a second and looked from David back to his mother before answering.

"That's exactly what I was getting at. Specifying that palliative medications should not be withdrawn will not cause any problem of itself. In fact, if anything it should greatly help our case."

"Alright then, what's your biggest worry about this?"
"That the application will be rejected and gets thrown out of court. This is a big gamble you know, uncharted waters. Days in High Court cost a fortune."

"I suppose it will depend to some extent on what judge is appointed to hear the case." David spoke to nobody in particular.

"Not just to some extent David. The President of the High Court will appoint the judge because your sister is a Ward of Court. Who he appoints is absolutely pivotal to the outcome. And all of this is outside of our hands."

The consultation room went silent for a few seconds. The sound of two typewriters at work next door drifted into the room. David had a question for the solicitor:

"Tell us this much Tom. Without going into too much legalese, what roughly are the procedures from here?"

"In a nutshell David, through this office, we will issue a Plenary Summons to the High Court to be followed by a Notice of Motion seeking an Order from them allowing for the discontinuation of Linda's tube feeding and her medications other than those medications used for palliative purposes. The application will be made in your mother's name, as she is now the Committee. The application will need to be strongly supported by the family -- that is yourself and your sister Margaret."

"Oh, yes? And what will we have to do?" David sounded surprised.

"We are going to need Affidavits from both of you. These will carry a lot of weight because you are the only people who have lived with this down through the years."

"And will these be contested?"

Tom Brogan was surprised at the young man's naivety.

"Of course, they'll be contested David. Do you think the doctors and carers are just going to sit there like idiots and do nothing?"

"No, I suppose not."

"You're damn right they won't. The carers, the institution where Linda is been kept alive, the Attorney General, and the General Solicitor for the Ward of Court Office, acting as guardian 'ad litem' as they call it, will vigorously oppose this application. So, you can see there is going to be plenty of opposition to the notion that Linda be allowed to die with dignity!"

"Will we be needed to give evidence in Court, and will we be represented by Counsel?" Mary wanted to know.

"This is no push-over Mary. You will need to be prepared to give evidence in Court, and of course, you will be represented by Senior Counsel – probably David Lavelle again if that's alright with you. At least he is familiar with the case. I will just have to check out that he won't have any scruples about this kind of thing, but I do not think that should be a problem."

Summer had given way to autumn. Wet October winds swirled around Ely Place and blew against the door of number eight, the headquarters of the Order of the Knights of Saint Columbanus. Upstairs in the large reception room, the log fire within the Adams fireplace burned brightly. Three men dressed in ceremonial robes sat at the large mahogany conference table under the Waterford crystal chandelier. Their conversation had urgency to it. Worrying developments in the case of the woman in a persistent vegetative state had come to their attention, and The Knights were going to have to intervene if possible.

Thomas O'Leary was a High Court judge soon to retire. He also held the position of Supreme Advocate within the Knights. Seated across from him were two grey-haired semi-retired hospital consultants Deputy Supreme Knight Dr. Peter Newman, Obstetrician, and Gynaecologist, and Supreme Registrar Dr. Walter Malone, consultant Anaesthetist. O'Leary was speaking.

"It is over six years ago now, Brothers, since this matter came up before. Most of the things that I predicted might happen in this case at that time have, in fact, happened. Not that it gives me any joy that that should turn out to be the case because now, or so it seems to me, things have come to a critical stage."

The Supreme Advocate at this stage left the table and went to the Adams fireplace, from where he lit a cigarette using the tongs to hold a lump of burning charcoal against the cigarette end. The wood smoke drifted into the large room, giving off a sweet aroma. The Knight inhaled deeply before continuing to speak with his back turned to the fire and to the portrait of Saint Columbanus hanging on the wall behind him.

"First of all, her parents sued for damages, and they had every right to do so - on their daughter's behalf. You should be congratulated for the way you handled that situation. It was settled out of court, and that was clever. Had it gone into court, the publicity would not have been good for the Pro-life movement. The so-called liberals might have asked questions as to why this patient was been kept alive, and an unsavoury debate might have ensued. Settling out of court avoided that happening."

Mr. Justice O'Leary turned around to flick his cigarette ash into the fire before proceeding:
"Following the damages award, your patient was made a Ward of Court, again as predictable. But now, and here is the really frightening bit, some six years later the patient's mother and family are seeking an Order from the High Court to allow for the discontinuation of feeding her via her gastrostomy tube. I will tell you Brothers this is the most outrageous suggestion that I have heard in a long time. If the High Court allows this to happen, it will open the floodgates to the legalization of euthanasia in Ireland. Now is that what we want to see happening? This could be legalized euthanasia through the back door, by legal precedent. If this happens it would be a body-blow to the whole Pro-life philosophy and might undermine the good work done to date by SPUC and PLAC in

265

keeping the twin evils of euthanasia and abortion well away from the shores of Ireland."

Flicking the half-smoked cigarette into the fireplace, O'Leary returned to his place at the table and continued:

"Your patient is receiving food and water, for God's sake. She is being given sustenance; she is being given what any decent human being would give to another. This is not medical treatment, for crying out loud! This is just ordinary, decent, life-respecting human behaviour. Is this not the feature of our behaviour that distinguishes us from other animals: that we support and help each other without stint or question?"

The other two Knights sitting at the table might have wanted to say something at this stage, but they had rules to obey, and The Supreme Advocate was not yet finished talking.

"What does this family want? Well, I have had a look at some of the papers lodged in the Four Courts, including affidavits sworn by the ward's mother, brother, and sister, and I can tell you what they want. They want the High Court of Ireland to declare that it would not be illegal if someone were to pull the ward's gastrostomy tube out and let her die of starvation and dehydration. Can you believe this, I ask you, Brothers? Can you believe what is happening today in our society and how respect for the dignity of human life does not seem to matter anymore? This is just euthanasia under another name. Killing off the weak and helpless! This is Dachau all over again."

"But it is even worse than that." Justice O'Leary now loudly tapped several times on the mahogany table in front of him with the knuckle of his right middle finger to give emphasis to what he was saying.

"If this heinous petition gets through our judicial system and, let's face it, there is a chance that it will, then what that means is that this woman will be condemned to death, not by hanging, not by lethal injection. Oh no, that might be too good for her. No, she will be condemned to be executed by starvation and dehydration. And for what crime, what has she done, who has tried her?"

The tapping on the table had suddenly stopped. The Supreme Advocate was extremely agitated and, on his feet again, heading for the Adams fireplace.

Dr. Peter Newman raised his right index finger a few inches off the mahogany boardroom table. As Deputy Supreme Knight, he held a rank above the current speaker and was therefore entitled to interrupt, although convention and good manners dictated that he should indicate his wish to speak first rather than just cut in.

"Yes, Brother, do you want to say something?"

Dr. Newman cleared his throat before he spoke:

"Brothers, I simply cannot accept that this is happening, ah. I simply cannot believe it. Walter and I have long known that Linda's family were unhappy with the way we were managing to keep their loved one alive. It must be, oh what, ten years ago anyway, that I had a run-in with Linda's old man, ah. He died a few years ago, ah. I can only hope that he made his peace with God Almighty before he departed this life because he had a black evil soul to him, ah. He wanted me to consider starving his daughter to death, ah! Our relationship with this family was never good down through the years. When the old fellow passed away, I expected that things might at least settle down. And now this, after so many years, they want us to just kill her off, ah. After all the care and minding and love that those good and dedicated nurses have heaped upon Linda Boyle for over fifteen years, is this to be their reward, to know that in the end of it all her family just killed her off, ah?"

The Supreme Registrar indicated that he wanted to say something, and Dr. Newman nodded in his direction to indicate that he was free to do so.

"Are we not perhaps worrying too much here, Brothers? I mean to say, the family may petition the High Court to allow for the discontinuation of food and water; they can petition the Courts for whatever they like, but that does not mean that the Courts will grant it, not in Ireland anyway. The UK is different, of course. They have legalized abortion over there since 1968, so it's hardly surprising that they allowed for the starvation of people in PVS in England. But this is

Ireland with a Pro-life constitution guaranteeing protection to every citizen, including the unborn, from the moment of conception. How can the Courts sanction murder, for Heaven's sake? Taking out Linda Boyle's gastrostomy tube, knowing that by doing so you are going to bring about her death, is an act of murder, surely, or of manslaughter at least? It is also, as our dear brother here has so eloquently put it, execution by starvation and without trial. What in the name of Sweet Jesus is this country coming to? Just when we thought that things were going well, this anti-life proposal raises its ugly head yet again and does so in a most public way."

The large reception room fell silent for a few seconds. Thomas O'Leary was still standing, back to the Adams fireplace. He threw on a birch log and lit another cigarette from a small lump of charcoal held at the end of the tongs. From there, he addressed his fellow Knights without asking permission to do so. He was a Justice of the High Court. His opinion in this company was the only one that mattered right now, and he knew that.

"I share and agree with everything that you have said, Brother Walter. In our eyes and in the eyes of Our Lord Jesus Christ and His Blessed Mother Mary, of course, it is cruel murder to deliberately cut off the food and drink supply to a person who is totally dependent on you for everything. It would be an unspeakably evil act to starve the Ward to death. Food is not medicine; it is not given with an expectation that it will cure anything. In this particular case, it is not given as a

269

treatment for the persistent vegetative state. We always give food to those who can't help themselves. We give food and drink to babies. We give food and drink to the elderly and infirm. If it is drink and food by cup and spoon, it does not suddenly cease to be drink and food by virtue of it being given by a gastrostomy tube. I do not believe that any High Court Judge of this land would agree to allow the discontinuation of feeding in the case of the Ward of Court. You are right, Brothers, except for one thing."

The Supreme Advocate looked at his watch and returned to the table. There were ten minutes left before they must go into the general assembly. Mr. Justice O'Leary needed to wrap it up. To hell with the Knights' protocol, he needed to speak now:

"And that one thing is what judge will be drawn to hear this case. Who will hear this petition? That is the one single most crucial element in this case. Draw the wrong judge, and suddenly killing in this country will become respectable, and euthanasia will be legalized. The vast majority of judges down there in the High Court would throw this thing out of court and would never declare as legal a deliberate act that ended a person's life. Of course, they wouldn't. But I have had a sneak look at the Affidavits for the family and from their supporters, and they are presenting their case in terms of it's being the 'withdrawal of futile medical treatment' that they want. This is all about words, interpretation, and perception. Now your patient's gastrostomy tube was put in place by a surgical operation. Therefore, it could be argued that as such her feeding is a form of 'medical treatment,' and as such, it could be legally discontinued."

Pausing just long enough to allow his fellow Knights to absorb what he has just said, O'Leary continued:

"God be with the good old days when we had at least six Brothers on the Bench down in the Four Courts at any one given time. In those days you could almost depend on getting the kind of judgment that you were looking for. Now, as you know, we are down to two Knights in the Dublin judiciary that is Mr. Justice James Morrissey and I. So how can we make sure that one of us gets this so-called 'Right to Die' case in order to make sure that it is thrown out of court? It is not going to be easy; I can tell you that much. The more I think about this, the more I'm convinced that the only way to ensure that this Motion is defeated is for me to hear it myself. We cannot rely on Morrissey because, as you may know, he does not be well and is out sick half the time. I might have a word with the President of the High Court and see if anything can be swung. But as I say, it is not going to be easy. Nor is it without risk. The President is a cute whore of a Cork man, and I doubt if there is much love lost between us. But I will try."

"And finally----" The Supreme Advocate was about to wrap it up.

"If the unthinkable should happen and this thing is granted by the High Court, then you can, and I presume will, appeal to the Supreme Court. Between five judges on the bench there, not one of them is a Knight though I understand that one or two of them are in Opus Dei --- not that you could expect much from that shower. They fund up Youth Defence, and that's about all they do for the Pro-life Movement. Youth Defence my arse. Anyway, I would not place too much reliance on the Supreme Court. Our last port of call then might be The Medical Council. We have, as you know, a brother or two on the Fitness to Practise Committee of that venerable body. They could, speaking off the record of course, threaten to strike off any doctor who would cooperate with a High Court declaration injurious to the ward. We will just have to play this one along as best we can. But it is worrying I have to say."

With that, the three stood up and bowed respectfully at each other before leaving the room to attend the larger assembly mustering next door.

The Dining-hall in the Four Courts, Dublin, was a formidable place occupying the principal part of the North Wing of that building.

At the top of this hall, positioned two feet above the other diners in the room, the judges or benchers sat. The other diners assembled here were for the most part Senior Counsels. A clear pecking order existed in this room. Formally dressed waiters provided table service only for the benchers. Mere barristers were expected to line up at a carvery and help themselves. The food was of the plain and wholesome kind – roast beef and potatoes, bacon and cabbage, chicken vol-a-vent. Wine was available but not encouraged. After a glass or two of red wine, aging judges were known to fall asleep during afternoon hearings, thus bringing the judiciary into some disrepute and ridicule. No, wine was not encouraged.

It was 2:15 in the afternoon, and most judges had returned to their chambers. Mr. Justice Tom O'Leary found himself dining alone at the top judge's table in the ornate Dining-hall of the Four Courts. He was politely picking through his bacon and cabbage and new potatoes boiled in their jackets. White parsley sauce and a good blob of freshly made English mustard finished off the dish. He had just been poured a glass of Chardonnay, and Justice O'Leary was adding a knob of butter to the new potatoes when a colleague, wanting to know if he could join him, suddenly interrupted his thoughts.

"Ah, the hard man Tom. Do you mind if I join you? Dirty old day outside for the time of the year that's in it?"

Looking up and rising from his seat by a full one inch, Justice O'Leary saw that the man asking to join him was Justice Barry Long, President of the High Court. O'Leary could hardly believe his luck. This was precisely the man that he had been trying to 'run into' for the past week or so. He did not want to approach him directly because that would have been too obvious. No, just bumping into him like this at the dining table and with no one else there to be listening in was perfect. Had he tried to, he could hardly have orchestrated it any better himself.

But O'Leary knew that he must now tread carefully if he was not to spook his colleague. It was like playing a salmon. You don't try to horse it out of the water. You take your time. Take it nice and handy.

"Any holidays recently Barry?" O'Leary pretended he wanted to know.

The waiter in the morning jacket was taking Mr. Justice Long's luncheon order.

"I'll have the cream of mushroom and chicken soup, please, for a starter, Mick."

Long addresses himself again briefly to the menu before looking up.

"And I'll have a few slices of roast beef on the rare side, if possible, Mick. Thank you so much."

"And potatoes, Sir?"

"Yes, mashed, please, with gravy on the side."

"How about a glass of wine, Sir?"

"Water will be fine, Mick. A bit early in the day for the stronger stuff, don't you think?"

Barry Long spoke with a pronounced Cork accent.

"Sorry, what was that you were saying there, Tom?"

"I was asking you if you'd taken any holidays yet this year."

"Indeed. I have a bit of an old cottage there just outside Millstreet. Nothing fancy now, I assure you. You do a bit of fishing, don't you?"

"Oh yes, never any good at it, though. Haven't the patience for it, to be quite honest with you."

"Even so, you would have some idea of what is involved. Sheila and I went down to the cottage there for a week around Easter time. We have a rod on the Blackwater there. Well, would you look it, if we were to be there for the next year, it would make no difference. Never got a touch. Flogged the fucking thing from dawn to dusk every day. Tried every fly in the box and then a few more besides. Ah well, such are the joys of fly-fishing. No matter. We had a few right nights down at our local though. Some great musical talent around that part of the world."

O'Leary scooped up the last of the English mustard from the side of his plate with his knife and applied it lovingly to a slice of bacon like an oil painter using a palette knife. He smiled across at his colleague. He liked a man who could curse.

"Ah sure, it's not just about catching fish. It's more about being out in God's own fresh air and relaxing and the few scoops at night and a bit of a singsong. Isn't that it, Barry? Getting out of this place and clearing the old head, sure isn't that what it's all about at the end of the day?" O'Leary warmed to his topic.

Barry Long tipped his soup bowl outwards to spoon up the last of his cream of mushroom and chicken. You can tell if a man is educated or not by the way he finishes off his soup, O'Leary thought to himself. At the same time, Mick arrived with the rare roast beef, mashed potatoes, and a small jug of dark gravy.

"Thanks, Mick. Could you get me a bit of horseradish, like a good man?"

The pair fell silent for a minute to concentrate on the serious business of eating.

"This is a funny old job that we have, all the same, I often think to myself."

It was Justice O'Leary who had broken the silence. He was closing in on his target.

"I mean to say when a judge sits on the bench, he or she brings with them their own baggage, their prejudices, their own politics, their own opinions, their own sense of morality, religion, ethics, philosophy, and so on and so forth. We may not like to admit it to ourselves, but you know, and I know that these feelings and emotions that we bring with us onto the bench do, or at the very least can, have a direct bearing on the outcome of any case. We may like to think that it is all pure law and the persuasiveness of the arguments being put by either side that influences the final outcome, but that is not the whole story."

"You are right, of course, Tom. I think everyone accepts what you're saying. It may be an imperfect system, but it is the best that we have. And in any case, there is always the right of appeal."

Justice O'Leary nodded across the table at his colleague and thought it might be time to start closing in a bit more.

"Tell us this much, Barry, and tell me no more, how are you enjoying your stint as President of the High Court?"

"Oh, it has its moments like most things. It is a great job for making enemies. No matter what case you give to what judge someone will be unhappy and start griping and whinging about something or other. It is not so much a question of not being able to please all of the people all of the time; it is more a question of not being able to please any of the people any of the time. Anyway, why do you ask?"

O'Leary had to tread carefully now. Can he really trust this Cork man to keep this to himself? If any of his superiors got even a hint at what O'Leary was about to suggest, that would be the end of his career on the bench. Goodbye. Early retirement. Lots of time then to hone the old fly-fishing skills.

A judge can't be got rid of that easily, but rigging, fixing, or manipulating the justice system was one sure way of doing it.

But O'Leary reminded himself again that this case was about life and death. He was doing God's work now. This was about how we treat the most vulnerable in our society. This was about respect for human life itself. This was about safeguarding Ireland against those foreign forces of evil that would try to introduce euthanasia and abortion into this holy land. This was the essence of what it was to be truly Pro-life, and it was why O'Leary took certain solemn oaths on that day he was initiated into The Knights of Saint Columbanus. He knew then that being a Knight might sometimes mean having to take risks for Our Lord Jesus Christ. And now was such a time. Let's take a risk for God. This just might work.

"Oh, for no particular reason really," O'Leary lied. He went on:

"It is just that I was vaguely wondering about a case that's coming up next week and that is of some interest to me. It involves a woman in a persistent vegetative state and her right to die. Her family are seeking an Order that nutrition and hydration be discontinued. Since she is a Ward of Court, you, as President, will be required to nominate the judge. If I can be of any assistance to you, I would be happy to take a look at it."

Barry Long continued to apply a skim of creamy horseradish sauce to his rare roast beef. Mick finally delivered this in a silver sauceboat.

Ah, so here we go again now. Ah yes. Rumour had long been out and around the Four Courts that Mr. Justice Tom O'Leary was a member of the Order of the Knights of Saint Columbanus, or maybe he was a member of a similarly secretive society like Opus Dei. It didn't really matter. What was known for certain among the judiciary, however, was his propensity for handing down some pretty perverse rulings, most particularly if the case in question involved subjects like Family Planning, Right to Information on Abortion, Sex Education, or Family Law. Regardless of the merits or otherwise of the case, it was a pretty safe bet that O'Leary's judgments would invariably come down on the side of the Established Church. And here he was yet again, sniffing around in what he would call 'Pro-life' issues and hinting that he be appointed to a particular case.

Mr. Justice Barry Long popped a modest piece of roast beef and mashed potato into his mouth before putting down his knife and fork. He folded his hands in front of him and chewing, he observed his colleague across the table from him. Before speaking, he looked over his shoulder to his right and to his left. The Dining-hall was almost empty. Mick was down at the far end clearing off a table; nobody was within earshot. Thanks be to God for that much anyway.

"We have never had this conversation, right? For fuck's sake, you know the rules around here as well as anyone else. The matter that you have just mentioned will be given to a pair of safe hands to adjudicate on. Quite frankly, I would not let you within an ass's roar of it, and please do not ever, ever mention this again to me."

Both men then finished off their lunch deep in their thoughts. Justice O'Leary consoled himself with the thought that 'nothing ventured, nothing gained.'

The summer of 1995 was one of the finest on record in Ireland for fifty years. After a cold and wet spring came the middle of May, and fine sunny warm days followed each other in an unbroken succession for the next one hundred days or more. In May of that year, Mary Boyle and her two offspring, Margaret and David, were gathered in the, by now, too familiar environs of Dublin's Four Courts. Judgement day had finally arrived. They had been through the mill in the last few days. The High Court petition to allow for the discontinuation of the Ward's tube feeding was heard in camera and was a gruelling affair from start to finish, lasting all of three days. Mary Boyle had not had a decent night's sleep in over a week. On day two of the hearing, each family member, in turn, took to the witness stand and gave evidence, firstly before Senior Counsel David Lavelle and then, under cross-examination, to one or other barristers on the other side.

The evidence that they gave was roughly in line with their sworn affidavits, and that was:

A. That the Ward was in a Persistent Vegetative State or in a Near Persistent Vegetative State without any prospect whatsoever of her ever recovering. That she was doubly incontinent, could not move any muscle, and all limbs were severely contracted. She could not speak or communicate and showed no evidence of awareness of self or her environment.

B. That the Ward hated hospitals all her short life and if she had awareness now, she would not choose to live out her life confined to a hospital bed and being force-fed.

C. That when alive and well, the Ward often expressed the opinion that should she fall into a coma or have a terminal illness that she would not want to have extraordinary means taken to keep her alive.

D. That the food and drink now being given to the Ward was futile 'medical treatment.' It must be seen as medical treatment since it required a surgical procedure to initiate it and may require further surgery to maintain it.

E. That the Ward's constitutional rights to bodily integrity and to privacy were almost certainly being violated by her present treatment.

F. That the Ward might have some minimal cognition and awareness of her desperate situation and that if that were so it would be a tremendous burden to her.

G. That the nursing care that the Ward was receiving was excellent and had always been excellent.

H. That the family had persistently failed to persuade the carers to adopt any treatment strategy that might envisage allowing the Ward to die even at some distant date.

I. That the relationship between the family and the doctors responsible for the Ward's care was not good and never was good.

Against these points, the opposition presented equally compelling and forceful arguments. Throughout the hearing, they consistently argued that food and water, regardless of how they are administered, were not medical treatment but simply nutrition, essential for keeping the Ward alive and comfortable. Listening to these arguments was extremely distressing.

Now, they were gathered in Consultation Room 8. Mary Boyle and her two children, Margaret and David, looked tired and worried. Along with them were their solicitor, Tom Brogan, and his Senior Counsel, David Lavelle, and Junior Counsel, Catherine Mullins. Fr. Tom Lucy had also come along to give moral support and had sat with them throughout the entire hearing. In his black suit and high white collar, a good white head of hair, he looked the quintessential Roman Catholic priest. But his presence was much more than mere symbolism. By being at Mary's side, the family of the Ward of Court conveyed that the family took their responsibility to behave morally and ethically toward their loved one seriously.

Senior Counsel David Lavelle broke the uncomfortable silence:

"As I was saying yesterday, you never can tell what way a judgment is going to go. But I have to say that, in my years working in this place, I have always found Mr. Justice McGill a fair and reasonable man."

"Yes, he seemed to listen patiently to each side and certainly showed no outward signs of any bias either way."

"That's right Mary, and when necessary, he politely interrupted to seek clarification. The other side, to be fair about it, did a brilliant job too. We will know the answer in an hour or so, of course, but Catherine and I agree that we are in with a good chance here. I suggest that you go off and stretch the old legs now and get a cup of coffee or a bite to eat. Let us all be in Court No. 3 by five to eleven. Alright, everybody?"

At eleven o'clock on the dot, Mr. Justice McGill swept into Court No. 3 from the side entrance behind his bench well above the level of the body of the court.

"All Rise!"

The Court Clerk cried out as the tipstaff held back the high-backed chair for Your Honour to take up his position. A general scampering to their feet now as the fifty strong attendances stood up and awaited the judge to be seated. Not an empty seat remained inside the courtroom. The press benches were full of reporters, notebooks in hand. The Stenographer was poised for action. The Court Registrar and solicitors for each side were seated in a line just under the judge's bench facing out into the court. Senior and Junior Counsels representing the various interested bodies, wearing wigs with tassels, took up the space available in the barrister's benches. A landmark judgment was about to be delivered, and the courtroom was filled with a general air of expectation and controlled excitement. Relatives and friends of the Ward, the carers, the doctors, and the hospital administrators took up all the spaces around the walls. Everybody who had a seat sat down. Others stood inside the door and shuffled forward as still more people tried to enter the courtroom.

Mr. Justice McGill cleared his throat and began in a loud, clear voice. He was to speak for almost an hour and a half. A great deal of what he had to say made little sense to Mary, David, or Margaret Boyle. It contained a lot of legal language that was not always easy to follow, like *'aforementioned'*, *'aforesaid'*, and *'pursuant'* and *'parens patriae'*. A great deal of it concerned matters of jurisdiction and historical references to the Lord Chancellor of England and something called *'letters of lunacy'*.

The judge spent a great deal of time describing the Ward's condition, stating that he was satisfied she was in a 'near' rather than a 'full' persistent vegetative state, with no prospect of recovery or improvement. But the label 'near' rather than 'full' Vegetative State seemed to sway the judge towards the petitioners more so than towards those who argued that treatment should not be discontinued.

He said:

"But if such minimal cognition as she may have included an inkling of her catastrophic situation, then I am satisfied that that would be a terrible torment and burden for her to carry and her situation would be worse than if she were in a fully persistent vegetative state."

As he went on speaking, little by little, hint-by-hint, it began to become clearer what way Mr. Justice McGill was inclining. Mary Boyle could not believe what she was hearing. This was Ireland, after all. Judges did not speak like that in Ireland.

Towards the end of his judgment, he stated that he was satisfied nutrition via a surgically initiated and maintained gastrostomy tube amounted to medical treatment. From this point onwards, it became almost inevitable that the judgment was going to go in favour of allowing for the discontinuation of such medical treatment. The judge was careful to point out that this was not euthanasia, had nothing whatsoever to do with euthanasia, and that this was a standalone case unrelated to any debate on end-of-life management. Finally, he gave the Hospital and carers permission not to be involved in anything that ran contrary to their ethics and ethos and he put a stay on the Order to allow time in the event of an appeal. Then the judge sat down. Suddenly, the case concluded, and the courtroom emptied.

CHAPTER 9 - MERCIFUL DEATH AT LAST

Mary feels that she had been through the wringer. She is utterly spent. The build up to the High Court hearing and the proceedings themselves, have been among the most stressful few weeks in her entire long life. She needs to get away somewhere if only for a long relaxing weekend.

The evening after Mr Justice McGill delivered his unexpected judgement in the High Court, allowing for the discontinuation of Linda's tube feeding and antibiotics, the family gathered for an early supper at the Italian restaurant within walking distance of 16 Ashgrove Lane. They had ordered a bottle of Chianti Classico while waiting for the simple pasta dishes that each had chosen. David poured the wine for the three of them while his mother spoke.

"I suppose they'll say now that we 'won' the case."

"Can't you see it in tomorrow's headlines Mom? Family of Right to Die case *win* right to allow victim this and that. The tabloids will have a field day," Margaret said sounding exasperated.

"I don't have any sense of being a winner nor have I the slightest inclination to celebrate." Mary continued. "What we achieved for Linda was a right for her to die. That might be significant but hardly something to celebrate."

"You are damn right it's significant," David said, placing the wine bottle back onto its coaster.

"Look at it this way Mum. Suppose Your Honour had gone the other way this morning. And to be quite honest with you, this being Ireland, I was quite prepared for such a judgement. Now where would that have left us?" David took a sip of his Chianti before continuing. The pastas had started to arrive and each of them thanked the waitress in turn.

"I'll tell you where it would have left us. It would have left us in a right old mess that's where. We would now be in a no man's land and looking at whopping big legal fees."

"We could have appealed David," Margaret interjected.
"Of course, we would have appealed Margaret. But according to Tom Brogan, that's never a safe place to be, trying to overturn a previous High Court decision. What do you feel Margaret?"

"What do I feel? Oh, just tremendous relief, that's all. Relief that it's all over, relief that there is now an end in sight for Linda. You know --- just relief."

Margaret looks thoughtful before continuing:
"David Lavelle said something to me during one of those interminable waits in the consultation room that I thought quite extraordinary. I had forgotten about it until just now."

"And what was that dear?" Mary asked anxiously.

"He said to me that he had heard from an impeccable source that the judge for this case was handpicked by the President of the High Court. McGill, it appears, was well known for his impartiality in matters religious or moral."

The three ate in silence for a few minutes, each lost in their own thoughts.

"Just look at what we've been through Mother over the last twenty-one years." Margaret broke the silence. "All I can say is that you are some women, having to watch poor Linda struggle day in day out with never any sign or hope of improvement, and to do all that without breaking."

Mary is uncomfortable with Margaret's praise.

"Margaret love. I was never alone. Let us not forget your gentle late father. May he rest. The whole thing sent him off to an early grave and of that I have no doubt."

David emptied off the last of the bottle dividing it evenly between the three glasses, speaking while he poured:

"Do you know what you two ladies should do now?"
"No, what should we do?" Margaret wanted to know.

"You should go over to Connemara for a good long weekend break. Stay in Ballynahinch Castle. God knows you deserve it. Take the fly rods with you or maybe the hotel can lend you some tackle. I'll look after the booking for you. Is that alright?"

"David. That sounds like a really good idea."

The Ballynahinch River is only two and a half miles long. Emptying a system of small lakes and pools into Bertraghboy Bay on the Atlantic coast its waters are as clear as gin and free flowing all year round. It was the month of June and the middle of the sea trout fishing season. Mary and Margaret Boyle were on the fishing beat just below Ballynahinch Castle each standing out at the end of a casting pier that took them safely towards the middle of the river. They were dressed similarly wearing lightweight trekking boots with woollen stockings pulled up on to trouser ends. On top they wore fly vests with their myriads of pockets from which protruded a plethora of fly-fishing paraphernalia -- forceps, scissors, leader line, collapsible priest, and fly boxes.

Each woman cast with her back to the light southerly breeze and to the flow of the river. They were using light tackle hired from the hotel – floating lines on ten-foot single-handed fly rods. Mary had tied on a wet fly called a Bibio onto a light leader as recommended by the hotel's hall porter Peter Vahey. Margaret had taken her own advice and was using a sinking fly called The Yellow Pheasant Tail Nymph Fly that swirled and darted well below the river's surface twenty yards down from her. She could not see it but knew exactly where it was.

The day was overcast with the sun only managing an occasional fleeting appearance. Rain clouds threatened. Mary was glad that there was a fishing hut only a few yards away into which they could bolt in the event of a downpour. This was a fly fisherman's paradise, and the conditions were about ideal. Both women knew that dull days were best for fly-fishing.

Every now and then one or other of the women hauled their long floating lines out of the water, holding their rod vertical and motionless for the count of two whole seconds, allowed their line to make its long journey backwards over their heads before straightening out behind them. At that precise moment they flung the tip of their rod forwards again bringing the line back over their shoulder in a graceful arch to fall lightly on the water's surface before them in a line as straight as a die. Timing and precision were everything and the two women were well practised fly rod casters.

They were twenty yards apart. To communicate with each other and to be heard over the river's babble they had to shout. They did this only after long periods of silent concentration. They were lost to their tasks. Theirs was a contemplative pursuit and a mind cleansing exercise.

"What have you got on there, Mom?"

Margaret suspected that her mother might have made the wiser choice of lure than she had and did not want to be out done.

"A Blue Bibio as recommended by Peter Vahey the hall porter in there. He says it never fails on this beat."

"Well, he should know – he's fished here all his life. I love these casting piers, so much easier and safer than wading. In fact, come to think of it, my wading days are over. Give me dry land under my feet any day. Can't beat the old terra firma."

Margaret suddenly stopped talking. What was that? Suddenly and unexpectedly her line went tight, and the tip of the rod bent forwards and shuddered. Bang! She brought the end of the rod decisively into the vertical position and shrieked in delight. Her left hand went for the reel to stop it running. By the feel of things, she knew that she was into a decent sized fish. Hearing her hoops of delight Mary looked across at her daughter and shouted over some gratuitous advice.

"Well done love, well done! If it wants to run let it run! Don't try to horse it out of the water but still keep in touch with it! No slack! No slack! Keep the end of your rod up!"

All the while Mary was giving out this unsolicited advice she was reeling in her own line and running to the end of her casting pier to collect the landing net.

Now she was at her daughter's right-hand side with landing net poised above the rapidly flowing water. Both women craned their necks forwards trying to see what was on the end of the line twenty yards down the river in front of them. Then the dazzling silver speckled fish jumped six feet clear out of the water and fell back in again with an audible splash.

This brief appearance was enough to tell the anglers that they were into what might be a four-pound sea trout. They give off whoops of delight. The fish was now heading towards them, and the line went dangerously slack for a second time. Margaret reeled in for all her worth until all slack was taken up and the tip of her rod was bending forwards again. She was back in touch with the floundering sea trout.

Another run set the fly reel whirling with a high-pitched screech. Margaret's heart was pounding. If she loses this fish, she will never be allowed to forget it. After some time however the sea trout was running out of fight. Margaret lifted its head out of the water and gently brought it to a position directly above where her mother now could scoop the immersed landing net under it and in one movement lift the mighty fish out of the water. Both women congratulated themselves with a hug and agree to fish on for another hour.

A woman dressed in a long-waxed coat and waxed hat was standing on the far bank of the river fifty yards down from where Mary and Margaret were fishing. She was too far away for them to be able to make out any details of her facial features, but the situation was odd. What was odd about it was the way that this woman had now been standing there without moving a muscle for over five minutes just staring across at them. Had they not seen her move earlier they may have mistakenly taken her for a bronze sculpture standing there on the mowed lawn. But once they landed the fish and dispatch it with two sharp blows to the head with the priest the woman in the long-waxed coat turned around and walked away.

The angler's backdrop here were the spectacular rugged Connemara Mountains. Sea breezes with their hint of kelp and iodine constantly delighted their senses. While the gentle babble of the Ballynahinch River mixed with the contributions of the riverside songsters – blackbirds, thrushes and reed warblers, these delights fused into a milieu specifically designed to heal the soul of troubling thoughts. In a few weeks' time Linda would be dead. She will be dead as a direct result of the legal proceeding instigated by Mary and Margaret Boyle here and by David minding the house at home in Dublin. But for the moment at least, and for the first time in many months, those dark thoughts could be temporarily set aside.

Dinner in Ballynahinch Castle was a semi-formal affair. Gentlemen were asked to wear a jacket and tie. Mary and Margaret had pre-booked a table overlooking the river just above the spot where, only a few hours earlier, Margaret, with the help of her mother, had landed a three-and-a-half-pound sea trout. The fish had been weighed and was now safely hanging in the hotel's cold room.

"I believe congratulations might be in order?"

The smartly dressed waiter had materialised beside their table, note pad in hand. Both women beamed up at him. There was something deeply satisfying and amusing about these kinds of situations that can only be understood by fellow anglers.

"Do you mind me asking you Miss, Boyle but what did you catch him on?"

Margaret was enjoying this immensely.

"Not in the least little bit Con, you can ask me whatever you want to. I caught him on a sinker called The Yellow Pheasant Tail Nymph Fly."

"Ah be Jesus aye, is he a lad like this?"

The waiter drew a passable representation of the lure in question on his note pad and held it out for Margaret's inspection.

"That's him Con, well done. But it was not the fly that this hotel was recommending this morning. Peter Vahey the porter told Mother here to tie on a Blue Bibio on a fine leader!"

Mary leaned across to the waiter and in hushed tones said:

"I don't mean to be rude Con, but would you ever tell that fellow Peter Vahey, the next time you run into him, what I said he was to do with his Blue Bibios!"

All three erupted into spontaneous loud laughter that drew looks of surprise from some neighbouring tables.

When they eventually settled down both ordered seafood starters, Mary a prawn cocktail and Margaret half-dozen oysters lightly grilled. To follow they would have the rack of Connemara Mountain lamb with mint sauce and garlic potatoes and a half bottle of the house white to go with the fish and the house red with the lamb.

"That's grand now Con. And would you ever pull the cork on the red now and let it breathe for a while like a good man?"

"Of course, Mrs. Boyle."

The food was scrumptious. Over the meal they sipped
their wine, and the talk was about food and other places that
they had eaten and stayed in the West of Ireland and other
fishing trips that they could remember taking when Joseph was
alive. Margaret could recall her first ever fly-casting lesson that
she got from her father when she was only nine years of age.
The memory momentarily brought tears to her eyes.

Across the dining room from them there was a lady
dressed in a white blouse, with red silk neck scarf and red
slacks. She was a lone diner. Mary noticed that this loan diner
had been staring across at them frequently as they ate and
chatted. When they were having the laugh with the waiter
earlier about The Blue Bibio, Mary noticed that this lady smiled
across at them. She seemed vaguely familiar somehow. Could
she be the same lady dressed in the long-waxed coat and waxed
hat that was so unnervingly staring across the river at them this
afternoon when they caught the fish? But just as Margaret was
beginning to feel slightly annoyed by this nosey person the lone
diner stood up and approached Mary and Margaret's table.
They guessed her age to be in her early sixties.

"Hello, you are Mrs. Mary Boyle are you not? I am
sorry if I seem to be intruding."

Margaret was beginning to feel annoyed. Although
Linda's so called 'Right to Die' case was kept pretty much out
of the limelight down through the years her mother's face had
appeared in newspapers from time to time, such that

occasionally people might recognise her but only rarely actually talk to her. This woman was being far too audacious altogether!

"Yes, I am sorry too, but you are intruding. My mother and I were just having a private conversation and if you don't mind now, we would like to continue with it."

It was unlike Margaret to be rude but really this woman was out of order.

Ignoring Margaret's rebuke, the lady addressed Mary Boyle:

"My name is Ann Harris; I was in theatre the day Linda had a cardiac arrest. Listen, I am sorry if I'm annoying you but---"

Margaret and Mary instantly shared the same thoughts. Jesus, what did this woman say? Could they have misheard her, or did they actually hear her say that she was in theatre at the time of Linda's catastrophe? For almost twenty years now Mary Boyle had searched for the answers to many questions surrounding her daughter's devastation and for nearly twenty years she had received only half-truths, obfuscations and lies. And here they were now in Connemara and here was a woman standing beside their dinner table saying that she was actually in theatre at the time!

The stranger continues: "I just had to be sure I had the right people. It is a long, long time now since I used to see you coming in to visit poor Linda. But listen, if this is----"

297

Margaret now bitterly regretted her earlier rudeness.

"Oh no, no, no, please, please, pull up a chair and join us!" she said indicating a free chair at the next table.

"Would you like a glass of wine? Con! Bring us a wine glass please!"

Ann Harris brought a chair over to Margaret and Mary's table and sitting in she folded her hands in front of her on the white tablecloth.

"Well, as I was saying I was in the operating theatre in St Malachi's on the day that your lovely daughter got into such terrible difficulties. I was Theatre Sister on the day; I can remember it as if it were yesterday. But maybe you would prefer not to talk about it, I'm not sure-----"

Ann Harris moved as if about to stand up.

"No, no, no, no, please, it's alright Ms. Harris."

Mary gently restrained the Theatre Sister by the forearm for a second. Then she said:

"Talking about Linda and what happened to her was never a problem for us. Getting at the truth that lay behind what happened to her was always the problem, not talking about it. Can you believe Ms. Harris, that nobody ever told us what really happened in theatre that terrible day?"

"Yes, I'm afraid I can believe that. We know now that the doctor's professional indemnity insurer had advised them not to speak to you. But to be quite honest with you, I believe that Newman and most certainly Malone used that as an excuse to hide behind. And both of them had things that they needed to hide."

"Oh yes Ms. Harris, like what? I would love to know."

Margaret too was finding it difficult to believe that after all these years they should by accident, suddenly run into someone who knew Linda's real story and who seemed not afraid to speak about it. Could this woman be for real?

"Well, as I think you may by now have learned, Linda's hysterosalpingogram was not necessary in the first place. A simple blood test for hormone levels would have sorted her out. But to this day I believe that Peter Newman is in denial on that point."

"Yes, over the years we gradually came to that conclusion ourselves. But, what about Malone?" It was the enigmatic anaesthetist that really interested Mary Boyle.

Ms. Harris continued: "Walter Malone! Well, he had, and still has, issues to do with alcoholism and self-medicating with prescription drugs. On the day that poor Linda arrested he was pathetically ineffective and lost precious minutes wasting time and fumbling around the place."

After nearly twenty years of being virtually stone walled it was hard now to credit that what Mary Boyle had long suspected, was proving to be true and that all was not well inside that operating theatre on that fateful black day back in the spring of 1974. And here now, in this dining room in this hotel in the West of Ireland so many years later was this stranger, this gentle and pleasant lady of mature years, confirming for her exactly what she had always suspected. This was incredible!

Ann Harris spoke in measured tones for the next ten minutes. She gave a detailed account of exactly what happened that day in theatre. She told how Malone was flustering about with the monitor leads and wasting time. She said how it was she herself who instigated cardiac resuscitation having to first push Malone out of the way. She related how Newman did his best and applied the defibrillator but that everyone in that operating room knew that Linda was without a circulation for far too long and most of them predicted the devastating consequences. From that moment onwards, she was doomed.

On the point of tears Ann Harris continued her voice breaking noticeably.
"Now I just want to tell you something else and this is difficult for me."

Mary hoped that this nice lady was not going to start crying because that would serve no purpose at all, and she desperately wanted to hear everything possible. But Ann Harris seemed to compose herself after about a minute and continued:

"I am retired out of St. Malachi's now for over eight years and yet I still feel that I am caught within the clutches of its culture of bullying and harassment in that workplace. In that hospital then, as in most hospitals in Ireland, then and to a less extent today, a strict hierarchical system was in place."

Now Ms. Harris held up three fingers, one at a time while continuing: "They were Consultant, Reverend Sister, and Nurse. If any nurse ever tried to challenge that system, then she could kiss goodbye to any promotional prospects forever."

"But what could they have done to you?" Mary was incredulous.

"You have no idea Mrs. Boyle. From the moment she started to complain a nurse's career prospects would be frozen like a block of ice. For example, for me to have blown the whistle on Malone would have been quite simply professional suicide. It would have been madness. And besides I would have got absolutely zero support from any of my nursing colleagues. I would not have been believed and I would have been ostracized and isolated. The Consultants would close rank and the Nuns would say nothing and Malone would continue to be dangerous as he continues to be dangerous to this day."

Ann Harris paused for a while and looked first at Mary and then at Margaret. This was difficult for all three women, but the truth must out now. She continued:

"I must say this to you Mrs. Boyle and say it sincerely. Many and many were the times that my colleagues Staff Nurse Jennifer Ryan and Theatre Sister Mary McGonagall and myself of course would see you and your late husband coming into the hospital to visit Linda. You wouldn't recognise us of course but we knew exactly who you were. And we would have only loved to have been able to go up to you and to have said how sorry we were for what had happened to Linda and for what you were going through."

"Yes Ms. Harris, that might have helped." Margaret found it difficult to hide her annoyance.

"But Margaret, we could not go up to you and say sorry. That old bitch Sister Mary Assumpta specifically warned us not to and it was as much as our jobs were worth to disregard her orders. We knew what had happened in theatre that day. We knew you were looking for answers. We knew you were being told little or nothing. We knew that nobody had ever sat down and explained what had happened. We knew that nobody had ever apologised to you and still we could do nothing except watch on from the side-lines. We hated ourselves for it."

Here Ann Harris paused again and took a sip of red wine. The tears were welling up in her eyes again only this time they overflowed and ran in tiny rivulets down her cheeks. Mary Boyle handed her a tissue. She dried her eyes and composed herself before continuing:

"I want to therefore take this opportunity on behalf of the nurses in St Malachi's hospital to say that we are sincerely sorry for the hurt that was caused to you Mrs. Boyle, to your late and gentle husband and to your son and daughter. Obviously, I did not know that I was going to meet you here this weekend. Providence must have sent me."

Both Mary and Margaret were quietly crying at this stage, something that they had not done for quite some time.
"And can I say one last thing, or you would prefer if I stopped now?"

Mary took the tissue away from her eyes looked at Ann Harris and shook her head.

"No Ms. Harris please please go on for as long as it takes."

"It is about Linda's management, her being kept alive for almost twenty years even though such treatment was and remains manifestly futile. I want you to know that there were and there still are many nurses and doctors in St. Malachi's who think that such a management strategy is morally wrong and grotesquely cruel on the family and on Linda. Most nurses and doctors attached to St. Malachi's are privately delighted with the outcome of your recent High Court challenge and would want me to pass on their best wishes to you."

"Most nurses and doctors Ms. Harris?" Mary found this difficult to believe.

"Yes absolutely." Ann Harris continued, "I think I can tell you what motivated Newman and Malone."

"Yes, please Ms. Harris. Go on."

"In the first place, St. Malachi's is a hospital founded and run by a Religious Order of Catholic Nuns and they take a narrow perspective on what is called 'The Catholic Ethos' and the 'Pro-life' philosophy. The nuns believe that to allow Linda to die, when she can be kept alive, would be contrary to the said Catholic Ethos and might be seen as 'anti-life'."

Now Ms. Harris took a quick look over her shoulders to check for eavesdroppers before continuing:

"Then secondly: this also suits the Consultants --- Newman and Malone. They preferred to think of Linda as being 'alive' because in that way nobody could ever say that they had brought about her death. This absence of a death certificate allows for the lessening of their sense of guilt and responsibility for what happened to her."

"But at what cost to Linda?" Mary Boyle was visibly shocked. But Nurse Harris continued:

"I know Mrs. Boyle. A strong rumour has been going around the hospital that Newman and Malone are members of either Opus Dei or the Order of the Knights of Saint Columbanus. It is nearly impossible to establish this for a fact. All I do know is that one of the nurses saw the pair of them enter Ely House, the Knight's HQ, together about a month ago. If that is so, then these two consultants would never withhold food and water from anyone as that would run contrary to their fundamentalist values."

Now Ann Harris snapped open her handbag and rummaged around in its contents for a few seconds before producing a small card.

"Please take this Mrs. Boyle. My phone numbers and address are here. If for any reason in the future, you feel like contacting me then please do so without hesitation. Some other questions that I have not thought of may occur to you later. And now if you will excuse me, please. I am sure you could do with a bit of time to yourselves."

With that Ann Harris stood up and was about to leave. Mary restrained her momentarily by her right wrist.

"Ms. Harris, I doubt if you will ever fully appreciate how much it has meant to Margaret and me to have spoken to you and to have heard all you have had to say about that awful day and Linda's subsequent treatment."

"It's nothing Mrs. Boyle, believe me."

"Well, you may think so, but take my word for it. It's as if you have managed to pull back the clouds that have amassed over these events during the last twenty years. You have shone a light into some dark corners of Irish medicine. Thank you so much. It was very good of you to take the trouble."

Ann Harris smiled sweetly at the two women before walking out of the dining room. Just then Mary noticed that Con was heading their way. The waiter quietly approached their table and bending slightly at the waist addressed Mary:

"A telephone call for you Mrs. Boyle. You can take it from behind Reception."

Both women were brought suddenly back down to earth. Only one person at that time knew of their whereabouts.

"It must be David. I hope there's no bad news!"

Mary said as she left the table. Margaret decided that she may as well go along with her in case she might be needed for support.

Behind Reception the phone was lying on the table out of its cradle. She picked it up and sat down. Margaret heard her say:

"Yes, good evening, David. And what has you calling at this time of the evening?"

This was followed by long periods of Mary just listening and saying:

"Oh my God, I don't believe it. Oh my God, I don't believe it," over and over again like a mantra.

She was beginning to slump down, and Margaret feared that she might fall off the chair. Taking decisive action

Margaret walked in behind Reception, gently took the phone from her mother, and put it to her ear.

"David this is Margaret here, what's up?"

"What! They are going to appeal it. But Brogan said they had decided against that!"

"Jesus, this is really all we need right now."

David then did his best to reassure his sister.

"Come on Margaret, it's not the end of the world."

"Well, if you could see your mother right now you might think otherwise David."

"Will you *please* tell her that Brogan and Lavelle are not concerned, and that they are saying the doctors are only going through the motions? It's those two perverse consultants again. I mean to say, what would you expect?"

"Alright David, I'll do my best. We'll be home tomorrow evening, see you then."

Margaret placed the receiver back in its cradle. She helped her mother to her feet, and both crossed to the lounge where an open log fire was burning slowly. They ordered a couple of brandies. The drinks quickly arrived served in large bulbous brandy snifters. Neither woman spoke for a full two minutes. Margaret picked up the snifter and holding it in the palm of her right hand she swirled the contents around slowly gently warming it.

"We shouldn't be too surprised I suppose. I mean this is completely compatible with the way those doctors have behaved all along."

Margaret now desperately needed to reassure her mother and to buoyed her up for what was surly to be the final hurdle.

"No, no you're right dear. You're right. It's just the initial shock, that's all."

"We have come too long a way at this stage to let this defeat us."

Margaret paused for a tiny sip of her brandy before continuing.

"So, all right then, we thought, because that's what we were being told, that there was not going to be any appeal. And now we know differently. But it is no big deal really. And what would you expect anyway from the likes of Malone and Newman. Appealing to the Supreme Court is consistent with their usual horrible behaviour down through the years. May God forgive me, but I really have come to hate those two doctors."

Margaret paused again for another sip of her drink and replacing the snifter on the table in front of her reached across and gently held her mother's left forearm and shook it slightly to emphasise what she was saying:

"I listened carefully to every word that David said outside on the phone."

Mary said: "So did I. His reading of the situation is that these doctors are just going through the motions with this Supreme Court Appeal."

"Yes, but more importantly that's the view of Brogan and Lavelle."

Soon the two women finished their drinks and were ready to retire for the evening. It had been a long day.

The Irish Supreme Court is the highest judicial authority in the State and the court of final appeal. If the High Court ruling on this so-called 'Right to Die' case was to be upheld here, then the carers and doctors would have nowhere else to turn. They could in theory bring their case before The European Court of Human Rights, but their advisers would have told them that such an action would be a waste of time and extremely expensive.

"The Supreme Court hears arguments on matters of law not on matters of evidence."

They were gathered once again in Brogan's office and their solicitor was speaking:

"What this means in effect Mary is that neither you nor David nor Margaret will be required to give evidence this time out."

Margaret looked relieved. "Well thanks be to God for small mercies."

Brogan continued: "All you need do is to sit back and relax and listen to the various arguments being put forwards. Or stay away altogether if you like. It is entirely up to yourselves."

"I don't think we'll be doing that Tom." Mary thought to herself as he spoke. It was all very well for old Brogan here to try and make light of it. But by now the Boyle family were only too well aware of the vagrancies of the legal system. Nothing was certain. Nothing was ever guaranteed. Even seasoned Senior Counsels never tried to second-guess the system. When asked their opinion about what the most likely outcome was, they invariably hedged their bets.

The Supreme Court judges wore longer wigs than their High Court colleagues. This was one of the first things Mary Boyle noticed as she stood up to the 'All Rise' from the Court Clerk. All five judges, four men and one woman, filed in behind the long desk that ran almost the full width of the courtroom. This was raised six feet above the body of the court. The judges were led in by the Chief Justice the President of the Supreme Court. They took up their positions in front of their green leather high-backed chairs. Each chair had a gold harp embossed into the leather halfway down the back. The chairs were held out by court attendants and shoved in under each judge as they sat down. Only then did the rest of the attendances sit down.

David and Margaret had joined their mother for this the final saga of what had been a marathon legal battle to gain justice for their loved one Linda who has lain moribund in a persistent vegetative state now for just under twenty years.

In attendance also was the Rev Doctor Tom Lucy the Moral Theologian who had stood by the family through these recent legal proceedings. Looking at this theatre now being enacted out in front of her Mary reflected on just how unnecessary the whole thing had been. Had the doctors and the carers taken the family into their confidence and discussed with them a long-term strategy for Linda's care then none of them would be here in this courtroom today. Simple good manners and common sense could have avoided most if not all of this. Sensible and educated people should not need the Courts to decide for them what is best to do in the circumstances like these. Sensible and educated people like doctors and nurses and Linda's family should, had there just been the will, have reached amicable compromised arrangements about Linda's care that everyone could have lived with. But alas, that was not to be. At least now, since Mary and Margaret had fortuitously met Ann Harris, some considerable light had been shone into the darker shadowy corners of this unfolding tragedy.

The Supreme Court hearing lasted three full days. Two of these were given to hearing argument from Senior Counsel for each side and the third day was taken up by each of the five judges delivering their judgement.

The arguments that were trotted out by Counsel for the doctors, the carers and the institute were broadly in line with those used in the High Court four weeks earlier with a few novel additions. One innovation was the introduction of the concept that this was not a matter for the Courts to decide in the first place. They argued that only the doctors could properly decide any alterations in Linda's care since they were the only ones medically competent to make such judgements on clinical grounds.

Listening to this classical clash between Medicine and Law being introduced into the lion's den of the legal profession Mary, Margaret and David were agreed that it was a pathetic last-ditch attempt to turn the tables on McGill's judgement. The 'Doctor Knows Best' argument might have been good enough many years ago and in some other setting. But here in the Supreme Court it was cutting little ice and the body language of the five judges sitting in a row made that clear.

One other brief exchange during the two-day hearing was unusual and something of a giveaway as to how the judges were feeling. Counsel for the carers was going on at considerably length about how the Ward had a constitutional right to life and that thus the carers had a duty under that constitutional provision to keep the Ward alive. Senior Counsel was in full flight along these lines when none other than the Chief Justice himself suddenly interrupted him:

"But what is the point of keeping her alive?" the judge wanted to know.

Indignation was written over the judge's face and reflected in the sound of his voice. It was of course a rhetorical question, but it also was an interjection from the bench that was somewhat out of character with the rest of the hearing. It also set down a marker. It clearly showed what way the Chief Justice was thinking, and it was a safe bet that the majority of his colleagues would concur with whatever way he was thinking.

And that in fact was what happened. On the third day of the Supreme Court hearing each of the five judges delivered their lengthy judgements taking on average one hour each to do so. Four of the judges dismissed the appeal while only one upheld it. All of Linda Boyle's medical treatments, including her tube feeding, could be lawfully discontinued and this was now coming from the highest court in the land. The end of the road had finally, finally, been reached. Mary, Margaret, and David Boyle each breathed a silent sigh of relief. Fr. Tom Lucy reaches across to each of them in turn and solemnly shook them by the hand.

That night Mary Boyle took a mild sedative along with her night-cap of brandy and for the first time in many, many, weeks slept the sleep of the just. The next day there was to be an important meeting with the family solicitor, and it was vital that everyone there was well rested and had their wits about them.

Tom Brogan lent back on his high-backed swivel office chair his thumbs hooked into the arm outlets of his blue pinstriped waistcoat. From that vantage point he surveyed his three clients sitting across the desk from him. The atmosphere in this office was a strange mix of relief, happiness, sadness, and apprehension. Brogan, a hardboiled lawyer of many years' experiences, had long rated this case that had just concluded, this case that the papers were front paging as 'The Right to Die' case, as being emotionally the most draining that he had ever been part of. Everyone in this office this morning had been through a great deal but nobody more so than that feisty fighter Mary Boyle. And they still had some way to go yet. Brogan was speaking:

"Just a few minutes ago I had a spokesperson on to me from the institution, Sister Mary Assumpta she called herself and a right frosty old bitch she sounded like too. I think you know her from the past Mary?"

"Oh, indeed I do Tom, only too well. In the early years of Linda's illness Joseph and I had many a good old barney with the same Sister Assumpta. As relationships with the institution deteriorated, our run ins with that long old streak of sanctimonious misery increased. What's eating her now?"

The windows of Brogan's office were flung wide open against this sultry late August day. Traffic noise coming in from the narrow street outside meant that those inside at this meeting had to occasionally raise their voices to be heard.

Tom Brogan stood up and pulled down the windows before replying to Mary's question. The noise levels of traffic outside subsided significantly and raising one's voice to a near shout was no longer necessary. Tom, turning back into the room, remained standing while resting his arms on the back of his chair.

"As you know in the High Court and Supreme Court hearings the carers and the institute were allowed to disassociate themselves from any future actions that might run contrary to their conscience."

"Like what?" Margaret wanted clarification.

"Well for example they were given leave to not have to do anything that might run contrary to their Catholic Ethos, like stopping nutrition."

"Which is fair enough I suppose," Margaret said.

"Yes, which is fair enough. But now the nuns and their hospital seem to have gone into overdrive all of a sudden and there is suddenly great urgency about discharging Linda out of their care."

"But this is nonsense." Margaret said looking to her mother for clarification.

"Of course, it's nonsense Margaret. But hardly surprising. Newman and Malone are behind this. Can't you just see them?" Brogan said while straitening himself up.

"But they are the people who claimed to love Linda and here they are now threatening to throw her out on the street." Mary sounded incensed.

Brogan interjected again:

"Do you know what I think this is about? I really think that this is pure vindictiveness, pure spite. This is the last chance that these doctors have to get back at you and make you suffer, and it now looks as though they are prepared to use Linda's broken body as one way to get back at you while they still can. How cynical and sick can these people really be?"

Mary, looking up at the solicitor said: "They can be very cynical and sick, and I have always known that. But we must stand up to them Tom. They can hardly put her out on the side of the street. I am going home now, and I will immediately start looking for a private hospital or nursing home that might be willing to help us. I will need your help too David please."

David Boyle nodded quickly in his mother's direction.

Brogan still felt more caution was needed: "They might not put her out on the street Mary but there is nothing stopping them from putting her into an ambulance and having her turn up on your doorstep."

"Just hold on there now a second Tom will you please?" Mary sounded aghast at what she judged to be her solicitor's windy response to the institute's implied threats. She was having none of it.

"We simply must continue to stand up to these people. If Sister Assumpta calls you again and threaten to move Linda before we have had a chance to find a home to place her in then tell her that if she does that, we will sue her personally for negligence or for dereliction of duty and for whatever else that you and Lavelle can dream up." Mary looked around before continuing.

"Tell them also that if they make any untoward moves that would be damaging to Linda's wellbeing, then we will personally see to it that each of their names and the name of their institution will be on radio, television and in the national newspapers. That should soften their cough for them. In fact, come to think of it, Tom, maybe you'd give them that message anyway please over the phone as soon as I have left."

Margaret looked across at her mother and slowly shook her head from side to side. By God, she never lost it did she? But she was right.

"Good on you Mother. That's called a pre-emptive strike."

"Is that what it's called? Good. Let's have a pre-emptive strike then Tom like a good fellow. The only way to deal with bullies is to bully them back. Capitulation or appeasement is simply useless and only encourages the bully to try harder."

David and his mother sat on opposite sides from each other at the pine kitchen table in number 16 Ashgrove Lane, Rathfarnham, Dublin. They each had a copy of the 01 Golden Pages in front of them and had it opened at the section headed 'Hospitals'. Linda did not need a hospital as such, but they had agreed that they had better spread their nets as wide as possible and include nursing homes and hospitals. Finding a place to take Linda in and to remove her gastrostomy tube and to let her die with dignity may not be as easy a task as one might first think. This despite the fact that the highest court in the land had just declared that such as action would not be unlawful.

After about half an hour of searching they had managed to phone up two nursing homes and one hospital each and already a worrying trend was beginning to emerge. When they got on to the person in charge of admissions there was initially no problem. Yes, they had a bed or will have one in a day or so. And no, PVS was not of itself a problem. Given a few days they can put together the team of nurses that will be required to nurse Linda twenty-four hours a day seven days a week.

"No problem, Mrs. Boyle we can do that for you." Mrs. Cunningham, Matron of Allen View Nursing Home sounded confident, professional.

"Just give me a day or so. Of course, we will need a summary of her hospital records, a doctor's note, and a list of her medications. I will need to go into St. Malachi's and personally speak to my colleagues there to see how they have nursed Linda over the years and so on like that so as her transfer from the hospital to my nursing home here will be as seamless as possible."

Mary did not like the requirement of a doctor's note and a list of medications. She could see that while it might be sensible to have these things of course, getting them from these people who had suddenly turned hostile, and nasty was not going to be so easy. Anyway, she would cross that bridge later. Time now to move on to the 'substantive' issue as they might call it.

"Thank you. That sounds reassuring." Mary now braced herself for the really difficult bit.

"Mrs. Cunningham, you should know that I am the mother of the so-called Right to Die case. I suppose you have been following it in the various media lately. Indeed, there was a special documentary on it last night?"

A long silence now followed on the other end of the phone during which the proprietor of Allen View Nursing

Home grappled to come to terms with what she had just been told.

"Mrs. Cunningham, are you there?"

"Yes Mrs. Boyle, I'm still here. Sorry, I was just trying to come to terms with what you have just said there. Of course, I am familiar with the Right to Die case and have been following it with great interest all along since it came to court a number of weeks ago."

Mary could sense the doubts in the Matrons tone of voice. "And do you have any problems with the Court's recommendations?"

"Please do not get me wrong here Mrs. Boyle. I have every possible sympathy for you and for your daughter and the way that she was kept alive artificially for all of those years was nothing short of scandalous. I believe that you and your family have been most courageous in fighting this thing through the courts for your daughter's rights. I want to say congratulations to you and to your family and to say how delighted my husband and I were with the result. It is a privilege to talk to you. But there may be a problem."

Mary Boyle's heart sank at the sound of the word 'problem'.

Here we go again. 'I really should have anticipated this,' she thought to herself. The trouble is that when you are wrapped up in a lengthy High Court hearing followed by an equally stressful Supreme Court Appeal you really can only deal with issues on a daily basis as they turn up. Mary could not have anticipated that problems would go on even beyond the successful Supreme Court outcome. But now she knew exactly what Mrs. Cunningham was going to say on the other end of the line.

"If you were to ask me, I would have no problems in removing Linda's gastrostomy tube and letting her die in peace here in Allen View Nursing Home. I would consider it a privilege to have been able to help. But this is not just about me and that is the problem."

Here the Matron paused but Mary already knew what was coming:
"We have eight full-time Senior Registered Nurses and four part-time Registered Nurses working here in Allen View. Several general practitioners have patients here and we rely on them to refer patients into us. And then there are the thirty-six patients in residence here at the moment and of course their relatives. The sensitivities of all these people have to be considered, as have those of the broader community. I'm afraid Mrs. Boyle, even with the best will in the world, taking your daughter in here and allowing her to die by withholding hydration and nutrition is just not possible. The negative consequences are simply not calculable. I am so sorry."

"It's all right, Mrs. Cunningham. I understand. Thanks anyway."

Within a further hour David and Mary had between them managed to get through to the proprietors of seven more Nursing Homes or Private Hospitals. In some cases, when the person at the other end of the phone learned that the call was directly connected to the recently heard Supreme Court Right to Die case, their reaction was to get the caller off the line as quickly as possible. One Nursing Home that David called actually put down the phone on him when he was mid-sentence. Most institutions however, to be fair about it, listened courteously first and then declined giving as an explanation more or less the same as Mrs. Cunningham had done --- third party's sensitivities.

"David love, this is not going to work. We are getting nowhere. Let's just stop for now and have a think about it."

Mary was beginning to see that the practicalities of finding someone to help her let her daughter die with dignity was a great deal more difficult than she had first realised.

David closed the Golden Pages in front of him. Returning the portable phone, he had been using to its housing out in the hallway he returned to the kitchen and put the kettle onto the AGA's hot plate. Mary stayed at the pine table chin in hands elbows on the table deep in thought.

The kettle was boiling, and David tossed a round shaped teabag into each of the yellow mugs that he had ready, poured in the scalding water on top of these and swished around the teabags, squeezed their contents against the side of the mug before tossing the spent bag into the foot-peddled waste bin. Then, adding milk and sugar he passed his mother her tea.

"Have you thought of Northern Ireland at all Mum or even of the UK? They may not suffer from quite the same scruples given that they legalised the discontinuation of tube feeding themselves two years ago."

"No David. It is not really a question of individual scruples; it is more a question of institutional scruples. Even in England you will find the same sorts of so-called conscientious objectors that can make life impossible for everyone. And in any case, the thoughts of poor Linda having to be moved to another country in order to be allowed to die, is just too much. There simply has to be a better way."

Mary gave her tea a gentle stirring before taking a sip. Placing the yellow mug in front of her she continued.

"Do you know what I was thinking while you were making the tea there? We may as well just face up to it here and now and not be trying to further fool ourselves. Let's face it, we are simply not going to be able to locate a hospital or a nursing home that will take Linda in and remove her gastrostomy tube --- and, by the way, that is what I want for her. I do not just want people to stop feeding her through that damn tube, I want the abomination removed from her body altogether."

"No, no. I understand that, Mum."

"Anyway, as I was saying, finding an institution that might help is simply not on. St. Malachi's and that old bitch of a nun, aided and abetted you may have little doubt by those two creeps of doctors, are putting pressure on us to take Linda out of there. Therefore, everything considered and having thought about it now for a while, I think that the best place for Linda would be right here in this house upstairs in her own bedroom. What do you think David?"

David tossed back the last of his tea and looked across the table at his mother.

"I think that that is a fantastic idea, Mum. I must confess that I had thought of that also, a thought that was reinforced a few minutes ago when one of those institutions slammed the phone down on me when I mentioned the two words 'discontinue nutrition'."

"You think it would work then?"

"Yes, I do. This is the perfect peaceful place for Linda to die in the comfort of being surrounded by her own friends and family. There are of course a few snags or at least potential snags. For one thing we are going to need a doctor to remove the tube, oversee Linda's medical care and issue a Death Certificate when she dies."

Mary nodded: "Yes, I know. A doctor would be nice and of course I can see how you could not take up that role yourself. But if we cannot find one does that mean that we should abandon the whole thing altogether?"

"No, no we could manage at a pinch without any doctor. We may have to yet."

Mary drained her cup. "Anyway, the truth of the matter is that there is no going back now. St. Malachi's is pushing us to get Linda out of their hospital and we cannot find an alternative institution to help. So, at home it has to be."

David agreed: "We can only do our best. If necessary, we will ask a nurse to remove the tube and get a Death Cert from a local GP. I know that that is far from a satisfactory solution but, as I say, it is a question of 'what needs must'."

"David, I have one last string to my bow," Mary said while standing up. "After the Supreme Court hearing the other day, I met a doctor who had been covering the case as a medical journalist. I am not sure of course but I have a feeling that this man might help. He approached me, gave me his card, and said that if there was anything that he could do for me that I was not to hesitate to ask him. He does not know it yet, but I think I may have to take him up on his offer."

It was the end of August 1995, and the long hot summer went on unabated. Bright blue-sky days followed each other with an almost monotonous regularity. It was

Mediterranean weather and unusual for this island. People had been asked to preserve dwindling water supplies by not washing their cars or watering their lawns. Swifts circled high above Saint Stephen's Green with little thought of returning to their homelands in darkest Africa. Their first cousins the swallows and the house martins circled and weaved at a much lower level above the rooftops on either side of Ely Place and over number eight the headquarters of the Order of the Knights of Saint Columbanus. These summer visiting birds swooped and dived giving off the occasional short sharp shriek as they hovered up insects while in full flight.

For once there was no fire lit in the grate of the massive Adams fireplace in the elegant reception room located upstairs on the first floor. Four Knights, each dressed in the ceremonial colourful cloak of his rank within the Order were seated at the long mahogany boardroom table under the Waterford crystal chandelier. Under their cloaks they each wore dark pinstriped double-breasted suits. All had white double shirt cuffs showing with the gold cufflinks peculiar to the Order. Under the table was a row of shiny black shoes and black stockings. The windows had been thrown open and the mid-afternoon Dublin traffic rumpled far below. An occasional car-horn beeped, or seabird cried.

The assembled Knights were:
- Supreme Knight Thomas O'Leary a High Court judge by profession and one of the most influential Knights in Ireland of the day.

- Supreme Secretary Peter Newman Consultant Obstetrician Gynaecologist.
- Supreme Warden Walter Malone Consultant Anaesthetist St. Malachi's Hospital.
- Deputy Supreme Knight Stephen Ennis retired Consultant Endocrinologist and Chairman of the Medical Council's Fitness to Practise Committee.

It had just been agreed that Tom O'Leary be given the floor first. As is customary at these formal sessions, speakers are asked to stand at the head of the table while speaking. O'Leary took up his position with his back to the unlit fireplace and the large portrait of Saint Columbanus in the ornate gild frame hanging above the mantelpiece. The Knight leaned forward and placing the palms of his hands out on the table before him to give himself some support. He looked around at his little audience:

"Brothers." O'Leary paused for a full ten seconds.

"So now it has come to this sorry pass, has it?" O'Leary straightened himself up and raised his voice.

"It has come to this sorry pass that in Ireland, in Ireland I ask you, the highest court in this land has sentenced an innocent and helpless woman to death. It is quite simply outrageous and unbelievable Brothers that this should have happened in a country that has long prided itself in being Pro-life and in resisting for all time those twin evils of abortion and euthanasia. We have pledged our lives to the protection of human life and it's a pledge that we hold to be sacred. But above everything else we pledged our lives to protect the lives of those who are most vulnerable, the unborn baby in its mother's womb, the sick and elderly."

The Supreme Knight now stepped back to the fireplace and with his right elbow resting on the white marble mantelpiece he stabbed the air with his left index finger to give more theatre to his performance.

"What Brothers, can any one of you tell me in the name of Jesus Christ and His Holy Mother Mary, did this woman do to deserve the death sentence handed down last week by four out of five of His Lordships down there in those Four Courts?"

Tom O'Leary jabbed his left index finger in a direction exactly indicating the location of the Four Courts across the city.

"I'll tell you what she did. She did nothing, nothing whatsoever. For the past twenty years she has lain quietly in her hospital bed in a coma. She has never offended anyone. She has never hurt another soul. She has never done anything illegal. All she asked of us and of you doctors was that she be given food and water. Not much to ask for now, was it?"

The other Knights remained silent; heads bowed. O'Leary went on:

"And now, notwithstanding the fact that she has done nothing wrong, she is condemned by our Supreme Court to be executed. Her life is deemed not to be worth saving anymore, is that what we are being asked to accept? Capital punishment has been reintroduced into Ireland. They can pull out her feeding tube and watch her die a slow and painful death. Now just watch the floodgates of euthanasia open up in this country. This, my brothers in Christ, is quite simply unbelievable. It is one of the darkest days in the history of this State."

Tom O'Leary returned to the long mahogany table and leaning forwards placed the palms of his hands flat down again. He lowered his voice to a loud whisper.

"And what mode of execution do you think that our Lordships of the Supreme Court have so carefully selected for the Ward? Lethal Injection? No. Hanging by the neck maybe? No, wrong again. How about the electric chair or gassing, a firing squad maybe? No, no, no, nothing so pedantic. After two days of deliberation a majority of four out of five have decreed that your patient should be starved to death. I hope they are proud of themselves. I curse them before my Almighty God. May each of them fester in hell for all time! I never thought that I would hear myself say this, but the truth is that I am now deeply ashamed of our judiciary and equally ashamed to call myself a judge."

The elegant reception room fell silent but for the hum of traffic drifting up from the street. None of the seated three Knights had given an indication that they wished to speak at this juncture. Brother O'Leary was therefore free to carry on:

"I did my best to intervene and see if I could be given this case at the High Court stage. That stupid cute whore of a Corkman, Barry Long, of course would not hear of it. No chance at all and I nearly got into trouble for just asking. But of course, this being a Ward of Court case the judge was always going to be a nominee of the President of the High Court a gentleman for whom I don't mind telling you I have no respect and little time. What else would you expect from a Corkman? In the end he appointed that snivelling bastard McGill to take the case!"

The Supreme Knight now addressed his remarks in the direction of his deputy Dr. Stephen Ennis.

"Brother, I asked that you sit into this meeting with us this afternoon because you may be our last chance to at least bring about a stay of execution for this unfortunate woman. You are a member of the Fitness to Practise Committee of the Medical Council. That is a powerful position to be in. If the family are going to carry out this killing, then they are going to have to elicit the help of a doctor isn't that so? Pray speak up Brother and give us some comfort on this bleakest of days."

The Deputy Supreme Knight Dr. Stephen Ennis shuffled to his feet and cleared his throat while Tom O'Leary resumed his seat back at the long shiny mahogany table. The Deputy was an old man and slightly stooped. Convention within the Knights dictated that older men are exempt from rules like having to go to the top of the table to speak. Dr. Ennis spoke from where he was in a quiet husky voice:

"Yes, I believe that they are going to need a doctor to remove the gastrostomy tube and to oversee this execution by starvation that might take up to two weeks to complete. It is my personal and deep-felt belief that such a doctor is little better than a murderer, is a disgrace to his profession and should be struck off immediately."

Three heads across the shiny table nodded up and down approvingly. Brother Ennis was making the right noises. He continued in his quiet husky voice:

"That of course is my own personal view. It may also be one that many of my colleagues on the Committee share. But I do not think that we could put it out as the official position of the Medical Council at this point in time. To do so would be to invite some dissent from within the ranks of the Council and we certainly don't want that right now."

What I would propose then is this. I will put the word out through my friends in the media that I would like to make a statement to the press radio and television as a member of the Fitness to Practise Committee of The Irish Medical Council but speaking in a personal capacity. That always confuses them. They will think it is the Council speaking even if I make it clear to them that that is not the case. What I would propose saying to the media is something like this:

"A distinction exists between the laws of the land and medical ethics. Just because a certain action is legal, does not mean that it is ethically acceptable. Any doctor who might involve themselves in complying with the recent so called Right to Die case might find that they have questions to answer before the Medical Council."

"I would not want to put it any stronger than that for fear it might draw contradiction from the handful of so-called liberals within the Council. This is a delicate situation, and we need to be careful about over kill. It would be only asking for trouble if, for example, I was to say that such a doctor would be struck off."

Supreme Warden Malone had his hand raised a few inches above the table's surface indicating that he would like to say something. Dr. Ennis on seeing this nodded in the Warden's direction.

"Yes Sir, you want to say something? Please say."

"Thank you. I was just wondering there while you were speaking Doctor. Two things actually: Is it your belief Sir that there are so-called doctors in this country who would actually oversee a fellow human being, being, starved to death? That's one thing. And secondly, I was wondering if threats from the Medical Council would deter them in fact?"

"On your first question there about whether or not there are doctors who would do a thing like this. Have no doubt about it Brother Walter there are indeed such so-called doctors. We already know in fact who they are. Some of them make no secret about their attitude to so-called mercy killing. They are out there alright; you need have little doubt. Now as to the second part of your question, would Medical Council warnings deter them? I believe that they would almost certainly. It is every doctor's nightmare that he might be struck off the medical register, that he might be defrocked and disgraced. Any doctor with that kind of thing hanging over his head would think long and hard before taking an action that would put him at risk of being stuck off. In any case it is the best that we can do at this late stage. If anyone here has any better ideas, please speak up now."

The room fell quiet. It was an uneasy quiet. Suddenly the meeting was over, and four Knights pushed back from the table and standing gathered their ceremonial silk robes about them. Led by the Supreme Knight they shuffled out of the room in single file bowing to each other as they went along.

Mary Boyle was standing over the pine kitchen table ironing a few things that she had just taken off the clothesline outside. The radio was playing quietly in the background. It was coming up to the One o'clock News time. Things at long last were beginning to fall into place since the Supreme Court appeal ten days ago. The family were agreed that the best thing to do would be to take Linda home to be allowed to die in peace and with dignity in the loving surroundings of her family and friends. A team of six Senior Registered Nurses had been put in place to give Linda the around the clock nursing that she was going to need. Two days ago, Mary had phoned the GP who had approached her earlier after the Supreme Court hearing offering his help. True to his word he now had agreed to take Linda on as his patient and to oversee her care when the tube feeding had been discontinued at home.

Two minutes into the One o'clock News and an item was announced that struck Mary like a bolt of lightning from the sky:

'In a statement made this morning a spokesperson for the Fitness to Practise Committee of the Medical Council said that any doctor who cooperated with last week's controversial Supreme Court judgement allowing for the discontinuation of tube feeding a woman in a permanent coma may have questions to answer before the Council.'

Mary Boyle was rooted to the spot iron held in mid-air poised over the ironing board. She could not believe what she had just heard.

She unplugged the iron immediately and went directly to the phone in the hall. The GP's mobile number was on a card wedged into a corner of the hall mirror.

"Hallo is that you doctor? Listen, sorry to disturb you but I must know if you have heard the latest from the Medical Council and if so, how do you react to it?"

"Yes Mrs. Boyle. I actually heard that on the twelve o'clock news headlines on the car radio earlier and again just now. I don't think we should discuss this over the phone as I am sure you will understand. Listen, I will need to call around and talk to you face to face. How about in an hour's time? That will be fine then Mrs. Boyle. See you shortly. Bye for now."

As Mary was putting down the phone a key was turning in the hall door. It was David.

"David, did you hear?"

"Yes, on the car radio just now. God Almighty is there to be no end to it?"

"Listen David, the GP is coming around in an hour's time. He wants to discuss this with me face to face and I would like it if you could be here as well so as we all understand what's involved and where we are going."

"That's not a problem Mum. When I heard the news, I asked the boss for the afternoon off. There's no problem. How did the doctor sound?"

"It is hard to say. But he didn't sound upset or anything. He was just kind of relaxed and casual. Couldn't discuss it over the phone, that's all he'd say."

Fifty-five minutes later the GP was on Mary's doorstep ringing the doorbell.

"Come in doctor, take a seat. Would you like a cup of tea or coffee?"

"Tea please if it's not too much trouble. One teaspoonful of sugar and plenty of milk thanks."

The doctor lowered himself onto the couch and crossed his legs. David had the kettle going on the Aga.

"Alright Mrs. Boyle I will come straight to the point because I'm sure you are anxious about this. I heard that idiot from the Medical Council on the radio this morning and when I heard him, far from his making me fearful about what we were proposing here, what he did in fact was to make me all the more resolute to carry on."

"But surely you must be worried about the possibility of disciplinary proceedings being taken against you or even a remote possibility of such proceedings being taken against you. You could even be struck off you know."

David put the mug of tea down in front of the GP who thanked him before replying to Mary.

"I appreciate your concern Mrs. Boyle. I mean really, but to be perfectly frank with you I do not care about the Medical Council or their threats."

"How do you mean you don't care about them? Surely you have to care about your own professional life, about continuing to be a doctor and that kind of thing?"

The GP took a good sip of the hot tea before replying.

"Yes Mrs. Boyle, of course I care about my professional life, and I would absolutely hate to be dragged in front of the Council and be made accountable for my actions. But I do not believe for one second that the Medical Council would lift a finger against me or any other doctor. Not a snowball's chance in hell. Look it's very simple------"

The GP put his cup down before going on.

"Firstly, that fellow on the wireless this morning was not a spokesperson for the Medical Council. He is chairman of the Fitness to Practise Committee but, and he said so himself this morning, he was not speaking for the Council but in his own personal capacity. He is in fact quite an elderly man, long retired and well known within the profession as something of a right-wing maverick."

"But secondly," the GP continued, "and this is more to the point, the Council could not strike off a doctor for doing something that the Supreme Court had already adjudged as being lawful. If they attempted to move against the doctor in question, he in turn could take an injunction against them and the whole thing would become a legal nightmare. After all doctors have rights too and one of those basic rights is the right to make a living. The Medical Council may be many things but stupid they are not. They simply would not go there Mrs. Boyle, trust me."

"Oh, I do trust you doctor. But I could not live with it if you, or any other doctor for that matter, were to be dragged before any disciplinary committee because of something that I had asked you to do. Do you follow me?"

The GP stood up and finished off his mug of tea before asking David to join them.

"David, could you come in here for a second please? I just want you to hear me say this to your mother so as you can be a witness if ever the need should arise. Thanks."

"Mrs. Boyle, last week I offered to help and to take Linda on as a patient of mine and to remove her gastrostomy tube and oversee her last days in this life. That offer still stands. I appreciate that there might be some slight professional risks involved for me in doing this but if there are then that is entirely my responsibility, and you must be exonerated from any blame whatsoever."

With that the GP extended his right hand to Mary and smiling broadly shook hands with her warmly.

"Just before you go doctor, why are you doing this?"

"From what you have told me and from what I have learned myself in covering this case over the last few months I believe that the treatment that you and your family and of course most of all Linda has received from the medical profession has been nothing short of scandalous. Hearing and now knowing about it makes me feel deeply ashamed to call myself a doctor. If there is even the smallest little thing that I can do to atone in some way for that hurt and wrong, then that is what I should do. It is really that simple."

And with those few words the GP was out the door and asking them to call him as soon as Linda was taken home. He also added that if the institution makes an issue of releasing records of Linda's medication and nursing routines then not to push them too much on it because they were not essential.

His words were to prove prophetic. The institution did make a song and dance about releasing Linda's hospital notes and claimed that they could only do so if they were given the name of the doctor into whose care Linda was being discharged. True to form the institution was being as perverse as always. On the one hand they were putting almost unbearable pressure on the family to remove Linda out of their hospital. And they were doing this in the full knowledge of the enormous difficulties that the family were having in finding a hospital or home that would take Linda in and allow her to die in peace. And then on the other hand the institution was putting every kind of barrier in the family's way to make it as difficult as they possibly could for them to transfer her home. In the end their solicitor Tom Brogan had to intervene and ask that the institution be reasonable and waive a few of their rules and regulations for just this once. Hostilities remained up to the very end, to the point even where Mary and Margaret were refused permission to visit Linda for an hour before the ambulance came to take her home. No reason was given for this bizarre ruling and Mary and Margaret decided to let it go unchallenged. They had had enough.

Ten stressful days after the Supreme Court judgement and twenty equally stressful years after her unnecessary hysterosalpingogram, Linda Boyle was being gently lifted out of the back of the ambulance on a stainless-steel wheeled stretcher and was carried up the winding stairway with great difficulty by two strong ambulance men. Three Senior Registered Nurses were immediately in attendance. Closure was within sight.

Fr. Tom Lucy called in first. With great solemnity he administered the Last Sacraments to Linda and with the nurses and family present he celebrated Mass. The mood in the house was now one of sadness mixed with a sombre resolution and an absolute assuredness that what was taking place was right and fitting and utterly dignified.

The next morning the GP arrived as requested. Using a ten-cc syringe he deflated the retaining balloon at the end of the gastrostomy tube and slowly withdrew it from deep inside Linda's stomach. While the doctor did this, two nurses gently stroked Linda's face and brow and whispered gentle reassurances into her ear. The withdrawal of the feeding tube caused no apparent distress to the patient. All was calm and quiet.

During this their final ordeal, Mary, Margaret, and David each had to deal privately with their own particular set of mixed emotions. They cried silently together quite a lot. How could they ever be one hundred percent certain that what they were now doing was absolutely the right thing for Linda? They could never have such certainty in fact. At best they had feelings and instincts that informed that what they were doing was correct and these feelings and instincts, in the main, all three of them shared in common.

Their other feelings ranged from profound sadness and loss and to anger at what had befallen their loved one lying unconscious in her bed upstairs. The anger was still raw and was directed against those who had brought about Linda's calamity, a calamity that was utterly unnecessary and futile and one for which no formal explanation or apology was ever offered. Although she was forced to live on for another twenty years Linda's real life was stolen from her that day in Theatre Number Two in St. Malachi's General Hospital away back in January 1974.

Over the next eight days everything remained peaceful, sad, and dignified. No more moaning, no more distressful cries escaped from Linda's lips. The nurses worked their magic as only nurses could. They kept Linda's lips and mouth moist throughout with a damp sponge. No sedatives or morphine were administered simply because there seemed to be no need for any such medication. Only her quiet rhythmic breathing could be heard. This gradually grew shallower and shallower over the days until, eight days and two hours after the gastrostomy tube was withdrawn, her breathing ceased altogether. Linda's soul slipped quietly away leaving her wrecked body at peace at long long last.

At that precise moment also, in the small garden of 16 Ashgrove Lane the early autumn breeze suddenly ceased to toss the yellow flowering heads of the tea roses beside the clothesline. Now for one full minute they stood absolutely motionless and splendid. Just then too, halfway up the mature silver birch tree the blackbird fell silent. Up until now he had been giving forth bursts of crystal-clear notes in short sharp phrases given generously in measured succession each delightful phrase freshly composed, original and inspired. But now there was absolute silence. No bird could sing nor could breeze blow. In a short while the gentle autumn wind gathered itself up again to toss the yellow flowering heads on the tea roses. The blackbird from halfway up the mature silver birch resumed his repertoire from where he had left off; for all now seemed well again with the world.